A Tracy Brubaker Mystery

PRACTICE TO DECEIVE

Book 4

John Carter Stell

Midnight Marquee Press
Baltimore, MD, USA

The Tracy Brubaker Mystery Series

#1 The Big Nap
#2 Crossed Stitch
#3 Murder Me Twice

ISBN 978-1-64430-084-8
Library of Congress Catalog Card Number 2019951456
First Printing October 2019

Dedication

For my children: the best audience Tracy ever had.

Here's another nice mess I got you into. – Stan Laurel

Chapter 1

Merlin's Manor of Mirth and Magic was the new "it" place of Baltimore City. It had opened last summer in a renovated building close to the Inner Harbor as an attempt to bring the once popular art of stand-up comedy back to the forefront, and, as an added bonus, throw in the time-honored entertainment of illusion. Edgy laugh masters mixed it up with seasoned practitioners of sleight of hand, while patrons could imbibe to their heart's content while snacking on the establishment's light fare offerings. The experiment had been a sensation; reservations were a must.

Attorney Tracy Brubaker loved magic, had loved it all her life. She loved trying to figure out how the tricks were done even more. And everyone who knew her knew she loved a good laugh, too. Her fiancé, Brian Shane, certainly knew it. It was April 17— her 32nd birthday. He didn't tell her where he was taking her after the celebratory dinner had been consumed and enjoyed. They were passing the Inner Harbor shops, very close to the location where Tracy's condo building stood, as Tracy continued, unsuccessfully, to try and get Brian to spill the magic beans.

"How about a hint?" she asked, rubbing his arm.

"Nope."

"Oh come on, just a little one."

"Nope."

"I'll be your best friend."

"You already *are* my best friend."

"But I'll be even *bester*."

"Bester? Is that even a word?"

"Come on, just one clue, honey." She batted her eyes at him.

"You'll get nothing from me, dear."

"Brian," she cooed, "please tell me. Please oh please oh please. I'll *thank* you later." She started rubbing his leg.

"Don't even try it, temptress. I am immune to your charms—at least for the next few minutes or so."

Tracy snorted. "Has the magic left us already?" And then Brian started laughing heartily. She had inadvertently given *herself* a clue and didn't even realize it.

"No, my love, the magic is just beginning!" he told her.

Tracy folded her arms and made a grumpy face. She looked out her window. And then she saw it: the bright neon letters that spelled out the location's name. The sign was bookended with flashing chattering teeth and a blinking top hat.

"OH MY GOD!" Tracy screamed, clapping her hands. "Is that it?! We're going to *Merlin's*?!" Brian looked over to give her a quick smile. "Oh, Brian! What a great treat!"

"I thought you might like it," he said nonchalantly as he prepared to pull into the parking lot.

Tracy was clearly thrilled, so much so that she couldn't stop talking. "Who's here tonight? I don't even know! Do you, Brian?"

"To be honest, Tracy, I'm not sure either. I mean, I figured since I was able to get us tickets for tonight, for your birthday, you wouldn't care who was here."

Tracy nodded vigorously. "Brian, this is great! I can't believe it! I'm so excited! I just never suspected…"

"So I fooled the great lawyer-cum-detective? Ha!"

She smiled widely and leaned over to kiss his cheek. "I love you Brian; you're the best."

"You deserve the best, Tracy," he said softly. She rubbed his arm as they approached the pay lot gate. Brian grabbed the ticket when the machine spat it out, and then proceeded when the gate lifted. Soon they were making their way to the *Merlin's* entrance. Tracy was holding onto Brian's arm, leaning her head on his shoulder. Mentally, she was preparing for one of the best nights of her life. When all was said and done, it *would* prove memorable.

The lobby of *Merlin's Manor of Mirth and Magic* was a scene of chaos. The bright red carpeting could barely be seen because of the crowd that was constantly in motion. The 7:00 p.m. show had just let out, and those who wanted to arrive early for the 9:30 p.m. performance were piling in. Waiters were entering the main auditorium and moving about to take drink and food orders, while others were navigating the crowd with dirty dishes and glasses on their way back to the kitchen. On the right side of the lobby were various lines for ticket holders and would-be purchasers. Fat chance of getting anything for tonight; the show had been sold out for over a month. On the left was the bar; behind that was the kitchen. People were shouting loudly so they could be heard over the other people who were also shouting loudly. Some fools were even trying to talk on their cell phones. All Tracy heard were the callers yelling, "What? What did you just say?"

"There's supposed to be a reservation ticket booth around here somewhere," Brian told her while looking around.

"There!" Tracy pointed, "That marquee sign on the right down there!"

Brian took notice and then grabbed Tracy's hand; the two of them moved in the direction of the stand. "I guess this is the end of the line," Brian said when he found he could no longer move forward.

  Practice to Deceive

"We have time Brian," Tracy smiled. "It's not too much past nine."

"I hope this line moves quickly though," he said.

Tracy looked around the lobby. "Oh, this is so exciting!" Tracy was grinning from ear to ear and squeezing Brian's arm.

Brian laughed. He loved seeing her so happy; her joy was contagious. "Wow, you really *are* stoked for this."

"I haven't been to a magic show in forever. In fact, I think…" She trailed off.

"The last time was with me, wasn't it?" Brian asked ruefully. He and Tracy had dated in college, fallen in love, and made plans for a future together. But circumstances had conspired against them and they broke up. Now, 12 years later, they were back together and engaged to be married. But the painful memories were still there, at least for Brian: the guilt he felt about the breakup, anyway. He promised himself he would spend the rest of his life making things up to her.

Tracy was still smiling. "Yes, Brian. That time was fun, but this is going to be incredibly *awesome*!"

Another minute—probably less—passed. Brian grumbled, "We're not moving."

"They're probably still clearing out people from the other show. I'm sure once things get going we'll fly right through this thing."

Brian always found Tracy irresistible, especially when she was in such high spirits. "I love you Tracy," he said, and he leaned over and kissed her.

After their kiss, Tracy asked, "Hey, why don't I go to that bar over there and get us something? Want a ginger ale?"

Brian smiled. "Sure, Tracy, that'd be great."

"Back in a flash," she told him as she exited the line. Tracy twisted her body every which way as she negotiated the crowded path to the bar. She had a close call with a basket of cheddar fries and honey mustard sauce. But she arrived at her destination safely and unstained. Once there, she found an open space in which she could fit her five-foot-five frame and await her turn.

"Hey, what is this, last call on the Titanic?!" The question came from a casually dressed, curly haired late-twentyish fellow who was pushing his way to the counter.

"Hey, it's Woody Williams!" someone else screamed.

"Hey, sweetheart, wanna buy Woody a drink?" he asked the suddenly starstruck female. "I got some time."

"She ain't buying you nothin,' pal!" a stern-looking gentleman told the freeloader. The sour-faced fellow then put his arm around his date as if claiming his territory.

"Andy, he's the stand-up comic at the show!" the lady said excitedly.

"I don't care *who* he is."

"Alright, Stallone, calm down," Woody said, motioning with his hands. Then, the thirsty jokester called out, "Hey, I'm on in less than half an hour—I need some refreshment over here!" Not long after, a glass of draft beer was being offered to the noisy Williams. "See you at the show, folks!" he called out as he gave a quick wink to the lady. who was still smiling at him. "Hey, toots, ditch Kronk here and maybe you can buy me a drink later." He winked at Andy, too, as he headed toward the show doors.

"Hitting on women at the bar?" Tracy thought. "Titanic and Stallone jokes? The stand-up part is going to be a chore." Tracy leaned her head over the bar and then realized why she had found a place relatively easily to wait: the lone bartender was at the opposite end of the counter. She frowned.

"The show was incredible!" Tracy heard one man tell another while trying to be patient. "The magic part of it, I mean. I don't find a lot of these comedians today to be that funny. In fact, most of them are downright offensive."

"Yeah," the other guy agreed. "I like Tim Allen and Ray Romano. Those guys are hilarious."

"What?" the original speaker asked incredulously. "*Those guys*? No way—I'm talking your vaudeville and classic comedy teams: The Marx Brothers, Abbott and Costello, Laurel and Hardy. *Those* guys were funny without being nasty. *That's* comedy!"

"Never heard of them," said the other flatly, sipping his beer.

"Never?!…you never?! Oh you young people have *no* clue!"

"I know them!" Tracy piped in, feeling chatty and friendly. She might as well pass the time somehow. "*I* love those guys!"

The older gentleman turned, smiling. "You *do*?"

"You bet. I love Groucho's monologues, Chico's language mangling, and Harpo's sight gags. I never get tired of the 'Who's On First?' routine. And how could one not feel the warmth and love between Stan and Ollie, even when the latter is yelling at the former? And we haven't even gotten into the silent comedy stars: Chaplin, Keaton, Arbuckle, Lloyd…"

Tracy's audience of one was briefly speechless, maybe even shocked, as the names had seemed to come forth from her so easily. Then he smiled widely. "Young lady, let me buy *you* a drink. YOU, dear, have made my night!"

Tracy laughed. "Thanks, but you don't have to do that. I'm here buying drinks for two."

"Well, then, I'll buy you *two* drinks." The friendly purchaser leaned over the counter. "Hey, barkeep!" he shouted. "Some service for this young lady down here who's been *more* than patient!"

A harried but smiling server appeared fairly quickly. "What will it be for you, ma'am?"

"Two ginger ales, please." He nodded and was off.

Tracy turned to her new friend. "I'm Tracy Brubaker," she said, offering her hand.

"Dan Scarborough," he told her, accepting it. "You here for the next show, I take it?"

"Yup! Are you?"

"No—I just saw the seven o' clock. But I ain't in no hurry to leave, not with this mad crowd about me. Getting out of the parking lot is going to be a nightmare." Tracy nodded and smiled. "What do you do, Tracy?"

"I'm an attorney."

"No kidding! I'm in banking myself, manage a branch in Gaithersburg."

"Wow! You live out there and you came all the way to the city?"

"You bet! I love this stuff, magic, I mean. I *finally* managed to get a ticket."

"That will be $9.50, ma'am," the bartender announced as he returned, drinks in hand.

Before Tracy could act, Scarborough was handing him $11.00. "Here, keep it." The server smiled and thanked his customer.

"Thanks, Dan. That was very sweet of you."

"It's nothing! You're going to love this show, the magic part, anyway."

"I love magic shows myself, Dan!" Tracy enthused. "I've loved them since as far back as I can remember." Then she looked at her drinks. "I should deliver this to my fella; he's waiting in line for our tickets."

"Don't let me keep you! You go enjoy yourself, Tracy, you *and* your fella."

"Thanks again, Dan, it was really nice chatting with you."

"Hey, you too; it's always great to meet a young person who appreciates the classics!"

Tracy gave her benefactor another smile and then headed back to Brian. He had moved a little ahead, but not much.

"Look, I have a confirmation number!" someone was yelling. "So, *Rose*, you must have a ticket back there waiting for me. Find it!"

Tracy rejoined her fiancé and handed him his drink. "What's going on?" she asked.

"I guess they can't find this guy's ticket, and he won't stop complaining about it."

"Oh."

"He won't get out of the line, either; he's been there practically the whole time you were away. Seriously, this is starting to really piss me off."

"Easy there, Kronk," Tracy said handing Brian his drink.

"What did you call me?"

Tracy started laughing. "Just prepping you for the kind of comedy we'll be hearing tonight, honey."

"We'll refund your money, sir," the woman at the booth continued. "But the show is completely sold out."

"I don't *want* a refund! I came here to the *see* the show! Do you know how long I've been looking forward to this? You can't just send me away! I HAVE A CONFIRMATION NUMBER!"

"Sir, there's nothing I can do. You can move to the side, and if I get word of a cancellation, I will let you have a ticket. If someone hasn't shown up by 9:45 p.m., our policy is that the tickets are forfeited, so you might get a ticket that way too."

"Then I would miss part of the comedy act!"

"You wouldn't be missing much," Tracy thought.

"Sir, I am going to have to ask you to stand aside so I can help these other people. In the meantime, the manager is on her way to help you further."

"This is pathetic!" he cried out. Then, the angry patron grunted and moved to the side as requested, folding his arms like a spoiled child who didn't get his way. The three customers who were in front of Brian and Tracy were quickly handed their tickets.

"Two tickets for Brian Shane," Tracy's beau said to Rose, who was dressed in a top hat and glittery dress.

Rose flipped through some envelopes in front of her. "Right here, Mr. Shane." She looked in the envelope, grinned, and then handed the package to Brian.

"Let's go, Tracy!" he said moving toward the entrance doors. Tracy followed. The usher looked at the couple's tickets, tore them in two, and then led them through the auditorium to a table that was situated very close to the main stage.

"Too close," Tracy thought. Tracy made herself comfortable in the chair Brian pulled out for her, and then he sat down. She leaned close to him. "Brian, this is awfully close."

"Yeah, so?"

"Well, I just hope…"

     Practice to Deceive

"You hope what, love?"

"I'm not into audience participation, Brian. I'm here to *see* the show, not be *in* it. I don't want to suddenly find myself…Well, I'm just here to watch and enjoy."

Brian grinned. "What? *You're* nervous? You who deals with juries? You who arranges morning dinner parties and exposes murderers?"

"That's different. That's my *job*. Besides, there are what, 500 people here?"

"I think that's about right."

Tracy looked at Brian closely. "Why are you grinning like that?"

"Like what?"

Tracy's eyes narrowed. "What are you up to Brian?"

"About 5'-11"."

"Hardy har har."

"Oh Tracy, relax. It's your birthday; have a good time. This is all about fun."

Tracy looked at him suspiciously, but then smiled. "Okay. Fun it will be."

"*That's* better." Brian looked at his watch and then around the room. "Full house tonight."

"It's Friday; no surprise there."

"Are you excited?"

She smiled again. "Oh, YEAH!" She looked around.

"I love you," he told her.

"I love you too," she returned.

"Good evening," a waiter said to them. "Can I get you something before the show starts? You can't order anything when the show is in progress. The comic is on for about 40 minutes, until the first intermission occurs, so you'll have to wait that long if you don't order anything now, unless you want to leave the auditorium and order from the bar."

Tracy shook her head; Brian shook *his* head. "We're good, thanks," Brian told him. "These ginger ales will tide us over." The server nodded and moved to the next table, where Tracy could hear him repeating verbatim what he had just told them.

"Five minutes or so," Brian said. Tracy reached her hands across the table. Brian smiled and grasped them.

"Thank you, Brian," she said. "This is really great. Dinner was supreme, and now this…I'm really excited."

He looked at her and smiled. And then he told her again that he loved her. The noise of the crowd, try as it might, could not drown out his words. She kissed his hands in response.

"May I have your attention, please?" The room's built-in ceiling speakers had come to audible life. "There is absolutely *no* recording permitted in any way, shape, or form of tonight's show. And, yes, this includes the use of cell phones, smart phones, or any other kind of phone to do so. Anyone caught recording *any* portion of tonight's show will be told to leave; there will be *no* refunds given under these circumstances, and you may find yourself subject to civil penalties. So please, no recording.

"Also, at this time, please turn off *all* electronic devices so as not to ruin the experience of those around you. If you need to take or make a call, please exit the auditorium and take care of your business in the lobby. We thank you in advance for your courtesy. And again: absolutely no recording is permitted. Lastly, please note the monitors throughout the auditorium that you may refer to so you can witness the magic of the evening up close, no matter where you are seated. Our show will begin shortly. Thank you for your attention, and enjoy your evening!"

"Good for them," Tracy said. "If I hear one digital ringtone at all tonight I'm gonna—"

"Easy, darling," Brian said laughing. Tracy smiled. Finally, the lights dimmed.

"Ladies and gentlemen!" a disembodied voice began. "Welcome one, welcome all to *Merlin's Manor of Mirth and Magic*!" Applause and cheering erupted throughout the room. Tracy, fingers in mouth, whistled. "Tonight, our comedy master is none other than the winner of television's *America's Next Legends*: Woody Williams!" More cheering, more noise. Tracy applauded lightly just to be polite. "And then, tonight's special guest, a legend himself for over 25 years! *Merlin's Manor of Mirth and Magic* is proud to welcome, as your magic headliner: Casper Montado!" Tracy truly joined in the merriment this time. She had seen Montado the Great, as he was once known, many times on television in her life, dating back to when she was eight or nine. He was a talk show regular and a grand entertainer. She couldn't be more excited. After the applause had finally subsided, the voice returned. "But first—ladies and gentlemen—we have an extra-special guest for you tonight."

Tracy looked at Brian. "Oh wow, I wonder who else is here?" Brian shrugged his shoulders. And then he turned, as did Tracy, to see a figure making its way toward them. Brian raised his arm, at which point a spotlight found its way to their table, and, more specifically, the young woman who was seated there.

The impeccably dressed man with the microphone and beaming smile approached Tracy, and then spoke into his mike. "Ladies and gentleman,

 Practice to Deceive

we have a birthday to celebrate tonight here at *Merlin's Manor of Mirth and Magic!*" Again, the crowd erupted. Tracy, on the other hand, panicked. She turned to Brian, who was grinning at her.

"Oh NO you *didn't*," she started to say before the roving speaker stopped in front of her.

"What is your name, dear?" he asked her as he moved the mike toward her. Her face went completely red.

"Uh, Tracy," she said softly.

"Is it your birthday today, Tracy?"

She gulped. "Yes." Cheers from the crowd!

"Want to tell us how old you are today, Tracy?"

"No," she answered firmly. The crowd broke out into laughter, as did the host.

"Maybe this gentleman here with you will tell us."

"Not if the *gentleman* knows what's good for him," Tracy growled. There was more laughter and a smattering of applause. Brian still managed to maintain his grin.

"Who is your companion tonight, Tracy?"

"My fiancé until further notice." There were some scattered chuckles. A woman seated near Tracy, however, found this whole episode so hysterical that she nearly fell out of her chair while carrying on like a hyena. This seemed only to make Tracy more hostile.

"An engaged couple, ladies and gentlemen: let's hear it for them!" The crowd hooted, hollered, and stamped their feet. "What your fiancée's name, Tracy?"

"Toast." There was more laughter and clapping.

"What was that, dear?"

"Brian Toast."

The MC moved the mike toward the seated toast. "Brian, how old is your fiancée today?" The smile left Brian's puss and he just shook his head. Those who saw him, his face on the various screens, laughed until tears were streaming. The MC gave each of them a last smile. "Well, let's hear it for the birthday girl anyway!" As the audience once again made noise, the young woman who was previously seated at the ticket reservation booth joined the spotlighted attorney and placed on her head a top hat adorned with red neon stitching in the shape of smiling lips. The announcer spoke again: "Our gift to you, Tracy, here at *Merlin's Manor of Mirth and Magic!*" The employees then made their way back to their previous positions near the entrance doors, and the spotlight was redirected toward the stage.

Tracy glared at Brian. "You are in SO much trouble."

Brian laughed. "That hat looks really cute on you." Tracy immediately removed the suddenly offensive topper and placed it under the table.

"So much trouble," she repeated.

"Ladies and gentlemen, please welcome to *Merlin's Manor of Mirth and Magic*: WOODY WILLIAMS!" Applause and shouts of "Woody!" filled the air as the previously thirsty bar patron took to the stage.

"HELLO BAL-TEE-MORE!" Williams shouted. Some people even stood and jumped up and down at this latest assault on silence. "Howz everyone feelin' to-night?!" Everyone apparently felt fine. "I understand we have a birthday girl out there somewhere."

"Oh *crap*," Tracy thought. And then the light was back on her. Soon Woody was right in front of her.

"Your name's Tracy, right?" She nodded. "Hey, no need to be shy here, Tracy. RIGHT FOLKS?"

"I hate you, Brian," she thought.

"So what do you do for a living, Tracy? I mean what do you do to put *toast* on the table?" Chuckle, snort.

Tracy cleared her throat. "I'm an attorney."

"An attorney? Really? Ooooooooooooooooooooo...." Guffaws, more snorting.

"Yes."

"Do you have your own law firm, or are you just a cog in someone else's spinning wheel?"

"My own firm."

"Holy smoke, folks! Do you realize what we have here? Someone else who makes a living practicing to deceive! Am I right?" Screams and fits of laughter, and then applause.

Tracy thought, "Brian, you are dead to me."

"And this is your fiancé?"

"I'll have to get back to you on that." Thunderous applause.

"Hey lady, I do the jokes here!" Chuckles.

"Well, just let me know when you've started, then, and I'll stop." And Tracy Brubaker got what would turn out to be the biggest laugh of the night.

Woody blinked and then smiled. "Hey, if you quit your day job you've a future in…well, something else, I guess. Folks, give it up for Tracy, the future Mrs. Toast!" And the spectators shouted out their approval. Tracy, however, was officially perturbed. She did not like being the center of attention unless she was in control; she was not in control tonight.

Brian reached for her. "Come on, Tracy, it was all in fun. You were great!"

"Don't touch me, toast boy," she barked at him. And then she looked over at her smiling fiancé, trying hard to maintain her glacial scowl. But when he started laughing, she couldn't keep it up, and joined in. "But you are still in SO much trouble," she advised him.

"Well, like most people on the road, I'm in a relationship," Woody started, now that he was back onstage. "Do you like that expression, folks: 'in' a relationship? I mean, is it like walking *into* a wall, or diving *into* a pool? Or is it more like you stepped *in* something, like a pile of dog poo?" Scattered laughs. Tracy shook her head. "Now my girl has all kinds of problems, so many, in fact, that I thought, being the caring, sensitive guy I am, that I should get her help."

Some audience members shouted, "Aww…" Tracy just finished her ginger ale.

"So I go to this doctor, and he asks me, What is the lady's issue? And I tell him, Hey, doc, this woman doesn't have just one issue, she has lots of issues. In fact, doc, she's got a full-blown subscription!" Scattered laughs. "I mean, do you offer something like a magazine does, doc: buy 12 issues, get four for free or something? Can I get a discount here, or what?" More scattered laughs, some sporadic applause.

"Then this doctor reminds me that *he's* the shrink here, not me, and that *he'll* do the diagnosing. And I'm like, Hey doc, when someone's naked on the floor rolling around in cherry Jell-O, singing 'Smoke on the Water,' I don't need to pay some pinhead $750 an hour to tell *me* this gal's mental elevator doesn't stop at each floor. Diagnose *that*, doc!" The crowd erupted into applause.

"Please let this be over," Tracy prayed. And after 40 minutes, her prayers were finally answered. As the lights came up for the intermission and waiters started appearing like ants, Tracy turned to Brian. "Now I know why they push alcohol so much at these things. If these people weren't lit up like that sign outside, people like Woody wouldn't get *any* laughs."

Brian chuckled and shook his head. "He wasn't *that* bad, Tracy. Try and relax."

"I *am* relaxed. *He* wasn't funny."

"Fine, Tracy. The magic part will start in about 15 minutes; that will put you in a good mood."

Tracy smiled. "Oh Brian, I *am* in a good mood, really. But you know I hate being in situations where people are staring at me, social ones I mean."

"You were great, though; you got bigger laughs than Williams. And you weren't even trying. I mean, 'let me know when you've started'." Brian chuckled.

"I think that's a pretty standard heckler line; I stole it from somebody, I'm sure."

Brian changed the subject. "Do you want anything to eat or drink? They have appetizer-like food." Brian was scanning the menu. "How about soft pretzel sticks and port wine cheese spread?"

"Hey, that *does* sound good! And some water to wash it down. I'm out of ale."

"Sure. I just have to find a waiter." Brian looked around until he made eye contact with one of the apron-clad figures moving about. Shortly thereafter, their order for the food and two glasses of water was in place.

"I used to watch Montado the Great all the time," Tracy started, her enthusiasm quickly returning, after their waiter departed.

"Really?"

"Yeah, he was on Letterman and Saturday Night Live a lot, had his own primetime specials. My dad and I would watch him whenever we knew he was on. I'd ask Dad how they did this or did that, and he'd just smile and shake his head. Then Mom would say, 'You see, your father doesn't know everything,' and Dad would just start laughing." When she finished sharing her memories, she smiled at Brian warmly.

He smiled back. He was glad that Tracy could recount a memory of her father with a smile on her face. Peter Brubaker had been a detective with the Baltimore Police Department and had been killed when Brian and Tracy were dating during college. It was a painful memory for him—being there that terrible night when she got the news and watching her completely break down. But Tracy showed no signs of sadness when sharing her recollection tonight.

"I don't think I've seen him before," Brian offered. "I'm pretty pumped for it." They both looked up as the food and drink arrived. Brian spread the cheese on the warm pretzel sticks and handed one to Tracy. They "clinked" their snacks together in a makeshift toast. "Happy birthday, beautiful," Brian told her.

"I wouldn't want to be here with anyone else," she told him sincerely. And then the lights dimmed again.

"Ladies and gentlemen, *Merlin's Manor of Mirth and Magic* is proud to present, for your amusement and befuddlement, for your entertainment and bewilderment, the amazing Casper 'the Great' MONTADO!" The audience's cheers this time were accompanied by the sounds of percussion, as the stage curtain was lifted. The auditorium thumped and bumped. The gathered slowly quieted down until only the drumbeats emanating from the built-in speakers could be heard, and then suddenly the entire stage was

 Practice to Deceive

filled with smoke. As it dissipated, the figure of a man in top hat and cape, arms outstretched, was revealed. An old-fashioned entrance, of course, and Tracy loved it. Judging by the applause that followed the materialization, so did most everyone else.

"Good evening, my friends," Montado greeted. "Let me introduce you to my lovely assistant for the evening, the beautiful Karine!" A striking young woman came onstage. Long, dark hair bobbed on her shoulders as she moved. She was dressed in a one-piece black leotard-like costume, with fishnet stockings that reached up to her hips, and high-heeled black shoes. There were catcalls aplenty filling the air, now. Montado took her hand, and they both bowed. When Montado quickly pulled his hand away—seemingly, out of nowhere—appeared a bouquet of roses. The audience applauded enthusiastically. Then, Montado smiled and moved toward one of the manor's guests. "For you, my dear," he said, handing the flowers to Tracy. She was so overcome with delight and surprise that she almost cried. As the magician returned to the stage, Tracy turned to look at Brian. The smile she gave him told him he was officially untoasted.

The evening continued with the expected but nevertheless entertaining staples, including coin illusions, vanishing liquids, transformed items, and the ubiquitous Chinese linking rings, all performed with the accompaniment of bouncy pop songs or urgent-sounding instrumental pieces that played over the loud speakers. After almost 50 minutes of dazzling trickery, Montado announced, "For my next humble attempt to entertain you, my kind friends, I will need a volunteer from the audience." Hands immediately filled the room, even Tracy Brubaker's. Brian laughed; apparently she didn't mind the spotlight *all* of the time.

The spotlight was surveying the room when it fell on a sourpuss-faced gentleman seated just three tables over from Tracy. He was dressed in a sport jacket, white shirt, and dark pants. His black mustache matched his full head of hair. But what caught Tracy's attention about him was that he had on sunglasses. "How can he even see the show?" she whispered to her companion.

"Maybe he has an eye condition or something," Brian offered.

"How about you, sir?" Montado asked the stoic audience member, moving in his direction.

"I don't think so," was the response.

"Oh, please," the illusionist implored, extending an inviting arm.

"No."

Montado wasn't ready to give up. "My friend, you have no smile on your face. You are here to have fun, no? Please, my friend, join us!" The audience started cheering again, and Karine went over to the hesitant helper and led him up onstage. Karine positioned the unenthusiastic volunteer so that he was facing the audience. As Karine retreated to the back, Montado took his place next to his temporary assistant. "That is more like it! What is your name, my friend?" Montado asked.

"Conrad," he murmured.

"Friends, this is Conrad!" And there was more applause. Montado noticed the large M that was emblazoned on the left breast pocket of Conrad's sport coat. "Is this *my* jacket?" he asked. "I see it has my initial on it!" The audience chuckled.

"Uh…" Conrad started to say.

"My friend, I am kidding with you," Montado said chuckling himself, the audience joining in. "Now, Conrad, you and I have never met before, correct?"

"No, but why should they believe that?" And the audience burst into applause and laughter. Tracy thought she now had some competition.

"Ah, you are right, of course. I need you to be my witness for what I am going to do. Will you do that for me, my friend?"

"Sure, I guess so."

"Karine, please bring me the cards." The assistant handed Montado a deck of standard playing cards. Montado then handed the deck to Conrad.

"Will you please show our friends in the audience this deck, Conrad? Show them the fronts and backs, so that they can all see this is nothing more than an ordinary deck of playing cards." After Conrad complied, the Great One asked, "Will you now please shuffle these cards to your heart's content, and then hand them to back me when you are satisfied?"

"Sure," Conrad said, starting to relax. He vigorously mixed the cards, cutting the deck several times. Conrad then looked at Montado.

"Will you please now hand me the deck?" Conrad did as asked. "Karine, will you please give the blindfold to our friend here?" She complied. "Conrad, will you please look through the blindfold and confirm for the audience that you cannot indeed see anything but total blackness." Conrad placed the blindfold over his glasses.

He said, "I can't see nothing."

Tracy laughed loudly at Conrad's remark. "Of course you can't," she thought. "You're wearing sunglasses in a mostly dark room."

"Now, Karine, will you please place the blindfold over *my* eyes and tie it tightly," was the next instruction given and followed. Montado fanned the deck. "Now, Conrad, I would like you to select any card you wish from this deck. Do not say aloud what it is. Instead, reveal it to the audience; walk

                    Practice to Deceive

amongst our friends if you wish. After you have done so, please return to the stage." Conrad left the stage and started showing the card to various eager onlookers: it was the 10 of diamonds. Tracy grinned at Brian.

Despite the card being displayed on the monitors for all to see, someone called out, "Hey, over here!" Conrad grunted but made sure the caller could see. "Thanks, Conrad!" he said; several found the informality chuckle-worthy.

"He has returned to the stage," Karine announced.

"Excellent!" Montado said. "Karine, will you please show our friend the table on which he is to place the chosen card?" Karine brought forth a small table that stood almost four feet tall. She smiled and motioned to the table with her hand. Conrad placed the card, facedown, on the stand.

"Now, Conrad my friend, do you remember the card you picked?"

"Yes," he answered.

"And do you, my seated friends, recall the selection?"

The audience screamed "YES!" practically in unison.

"Excellent! Then are you all ready for me to tell you what card our friend Conrad chose?" Another affirmative set of screams erupted. "My friends, the card that Conrad chose and then showed to you is: the two of hearts!"

Conrad turned to look at the still blindfolded Montado. The audience looked at each other, not sure if this was part of the act or if the legendary illusionist had just screwed up. "By your silence, I surmise that I have guessed incorrectly?" Montado finally asked.

Conrad cleared his throat. "Uh, I'm afraid so, buddy." There were some uncomfortable giggles at Conrad's response.

"But I insist it *was* the two of hearts."

"No it wasn't, sir," Conrad confirmed, sounding as though he may have actually felt bad for the great illusionist.

"My friend, I believe you are mistaken."

"No, my card was the 10 of diamonds."

Montado started chuckling. "I am afraid that it is *you* who have made a mistake here, my friend."

"No way." Now Conrad sounded irritated.

"You could not possibly have selected the 10 of diamonds, because it is here with me in this deck I am holding in my hands." At that point, Montado removed the top card of the stack, still blindfolded, and revealed it for the audience to see: it was, indeed, the 10 of diamonds.

The audience started applauding madly. Conrad shook his head. "What the...?"

"Karine, please remind our dear friend Conrad of the card he selected." Karine, smiling, nodded and went to the table. She lifted the card so that it was now displayed on the monitors, although Tracy was close enough to see the card herself. It was, as Montado had insisted, the two of hearts. Again, the crowd applauded and loudly expressed their delight as Karine helped Montado remove his blindfold. Montado smiled broadly. "My friends please let us show our thanks to Conrad for his assistance here tonight!" And the applause continued as Conrad sat back down, shaking his head. Tracy felt like she was in heaven.

"That was *awesome*," she told Brian. He didn't remember the last time he had seen her so happy. He was so filled with emotion he couldn't speak. He just watched her as she continued applauding. For about 10 minutes after the traveling 10 of diamonds trick, Montado continued to dazzle his audience with his sleight of hand. Then, he moved to the center of the stage.

"My friends, I wish to sincerely thank you for your generosity and kindness tonight. You have warmed my heart with your affections. And you have all made it a truly wonderful evening for me. But alas, my friends, it is time for me to bid you all farewell." Now it was sounds of disappointment that were making the rounds. "Perhaps you will come see me again soon. But I *do* have one more experience to share with you." At that point, two men, clad in black, masks on their faces to match, came into view. They were pushing a large container, about 10 feet tall, dimensions slightly larger than an old-fashioned phone booth. A black tarp covered the structure completely. The assistants stopped moving when the large assembly was centered just behind Montado. "My friends, it is time for the water tank illusion!" As the crowd cheered, the two helpers started walking backward to the rear of the stage, pulling the tarp away, slowly revealing the water inside. Karine was preparing to take her position and was soon facing the fully exposed tank.

And then Karine screamed—a loud, bloodcurdling scream. The audience was staring at the tank. Tracy stood up. There in the tank was a body, motionless except for the movement caused by the water. A jacket was also floating freely, a coat bearing an M on its left pocket.

"My God, it's Conrad," Tracy said aloud to no one in particular.

"Do you think this is part of the trick?" Tracy overheard a woman ask her companion. Tracy turned briefly in the voice's direction long enough to scowl. This, however, was no illusion, no trick of light. Conrad—who just 10 minutes earlier was on the platform, in many ways the life of the party—was now floating lifeless for all to see. The curtain on Conrad's brief moment on life's stage had come down.

Chapter 2

"I can't keep 500 people here!" Pamela Houston told Tracy, trying to be heard over the commotion. "You hear all this noise? I could get sued for creating a firetrap if I lock all of the doors! You're a lawyer! You should know that!"

"The police are going to want at least the names and addresses of the people who were here," Tracy explained loudly to the manager of *Merlin's Manor of Mirth and Magic*. "If you could start collecting that info, maybe that will help get the people out of here quicker. They're all witnesses."

"Some people managed to leave already," Pamela countered. "Besides, we have credit card records that should take care of that."

"But what about those who paid cash, or the people for whom tickets were purchased by others? My fiancé paid for everything tonight, so you wouldn't know I was here if I just up and left." Pamela gave Tracy a scowl. "Look, I realize this is an awful situation, but somebody's been murdered. And if you don't have audience member information to share with the police, they will focus on the staff."

Pamela blinked. "Oh, I see you what you mean."

"I already called 911 and explained the situation. The police should be here any minute with some extra people to conduct interviews. If we can just keep people in the auditorium for a little bit longer, that will make things go a lot more smoothly."

Pamela sighed. "Alright, Ms. Brubaker, I'll have Richard make another announcement over the sound system."

"Great—and please call me Tracy." The attorney then left Pamela, who was standing right outside of the auditorium entrance doors, and went to check on her date.

"Tracy, where have you been?" Brian asked her. "It's pretty tense around here."

"Just trying to be helpful. Look, I need you to do me a favor."

"Which is?"

"Keep an eye out for the police. I'm going to go check on Karine; she was literally shaking when they took her to the back."

He looked at her skeptically. "You just want to poke around, don't you?"

"Huh? No—well, maybe a little bit."

"Uh-huh. Just sit down, Tracy. They're not going to let you back there anyway."

"Sure they will; I'm the birthday girl!" And then she smiled and left Brian to his own devices. Tracy moved to the side of the arena where she had noticed some activity. The area was shielded with thick black curtains. As soon as she moved one aside, a figure appeared.

"You can't come back here, ma'am," a stern voice said. Tracy turned to see a beefy, almost six-foot-tall fellow mostly dressed in black.

"Oh, you must be one of the men who pushed the tank onstage."

"Yeah."

"Hi, I'm Tracy, the woman who had the birthday."

The stern-faced fellow looked at her curiously and then smiled. "Oh right, I saw you on the monitor."

"And your name is…?"

"Kurt."

"Well, Kurt, I'm an attorney, and I'm kind of helping out the police before they get here. I'm pretty familiar with procedure in a case like this, so I'm doing what I can to preserve the crime scene and, hopefully, get everybody out of here as quickly as possible."

"Oh."

"I'm worried about Karine, though. I saw—we all saw—how upset she was. I was just hoping I could speak with her so maybe the police won't have to, at least, not right away. Do you think that would be okay?"

Kurt thought a moment. "Um, sure, I guess." He looked around. "Hey, Ron," he finally called out, "can you take this lady back to see Ms. Bowers? But if Ms. Bowers doesn't want to talk to her, bring her right back here."

"Sure," Ron said as he approached the curtain. He was obviously the other figure in black Tracy had seen earlier pushing the tank. "Follow me, lady," Ron said to her. She obliged. When they arrived at Karine's dressing room, Ron gently knocked on the door.

"Yes?" a voice finally called out.

"There's a lady here to see you, Ms. Bowers." Tracy leaned over and whispered to Ron. "She says her name's Tracy and she thought you could use someone to talk to."

The door opened. Karine stood there with a tear-streaked face, tissue in hand. She studied Tracy a moment and then smiled. "Aren't you the woman whose birthday is today?"

"That's me. I just wanted to see how you're doing."

Karine managed a half-smile. "It's okay, Ron, she can come in."

"Sure, Ms. Bowers." And then Ron turned and left.

"Come in, Tracy, sit down." Tracy looked around the neat and tidy room for a place to sit. Her eyes, however, gravitated to the large framed movie poster that hung on the wall. She moved toward it.

"Is this an original poster?" Tracy asked.

                    Practice to Deceive

"What?" Karine responded. Then she saw Tracy studying the framed decoration. "Oh, no, I don't think so."

"I have a poster of *The Maltese Falcon* in my living room," Tracy told Karine. "I used to watch classic movies with my dad, and I'm still a fan—mainly of crime-type stuff. But this *42ⁿᵈ Street* sheet you have here is a beauty."

Karine managed another smile. "My brother gave that to me on my sixteenth birthday. I bring it with me everywhere. You see, I wanted to be a dancer once, had dreams of making it to Broadway someday."

"Oh, really?" Tracy asked. "Do you do any dancing now?"

"Oh no," Karine said quickly. "You see, there was a real big problem: I'm not a good dancer at all." Karine laughed at herself, and then she started crying again. When she sat down on the small sofa, Tracy went over to Karine and put her arm around her.

"I'm sorry, Karine. How awful that shock must have been for you."

Karine shook her head. "I don't know why I'm so upset. I mean, I just can't stop crying. That's crazy, isn't it?"

Tracy tilted her head slightly. "Of course not, Karine. There's no right or wrong way to react to seeing what you saw." Tracy pulled Karine closer, and then there was a knock on the door.

"Yes?" Karine sobbed. The door opened as a jingling man, some drink on the rocks in his hand, slightly entered. "Oh hi, Greg."

"Hi Karine. Who's this with you?"

"Oh, forgive me," Tracy said standing up. "My name's Tracy; I'm just here to be the proverbial shoulder to cry on."

Greg moved toward Tracy. "I'm Greg Bowers, Karine's brother."

"Hey, great poster."

"Huh? Oh, that. Thanks." Bowers smiled and then stepped toward his sister. He handed her the drink he was carrying, something that was no doubt much stronger than ginger ale. "Here Karine, I think you need this."

She smiled weakly while accepting the alcohol. She emptied the container rather quickly, making a sour face as she did so. "Thanks, Greggy."

"Sure." Greg looked at Tracy and then back at his sister. "The cops are here now."

Tracy perked up. "Oh, I should go talk to them." Tracy rose and started toward the door. "Nice meeting you guys. I hope you feel better soon, Karine." And then Tracy left the siblings alone.

"Now who exactly *was* that again?" Greg asked, returning his attention to his sister.

"She's the one who had the birthday tonight."

"Oh."

"She was just trying to be nice." Karine gulped and looked at her empty glass. "I don't suppose you could get me another one of these?"

"You bet," Bowers answered, taking the glass. "I'll be right back." Karine watched her brother leave and then turned to look at the poster on her wall. And then she started crying again.

"Where are the lead detectives?" Tracy asked Brian as she returned to her seat. She had noted several uniformed officers already talking to various patrons, taking statements and getting information. In short order, crime lab personnel were all over the stage area, working their own magic.

"Uh, I think they're in the lobby. They were looking for you not too long ago."

"I'll find them."

"Tracy—"

"I'll be right back, Brian. Keep an eye on my hat and flowers, will ya hon?" And then she was quickly moving toward the doorway.

"I'll wait here, then," Brian said to himself as he looked around.

Upon entering the doorway, Tracy saw who she was looking for: two figures in suits were speaking with Pamela Houston. Pamela, in turn, saw Tracy. "There she is!" Pamela pointed in Tracy's direction. The two inquisitors turned and looked at the attorney as she approached them.

"Hi guys," Tracy said. Then she came to a stop as she recognized one of the faces. "Hi, Detective Lucas, remember me?"

Detective Jim Lucas nodded. "I'm not likely to forget you." Lucas turned to his partner. "Debbie, this is Tracy Brubaker; Tracy, Detective Deborah Price."

Tracy extended her hand. "Nice to know you, Detective Price." Price smiled and shook hands.

"Nice to meet you too." Price looked at Lucas and then back at Tracy. "I think I've heard about you. Your father was Detective Tanner's partner, right?"

"Yes," Tracy said. "Detective Tanner and I are pretty close."

Price nodded. "I can certainly understand that."

"So why are you here tonight, Tracy?" Lucas asked.

"I *was* on a date with my fiancé. It's my birthday."

"Hey, happy birthday," Price smiled.

"Yeah," Lucas said. "Where's your fiancé now?"

"He's inside guarding my hat and flowers. You might remember him, Detective Lucas: Brian Shane."

Lucas blinked. "You're engaged to Shane?"

"Yup." Tracy turned to Price. "Once upon a time, Detective Price, Detective Lucas here thought Brian was a killer. I had to set him straight on that."

"Really?" Price asked grinning.

"Never mind all that," Lucas said. "Now: you were one of the people who called 911?" Tracy nodded. "And you managed to keep most of the customers here?" Another nod. "Okay, why don't you tell us what happened, then."

"The victim, Conrad, was up onstage helping with a card trick. Ten or so minutes later, Montado's—he's the magician—assistants were bringing in the water tank, which at this point was completely covered by a black tarp. When they pulled the tarp away, there in the tank, floating, was Conrad."

Price was taking notes. "How did you know it was Conrad? Wasn't it hard to make out?"

"The jacket that was floating in the tank had an M on it; it was the jacket Conrad was wearing onstage earlier." The detectives looked at each other. Tracy furrowed her brow. "Okay—what's going on?"

"Well, for one thing, there was no identification on the body," Price offered. Lucas looked at her sternly. Price must have seen the look out of the corner of her eye, because she turned to face him. "Oh come on, Jim, she's a witness who has a lot on the ball. She'll keep things quiet if we ask her to."

Tracy smiled; it seemed as if she'd just made a new friend on the police force. "You bet, detectives, mum's the word if you tell me."

Lucas cleared his throat. "We don't think this guy's name was Conrad."

"Why not?"

"He was wearing a disguise," Price answered.

"What do you mean?"

"In addition to the jacket floating in the tank, we also found a wig of black hair, a black mustache, and sunglasses. All of those things were floating too."

Tracy blinked. "So *that's* what was up with the sunglasses. I wondered about that. So you're going to run his prints, then?" Price nodded.

"Well, keep all this quiet for now, Tracy," Lucas told her.

"Sure. So you guys know what killed him, yet?"

"He was in a water tank," Lucas said, as if the answer to her question should be obvious.

Tracy pursed her lips. "Yes, but was he already dead when he was put in there is my question."

Price grinned again. "There *was* a rather large bump on the back of his head. But we won't know if that killed him or if he drowned until we get the ME's report."

Lucas shook his head. "That's private too."

"Yeah—I figured that out myself, Detective Lucas."

This time Price actually laughed. She said, "I think I'm going to enjoy seeing you two working together."

"Working together?" Lucas repeated. "I don't think so." He turned to Tracy. "You're a witness; you have no client. Therefore, you have no rights beyond those of any other witness."

Tracy folded her arms and narrowed her eyes. "Don't be a grump. I'm just trying to help." They stared silently at each other until a uniformed officer approached Lucas. Tracy saw the name Westmore on his ID plate.

"Detective Lucas…," Westmore started.

"Yes, what is it?"

"I found someone who may have seen something relevant to the investigation."

Tracy grinned.

"Alright, let's go speak with him," Lucas said. "Or is it a she?"

"It's a him, or it's a he… Uh, male, Detective."

Now Tracy laughed, as did Price. Lucas looked at them. He was not pleased. "Let's go," he grunted, and Price and Tracy followed Lucas. Westmore led the trio to a front-row seat that was close to the security curtains.

"This is Mr. Lindstrom, Detective Lucas," Westmore said.

Lindstrom stood up. "Harry Lindstrom," he said as he and Lucas shook hands.

"Jim Lucas. What did you see here tonight, Mr. Lindstrom?"

"Do you want me to tell you all about the show, or what I told this officer that seemed to be important?"

"Start with the latter."

"Sure. I was sitting here watching the monitor. That Conrad fellow had just sat down. Then, not long after that, I notice him standing over here." Lindstrom started pointing in the direction of the curtain. "He stays there a bit. And then he disappears behind the curtain." Lindstrom shook his head. "So I figured this guy *was* part of the act, after all. And then the tank came out and, well, I guess now I don't know what to think."

"How long was he standing by the curtain until he snuck back there?" Tracy called out.

Lucas turned, not having realized she had followed them. "Tracy, what the hell? You can go now."

Price spoke up. "That's an interesting question, though. Can you answer it, Mr. Lindstrom?"

 Practice to Deceive

"Uh, a minute, maybe; I'm not really sure."

"That's weird," Tracy said. "I mean, if he was part of the act, you'd think he'd be stealthier than standing around so long; it increased his risk of being seen." Lindstrom, Lucas, and Price looked at her. Tracy shrugged her shoulders. "Just sayin'…"

"Well, stop it," Lucas said. He turned back to his witness. "Anything else after that, Mr. Lindstrom? For example, did someone else enter or exit? Did you see Conrad after he went back there?"

"No," Lindstrom said, shaking his head. "That's it. I didn't see anyone else. Of course, I was focused on the show."

Lucas nodded. "Okay, Mr. Lindstrom. Thank you very much. I'd appreciate it if you kept this information to yourself for the time being."

"Certainly," Lindstrom agreed.

"If Officer Westmore has your contact information, you're free to go."

Lindstrom smiled and quickly moved to make his exit. Lucas then noticed Tracy was still among them. "Tracy, why don't you find your fiancé and the two of you can go. I know where to find you if I need you. Go have a birthday dessert or something."

Tracy made a hurtful expression. "What? I want to stay *here* and help."

"No, Tracy. This is a police investigation, and, with all due respect to you and your late father, you are *not* a cop. Now I've given you a lot of leeway here already, so don't push it. Go home."

"But it's my birthday," she said pleadingly. Price chuckled.

"Tracy: GO!" Lucas ordered, pointing to the group of seats where Brian was still waiting.

"Shucks," she pouted. And Price started laughing again. "Um, Detective Price, can I give you one of my cards? I mean, just in case you have more questions for me."

"Sure, Tracy. And I suppose I can give you one of mine, just in case you remember anything."

"Supreme! Thanks, Detective." Tracy's mood was greatly improved as she headed back to her date.

"I really like her," Tracy heard Price tell Lucas. "Why are you being such a jerk?"

"Hey, I'm not being a jerk. I'm following procedure."

"You were being hostile when there was no call for it. You know she's helped us before, right?"

"Detective, let's just do our jobs."

"Fine—let's do just that. And leave your personal history out of it, if that's why you behaved like you did, I mean."

Lucas shook his head. Nope: Price warming to Tracy Brubaker was not a good thing, as far as he was concerned. Not a good thing at all.

"Time to leave, honey," Tracy told Brian as she gathered together her hat and flowers. "I'm not wanted here."

Brian looked at her curiously. "What does that mean?"

"They have no more questions for me, so we're being evicted."

"Why are you bothered by it? You seem so—bothered."

"I thought they might let me stay and help with the interviews or something."

"Why would they do that?"

"No reason other than I could have helped them."

"Tracy, if you're thinking what I think you're thinking, then let's get out of here now."

Tracy looked at him, slightly annoyed. "Well, let's go then, if you're in such a hurry," she huffed.

"I've been sitting here for like an hour and a half," Brian complained. Tracy just shook her head and started for the exit. Her fiancé, still not sure what was going on with her, followed.

"I need a client," Tracy finally said, as Brian was navigating the traffic in the magic house's parking lot.

"You have plenty of clients," Brian said, confused.

"No, that's not what I'm talking about. I need a client connected with this case."

"What, the Conrad murder?"

"Yes."

"What? Why?"

"I want to know how all this ends, and unless I have a good reason to be poking around, I won't be allowed to."

"Tracy, you're not a cop."

"Yeah, and?"

"Well, the cops will figure this out."

"Oh, I'm sure they will. But I was *there*, Brian. I mean, right in front of me, a murder was committed. How often is that likely to happen in one's life?"

Brian turned to face her, a mild look of shock on his face. "I don't believe this," he said. "Tracy, don't you think you've had enough involvement with homicides this past year to last you the rest of your life?"

Tracy looked at him. "This is different."

Brian frowned. "That's what you said the last time."

 Practice to Deceive

Tracy frowned back. "So what if I did? It *was* different. And this time is different from the last. So what's your point?"

Brian tilted his head back and let out a large sigh. "My point is that you keep getting involved in these things when you shouldn't be."

"Hey, *you* brought me here, remember? I didn't show up on my own accord looking for trouble."

Brian shook his head. "So this is my fault?"

Tracy gave him a look of exasperation. "Fault has nothing to do with it." Tracy took a deep breath. "Look honey, maybe we were meant to be here tonight."

"We're here tonight because it's your birthday and I thought you'd like it."

"But still, maybe I was meant to be here so I could witness the crime and then help the police."

"Oh Tracy—"

"I've helped before; you know I have."

"Sure I do Tracy, but—"

"But what? Why not help again? They had me there: ready, willing, and able, and that Lucas jerk just sent me away. How ungrateful, how unappreciative can a person be? And besides, it's my birthday!"

"Um, technically it isn't, anymore."

"Technically, schmectically; he should have let me help out."

Brian shook his head. "You know what? I don't want to talk about this, anymore. I understand you want to play detective again, maybe brush shoulders with Montado. But that's not happening this time, because, as you've already so correctly pointed out, you have no client." Brian returned to looking out the window. They hadn't moved in almost five minutes. "Damn, I wish we could get out of here!" he yelled abruptly.

Tracy was looking straight ahead too. "I need a client in this case," she said again. Then she looked over at her fiancé. "Brian, hasn't it occurred to you what took place here tonight?"

Brian had a mild look of panic on his face as he turned and asked, "What are you talking about now?"

She grinned. "We saw a murder happen in a place of illusion and trickery, a place where you can't trust your own eyes, where reality is not what it appears to be."

"HUH?!"

"Brian, tell me, who, under the apparent circumstances, could not possibly have committed the murder?"

He thought a moment. "Uh, you and me?"

Tracy laughed. "Oh, stop; I'm serious. Who has the absolutely perfect alibi?"

Brian wriggled his nose. "Oh, everybody who was onstage or in the audience from the time Conrad sat back down until he was found."

"EXACTLY!"

"So, what?" Then his eyes widened. "Are you saying the killer is someone who was onstage?"

"Why not?"

"Because that's impossible, that's why not."

"No, Brian, not impossible. How did that 10 of diamonds become a two of hearts? It didn't; it's a trick. You get me?"

"Tracy, it's not the same thing. I can see how you could palm a card or something, but a body? Come on!"

"Well, I know something you don't."

"Oh really, what's that?"

"I can't tell you."

"You can't… Oh I give up!"

"I'm sorry, Brian. I promised the cops to keep my mouth shut."

"A first time for everything, I guess."

"OH! You are so toast right now!"

"Sure, whatever."

Tracy twisted her lips. "Why was Conrad's jacket off?"

"What is it, now?"

"Why do you think the killer took off Conrad's jacket before dumping him in the tank?"

"I…maybe they were looking for something in the jacket."

Tracy turned her body 90 degrees to face her fiancé. She was smiling. "That's it, Brian, get those gray cells working!" she said excitedly. "I mean, asking questions—that's what both cops and lawyers do, right? If someone just hit Conrad on the head and put him in the tank, maybe to hide the body while the killer made his escape, then why remove the coat? Like you said, did Conrad have something in his inside pocket?"

"How do you know he was hit on the head?"

"I can't tell you."

Brian rolled his eyes. "Well, why would you have to remove the whole coat to get to the inside pocket, anyway? You could just reach in and check."

Tracy put her hands together and practically squealed. "GREAT POINT! So where does *that* leave us?"

"Uh, I'm not sure."

"Isn't this fun, dear heart?"

  Practice to Deceive

Brian started laughing. "You know what? Next year, we're staying in. We're going to invite people over and have one of those role-play murder games. That way, you can play detective in the comfort and safety of your own home."

"Hey, that sounds great!"

"On second thought, knowing your luck, someone would probably really get killed, which would mean one of our friends is a killer, and that wouldn't be good. Maybe we'll just read murder mysteries to each other or something."

Tracy laughed and then leaned over and kissed Brian. "I'm sorry, hon. I can't help it. Why was his coat off?"

Brian smiled and sighed. "You're right, Tracy, you need a client." They kissed again until the honking from the car behind them got their attention. The vehicles in front were finally moving.

It was almost three in the early hours of Saturday when Brian was sent on his way. "In spite of everything, I had a wonderful birthday," Tracy said to him. They were embracing by the doorway, as they did almost every night since they started seeing each other again. "I love you."

"I still feel like I can't take you anywhere," he joked. "But you know I love you too."

"Call me tomorrow when you've finished your chores," she teased. "Now—"

"It's time for me to shoo; I know the drill."

"May 21, 2016…then you won't be doing this, anymore; leaving me, I mean."

"That's more than a year off," he said quietly.

"I know. Time will fly by, I'm sure."

Brian sighed. "I doubt it. I'll call you tomorrow, I guess."

"You 'guess'?" she asked teasingly.

He smiled and kissed her again, and then exited without saying another word. She gulped. Her goal was to remain chaste for the rest of their engagement, something that, at times, would no doubt prove to be a great challenge. Tonight, for example, she wanted the intimacy they had previously experienced, the togetherness that comes with fully joined bodies. It had been a wonderful evening, despite the crime, and she felt very close to him. But with marriage and, hopefully, children, on the horizon, she had recommitted to her Catholicism. She had always been a practicing Catholic, but she had not necessarily followed the faith's teachings in all areas. As a result, she knew the pleasures and the feelings of closeness during and afterward that physical intimacy brought, having previously given in to her desire and curiosity. She missed this. And the truth was, if Brian pushed the issue, she could see herself giving in. Luckily, he seemed to understand her struggle and had been, to put it delicately, well behaved, as of late. She sighed as she started toward her bedroom to change for bed. Shortly thereafter, staring at the ceiling, she did some quick math: 390 days to the wedding, give or take. That's what? Say, 400 times 24—that's about 9,600 hours. But we really only spend about 5 hours a day together, if that, during the week, so that's five times 400, or 2,000 hours. Of course, that goes up if you factor in weekends. Tracy turned over on her side and closed her eyes. She was hoping she could shave at least 6 hours off the total before she awoke later that morning.

The murder at *Merlin's Manor of Mirth and Magic* was all over the news when Tracy turned on her television around 8:30 Saturday morning. The police were being secretive about their investigation, as one would expect; very few details had been revealed. There wasn't even an official confirmation of who died, under the standard "identification of the victim being withheld pending notification of next of kin" excuse. Tracy shook her head. How desperately she wanted to know what was going on. Then, she grinned. She went over to her kitchen counter and picked up the business card she had placed there last night. She dialed Detective Deborah Price's number. "Debbie Price," a tired voice answered on the second ring.

"Good morning, Detective Price, it's Tracy Brubaker."

"Hi Tracy, sleep much last night?"

"About five hours or so, I think. Have you even been home yet?"

"No, but I didn't come on duty until four yesterday afternoon, so I have some energy left in me."

"Are you heading home now?"

"Maybe half an hour; depends on what we find before I decide to call it quits for the day."

"I see." Tracy paused briefly and then decided to come to the point. "So, are there any new developments you can share? Mum being the operative word and all."

Tracy heard Price chuckle. "Well, yes, but…"

"I won't tell anyone you told me, not even Lucas, if you want. I didn't tell my own fiancé when he interrogated me—how's that for remaining strong?" There was some more laughing from the other end.

"Okay, I mean it will be released shortly, anyway."

"What will?"

"The identity of the victim."

"Oh, DO tell!"

"We got a hit off the prints: Zachary Granger. Does that name mean anything to you?"

"I don't think so."

"Thirteen years ago, he and two others robbed the Washburn Community Bank in Gaithersburg, Maryland. The driver got away; the other guy was shot and killed when he opened fire on officers who responded to the silent alarm. So, the courts wound up giving Granger 15 years. He was paroled last November, after serving 12 of it."

"So they never caught the driver?"

"Nope."

"And Granger didn't give him up?"

"Nope. In fact, he said he hardly knew the guy."

"Did he tell the investigators *anything* about him?"

"Let me see here: guy was short, in his forties, and went by the name Buzz."

"Buzz?"

"Yup."

"Hmm…I guess the crew didn't get away with anything."

"Almost $90,000."

"What?! How?"

"This gunman, Christopher Pyle, tossed some bags into the awaiting car through an open window. When the officers approached, he turned and fired on them. And that's when the driver took off, leaving Pyle to fend for himself."

"Yikes."

"Now, Granger didn't have a gun on him, and, supposedly, Pyle shouldn't have brought a loaded one, either; that's what Granger told the investigating officers, anyway. Granger was lucky Pyle didn't kill anyone. Otherwise, he'd probably still be inside."

"Well, maybe he would have been safer behind bars, as it turns out."

"Yes, I guess you're right."

"And none of the money ever turned up?"

"Some of it did."

"How much?"

"About $40,000 or so. When the getaway car was found, there was some money in the back. I guess the driver just grabbed what he could and took off."

"But the other 50 thou didn't surface."

"Right. The driver probably contacted some money launderer so he at least got some cash out of the whole thing."

"Uh-huh. So, were Granger and Pyle longtime pals, or were they strangers to each other, like this Buzz fellow?"

"Actually, they were buddies. In fact, they had very few other friends; at least everyone the cops talked to, at the time, who supposedly knew them said they didn't *really* know them."

"I get you. If the so-called friends did know something, they weren't talking."

"You got it."

"So, Detective Price, do you think Granger may have been looking for Buzz?"

"Hard to say, at this point; it hasn't been that long that we've had all of this info. I've been reviewing the information and reports that the Gaithersburg police scanned and e-mailed to us."

"Of course, these things take time. I understand. So, do you have any suspects?"

There was silence. "I'm sorry, Tracy, I'm not going to discuss *that* with you. I hope you understand that too."

Tracy was disappointed. It sounded like maybe they were looking at someone in particular. "Oh, I completely understand, Detective. You've been very kind to speak with me, and I am very grateful. Thank you."

"Sure, Tracy; like I said, the name will be out soon enough, so it's not like I told you anything you wouldn't have learned about eventually."

"I still am grateful. Maybe I can buy you a beer sometime."

Price laughed. "Sure, that might be nice."

"Oh my God!" Tracy shouted suddenly.

"What? What is it, Tracy?" Price asked her, concern in her voice.

"I can't believe I forgot."

"Forgot what?"

"Last night, before the show, I got some drinks at the bar. There was a man there I talked to. He said he was in banking and that he was from Gaithersburg."

"Are you serious?" Price asked enthusiastically.

"Completely. Let me think—his name was Dan something—Dan Scarborough."

There was silence again. "Dan Scarborough," Price repeated.

"Yes, I'm sure that was it."

Price cleared her throat. "Tracy, Dan Scarborough was one of the bank employees on duty when Granger and Pyle robbed Washburn Community Bank 13 years ago."

 Practice to Deceive

After Detective Deborah Price received Tracy's news about Dan Scarborough, she wanted the eager attorney to come down to BPD and share her information more formally. Price, however, didn't want Lucas to know she had confided in someone not officially connected with the Granger murder. Tracy readily agreed. But she had to make a phone call, first. "Oh Tracy, not again," Brian whined.

"I'm doing my civic duty, love. They just want me to make a statement about the guy who bought me drinks."

"Wait—what? Who bought you drinks? What are you talking about?"

"Oh, this guy I spoke with at the bar last night paid for our drinks."

"Why?"

"Because I like the Marx Brothers."

Brian paused. "Tracy, do you know how bizarre that sounds? You're lucky I'm not the jealous type."

"Well, don't start being that type now. Anyway, this guy who paid for our ales has a history of sorts with the victim. I can't really talk about that right now. I have to go."

"Uh, okay. I guess you'll call me when you're all done."

"Of course I will. I gotta shoo. I love you, Brian."

"I love you too." And there was silence. "You still there, Tracy?" Apparently she wasn't. Brian shook his head. He looked around his empty apartment. And then he smiled and laughed. "What can I do?" he thought. "She'll probably solve this case before the cops do, anyway." And then he sat on his couch and turned on his television. For the life of him, he couldn't remember what he used to do on Saturday mornings before Tracy reentered his life.

Lucas had finished listening to Tracy's tale of Dan Scarborough. Then he looked at Tracy and Price skeptically. "So you just suddenly remembered this guy and called Price about it?"

Tracy hesitated; she wasn't one to lie if she could avoid it. Then Price showed mercy and spoke. "Look, Jim, she called about the case. I didn't tell her anything that isn't going to be made public in the near future. And it's a good thing, too, because now we can get a jump on Scarborough."

"Uh-huh," Lucas mumbled. "I guess we should go talk to him sooner rather than later."

"Yup," Tracy agreed.

Lucas stared at Tracy. "Wait a minute, *you're* not going. As I've stated repeatedly, you have no business sticking your nose in this thing."

But Tracy had planned her strategy as to how to address this minor point during her drive to the station. "I should go in case he requests legal advice."

"What?" Lucas practically shouted. "He's not under arrest."

"But what if he confesses? Wouldn't you want to protect your case against him by having someone like me there? I can make sure his rights are protected and that you guys are covered too." Price started laughing. "And besides," Tracy added, "I can positively ID him."

"That would actually be a bad thing, Tracy," Lucas told her, "if we would need you for a lineup and all. But then I think you know that."

"Well…"

"Let's go, Debbie," Lucas said, rising.

All right, Tracy thought; time to get tough. "Okay then," Tracy sighed. "I sure hope someone from your office hasn't leaked anything to the press yet. I mean, it would be a real shame if Scarborough got word of who died last night. He might clam up, especially if he spoke with someone who told him he should keep his mouth shut."

Lucas stopped in his tracks. He looked at Price, who was trying to maintain a straight face, and then met Tracy's eyes. "You wouldn't dare."

"What are you talking about? I never said *I* would do something like that. It's just those pesky anonymous calls can sometimes make your job *so* much harder."

"You're blackmailing a police officer!" Lucas yelled. And then Price could no longer retain her composure.

Price said, "Let's all go, then. If Scarborough doesn't want her there, she can wait out in the car. Right, Tracy?"

"Sure—I'll wait patiently in the car if I have to."

"I…oh, the hell with it. Let's go, then!" And Lucas stormed out with Price and Tracy following close behind.

Dan Scarborough lived in a single-family home that must have been at least 3,000 square feet in size and sat on two acres of perfectly maintained lawn; trees were plentiful. Lucas pulled into the long driveway that led up to the two-car garage. All exited the unmarked car. Lucas turned to Tracy. "Now, listen, you don't say a *word*. *We* ask any questions. And if Scarborough wants you to leave, you leave. Are we clear?"

"Yes, Daddy," Tracy said humbly. "If I'm good, maybe you'll get me an ice cream on the way home."

Lucas just shook his head. "Go ahead, keep it up."

"Let's go," Price said, taking the lead. Tracy stood behind them as Price pushed the doorbell button. The door soon opened; Tracy recognized the opener immediately but said nothing.

"Yes?" Scarborough asked.

"I'm Detective Lucas, this is Detective Price," Lucas began. "And this is Tracy Brubaker, the woman you met last night." Scarborough looked at her, and then he smiled.

"Oh sure, I remember you."

"Hi Dan," Tracy smiled.

"What's going on here, Tracy?"

Lucas frowned. "Have you heard what happened at *Merlin's Manor of Mirth and Magic* last night?"

"Oh, yes, I have; it's all over the news."

"I understand you were there for the 7:00 p.m. show, and that you spent some time at the bar afterward."

"Yes, that's all true."

"What time did you leave, Mr. Scarborough?"

"Well, let me think. It was shortly after the 9:30 p.m. show started, when the lobby was finally emptying out."

"I see," Lucas continued. "And where did you go after you left the club?"

"Straight home."

"What time did you get home?"

"Uh, I guess between a quarter of 11 and 11. The news hadn't started yet. Should I get my wife? She might have a better idea of the time. The kids were here last night, too, but they're both out right now."

"No, Mr. Scarborough. I don't think that will be necessary at this point."

Scarborough scanned the faces in front of him. "I don't think I understand. I thought the murder occurred during the later show. Are you talking to everyone who was at the earlier show too?"

"No sir," Lucas said.

"Well, why are you here then?"

"May we come in for a moment, Mr. Scarborough?" Price asked. "We'll tell you exactly why we're here."

"Oh, okay; I guess I've been rude not inviting you in already. Please, come in."

"Do you want Ms. Brubaker here? I can ask her to wait in the car, if you'd like," Lucas said.

Scarborough gave Lucas a confused look. "Why should I mind? Of course she can come in too."

"Thanks, Dan," Tracy said giving Lucas a brief glare. She wanted to stick her tongue out at him, too; how immature she felt, sometimes. Scarborough led them to the family living room. A white sofa was centered between two matching recliners, collectively forming a semicircle around the fireplace. A big-screen television monitor was mounted above the hearth, with a table centered between it and the sofa. The three guests seated themselves on the couch while Scarborough sat on one of the single chairs. The noise of the arriving visitors brought in Scarborough's wife, who came from upstairs.

"Who are our guests, Dan?"

"Oh, these are detectives and a nice young lady I met last night. You're an attorney, right?"

"Yes, Dan. I'm Tracy Brubaker, Mrs. Scarborough." She stood up and went to shake the hand of her hostess.

"Oh, call me Sheila."

"Okay, Sheila. She turned to the still-seated officers. He is Detective Lucas, and she is Detective Price." They nodded after the introduction.

"What's all this about?"

"They're here about what happened last night at the magic show," her husband answered her.

"Oh, wasn't that awful?" Sheila asked with a horrified look on her face.

"May we speak with your husband alone for a few moments, Mrs. Scarborough?" Lucas asked. "We shouldn't be too long." Tracy rolled her eyes. Lucas lacked people skills, in her opinion.

"Oh, of course. I'll go back upstairs, then. Call if you need me."

"Thanks, dear," Scarborough said.

Lucas began, "We've identified the victim, Mr. Scarborough."

"Oh?"

"Yes, his name was Zachary Granger. Recognize the name?"

Scarborough went pale; he swallowed hard. "Granger?" he asked, almost whispering.

"Yes," Price confirmed. "Did you see him last night?"

"I...I..."

"Just tell them the truth, Dan," Tracy said sympathetically. "They're not here to hurt you. I can advise you, if you want me to." Lucas exhaled loudly. Tracy just ignored him.

"Thank you, Tracy," Scarborough said. He turned toward the detectives. "I guess I should just tell you everything."

Price nodded. "Yes, Mr. Scarborough. That would be the best thing you could do. Maybe we wouldn't even need to bother you again with this."

     Practice to Deceive

Scarborough cleared his throat. Then he whispered, "Look, I told my wife I was going with a business associate last night and that's why she couldn't come with me this time."

"Oh?" Lucas asked. "And who did you go with, then?"

Scarborough looked at each of them. "Granger."

Eyes collectively widened. "You were there with Granger?" Lucas asked.

"Yes. He bought tickets for us. He contacted me a couple of months ago, said we needed to talk. He said if I turned him down, he'd go to the cops with what he knew. I didn't know what he was talking about, and I told him that. Then he brought Sheila and the kids into it; I thought he was threatening to *hurt* them. So, I agreed to meet him."

"And he picked the magic place?" Lucas asked.

"Yes."

"Do you know why?"

"No, I have no idea why he picked there."

"Okay, tell us, then, what you and Granger talked about. What was it he was threatening you with?"

Scarborough looked at the floor. Then he looked at Tracy. She smiled at him. "Um, Granger said I stole some money."

"*You* stole some money…" Lucas repeated.

"Yes. You see…well, you're here, so obviously you know that I was working at the bank on the day of the robbery. I guess Granger remembered me. They were wearing masks when they were inside, so I didn't recognize him until later, after the cops removed his mask, I mean."

"Wait," Tracy interrupted. "You recognized Granger after he'd been unmasked?"

"Yes, I had turned him down for a home loan a few weeks before the robbery."

"Oh," Tracy nodded.

"I was a loan officer at the time, you understand. Anyway, I thought he might still be mad at me for that. But it turned out he thought I stole some money."

"How much?" Price asked.

Scarborough gulped. "About $50,000." The detectives exchanged glances. "But I didn't! I swear I didn't! I don't know why he thought that I took any money!"

"Calm down, Mr. Scarborough," Lucas said with little emotion. "So he invites you out, makes the accusation, and then what happened?"

"Well, I told him I didn't steal the money. And I think he may have started to believe me."

"Why do you say that?" Price asked.

"Because just before the start of the show, he said he had someone else he had to talk to about things. Then he just left me. I sat there and waited for him, but he never came back. I was still so nervous after the show that I went to the bar to have a few drinks. That helped some."

"Did he give a clue as to who this someone else *was*?" Lucas asked.

Scarborough shook his head. "No. I'm sorry. If I knew, I would tell you." Scarborough looked around the room. "Well, maybe I wouldn't."

"Why not?" Lucas asked.

Tracy answered. "Because, obviously, Dan thinks this other person probably killed Granger. Maybe he's scared the same thing will happen to him or someone in his family." Scarborough nodded.

Lucas gave Tracy another glare and shake of his head. He returned his attention to the homeowner. "Has anyone threatened you today, Mr. Scarborough?"

"Oh no, nothing like that. Look, can you keep my name out of this? I know you put everything in your reports and all, but can you keep this quiet with respect to the media?"

"We can keep it quiet for now, most likely," Price offered. "But I can't make any promises for the long run."

"Dan," Tracy said, leaning in from her chair, "if anyone does call or threaten you, call the police. If not them, you can call me, and I can act as your liaison."

Lucas cleared his throat. "Let's not get ahead of ourselves here," he said. "Did you see Granger interact with anyone else last night, Mr. Scarborough? Another customer, one of the employees, perhaps?"

"No, I don't think so—unless you count the drink he ordered from the waiter."

"What drink was that?" Lucas asked.

"Club soda."

"Where were you and Granger sitting, Dan?" Tracy asked.

"Toward the back, right side of the stage if you're facing it."

"So you didn't see exactly where Granger went when he left?"

"No. I was just sitting there wondering what I was going to do. I really wasn't paying attention to anything going on. Before I knew it, the show had started. I just sat there, like I told you."

"Thanks, Dan," Tracy said.

The detectives each removed a business card and handed it to Scarborough. Tracy did the same. "If you think of anything else, Mr. Scarborough, please call us," Price said soothingly. "And if you do get some strange calls, let us know that, too. We'll do our best to keep you out of it, as I said."

Scarborough sighed and then stood up. "Well, thank you all for being so kind. If I think of something, I promise to call you." Scarborough rubbed his eyes. "I think I should go talk to my wife about all of this now."

Tracy moved close enough to Scarborough so she could rub his arm. "It will be okay, Dan, these detectives will find who did this. Try not to worry."

Scarborough smiled. "You're a very nice young lady. It's a pity you're so far away; the bank could always use good attorneys." Tracy blushed slightly.

"Let's go," Lucas said sternly. "I'm sure Mr. Scarborough has things he needs to take care of." Lucas then started moving toward the entrance hallway, followed by Price. Tracy gave Scarborough another quick smile and then followed suit. Soon, the visitors were headed back to the city.

"Alright, Tracy," Price said, breaking the silence. "What are you thinking?"

"Huh?" Tracy asked innocently.

"Come on, Tracy, I realize we've known each other for less than 24 hours, but you've awfully quiet back there. It's deafening, if you get my meaning."

Tracy laughed. "I doubt Detective Lucas cares what I think. I mean, we just passed the last chance for ice cream before we're back on the interstate."

Price laughed. Lucas didn't. "Well, just talk to me, then."

"Well, okay, if you really want me to. I guess we can start with the missing money."

"The 50K."

"Right. Now I thought the theory was that the driver, this Buzz dude, took it when he abandoned the vehicle."

"True."

"But it sounds like Granger thought that Scarborough may have taken the money, and then the bank reported a greatly inflated theft."

Price nodded. "So the thieves really got away with only $40,000, and then Scarborough helped himself to $50,000. The bank reports $90,000, and the whole thing is blamed on the Granger troupe."

"Yup, nice and tidy. But that would mean Buzz left the car without taking *anything*; that's a little strange too."

"I agree."

"Still, did you see Dan's house? That thing is incredible."

"Oh, we'll check on him, alright," Price assured Tracy. "Granger must have had some reason to think Scarborough took it. I must say, though, I thought you handled him nicely, being a friend to him in there. I think that helped."

"Thanks, Detective."

"Call me Debbie." Lucas turned just long enough to scowl at his partner. She scowled right back. "Anything else on your mind, Tracy?"

"Yes. Why do you think Granger picked *Merlin's Manor of Mirth and Magic* for his meeting with Dan?"

"I was wondering that too, especially when Dan told us that Granger had someone else to see."

"Yup. Granger stuck around for the later show. And then he snuck backstage; that's what Lindstrom told us."

Price was nodding. "Maybe the person he wanted to see was part of the Montado show or worked at *Merlin's*."

"Yup again. Background checks on all those guys who worked for either are in order, I think."

"We've already started that," Lucas snapped.

"I'm sure you have. Oh dammit!"

"What Tracy? What is it?" Price asked.

"We forgot to ask Dan how Granger was dressed. Was he wearing his disguise at the *first* show?"

Price looked toward Lucas. "She's right, Jim." Price picked up a file, glanced through it, and then pulled out her phone. Soon she was conversing with Scarborough again. When she was done, she looked back at Tracy. "Dan says Granger was wearing a white shirt and black slacks, from what he remembers. I asked him about a mustache, and Dan said Granger was clean-shaven. I didn't want to reveal more of the details, so I just ended it there."

"So Granger must also have had a ticket for the later show," Tracy began. "He leaves, puts on his disguise so he won't be recognized as a returning customer for the night, and then takes his seat for the next show."

"Interesting; that's certainly possible."

"And then the poor guy gets brought up onstage. No wonder he didn't want to go up, at first. Suddenly he's got this attention on him, and he has to choose between making a scene by refusing or going onstage and playing along. I wonder if the killer recognized him anyway and was waiting for him in the back."

"Yes, yes that's possible. You've got some good ideas there."

"Thanks, Debbie. I mean, I owe you something for letting me tag along today."

"I think it worked out for everyone, actually."

Lucas had tired of the mutual love fest. "Look, Debbie, please remember she is a civilian. We shouldn't be dealing with her."

Price shook her head. "I'm sure she understands that, Jim. Now let's be nice to each other for the rest of the ride, and then it can be business as usual when we get back. Besides, I've been up almost 24 hours and am ready to crash."

"Alright," Lucas said. Then he raised his voice. "We clear on that, Tracy?"

"Sure, Jimmy." Price started laughing.

"Don't call me that. It's Detective Lucas."

"But after today I feel so much *closer* to you."

Lucas grunted. "Unlike my partner I *like* it when you're quiet."

"Okay, okay, I know when I'm a third wheel. I'll just close my eyes and take a nap. Wake me when we get there." Price looked back at Tracy, who was grinning. The detective shook her head but smiled back. Then Tracy looked out the window, and allowed her mind to consider other theories. Her mental wheels were spinning at full speed.

"Tracy, you're staring into space again," Brian told his fiancée. They were both seated at the dining room table in Tracy's condo.

"Huh?"

"Exactly. Look we don't have to work on our lists if you don't want to."

"I'm sorry, Brian. How many names have you come up with?"

"Well, about 60. I mean, how big do you really want this thing to be?"

"I don't know. Maybe about 200 guests, max."

"Yeesh. I'd rather it be a little smaller."

"Look, hon, let's just make our lists. Then we'll weed out the people who probably wouldn't come anyway."

"Yeah, okay."

Tracy reached for Brian's hand and rubbed it. "Why *don't* you want a big wedding? It's a once in a lifetime thing, you know."

Brian smiled. "I know. I guess I just like things to be low-key these days. I can't explain it."

Tracy stood up and stood behind her beau, and then started massaging his shoulders. "We don't have to do this now if you don't want to. I just want to get these 'save the date' things in the mail so people have plenty of notice. My caseload is quite manageable at this point, so I want to take advantage of that. And, of course, I have to talk to Mom and see if she has some friends she wants to invite who I may be forgetting about."

"That feels really good," Brian told her, allowing his body to practically go limp.

She laughed. "Good, that's why I'm doing it."

"What do you want to do for dinner?"

"I can make something."

"You don't have to."

"I want to. I abandoned you last night when things got crazy, and I left you to your own devices for most of the day today. So let me make us something."

Brian reached back and put his hands on Tracy's. "I can help."

"Why not just sit here and finish your list? I'll get started; chicken okay?"

"Sure." Tracy bent over to kiss Brian on the head, and then moved toward the kitchen. Brian leaned back on his chair and watched her as she started grabbing things from cabinets and the refrigerator. He stood up and made his way to the kitchen. He stopped and looked at her.

"What is it, Brian?" she asked noting the serious expression on his face.

"Want to hear something funny?"

She smiled. "Sure!"

"This morning, after you called to tell me you had to take care of whatever it was you had to take care of, I just sat there. I didn't know what to do. It was like I couldn't remember what I used to do with my free time before we started seeing each other again. Isn't that weird?"

Tracy looked at him. "I guess not. I don't really know, though. I…"

He was close to her now; he put his hands on her cheeks. "Life is so boring when you're not next to me." He leaned in and kissed her. And then, in one of the rare instances in their relationship's history, Brian pulled away first. "I think I need to go."

"What? Why?" Tracy asked sounding a bit alarmed.

"Because I'm not strong like you."

"What does that mean?"

Brian sighed. "Can't you guess? Tracy, I want you. And I know that you don't want to hear that, but there are times when I feel…I guess the word is, overwhelmed."

She gave him a half-smile. "Brian, why don't I call you some bad names, and then you won't feel so kindly."

He frowned. "Tracy, I'm serious. I'm really struggling here. I thought I could handle it and be respectful of your wishes and all that. But Tracy, sometimes I just…I start thinking about us when we've been together. And I hate the idea that I might put pressure on you, and then you'd give in, and then you'd feel guilty, and then I'd feel like a real jerk. I don't know why I can't just deal with it." Brian gulped; he was near tears. "I don't want to hurt you, Tracy, you know that."

     Practice to Deceive

Tracy looked at him sympathetically, and then took him by the hand. She led him back to the couch and they sat down together. "Brian, are you debating whether or not to take a drink?"

He shook his head. "No, Tracy, I promise."

"Well, maybe these things you're feeling are tied into your addictive personality?"

"My what?"

"Well, maybe somehow you've replaced your desire for alcohol with your desire for physical contact with me."

"What are you saying, that I'm a sex addict?"

Tracy shook her head. "No, Brian, that is *not* what I'm saying."

Brian raised his voice slightly. "Then what *are* you saying, Tracy?"

Tracy sighed, and then she took Brian's hands and met his eyes. "Brian, remember after your father's murder was solved, and I told you that you had to get sober for yourself, not for me, not for us."

Brian nodded. "Sure I do."

"Well, this—what you're going through—is exactly what I was talking about."

"I told you Tracy: I don't want a drink."

"I realize that. But if you're struggling so much with your feelings that you're compelled just to leave…well, I just think that doesn't sound right. We dated for almost two years before we slept together. And you were so patient and understanding during that time. You never pressured me or anything like that. Now, I don't know. I don't understand why it's so bad that you think the only thing you can do is leave me. I don't want you to leave, Brian. I don't want you just abruptly leaving anytime you…well, you know what I mean."

Brian looked away from her. "Well, what do you think I should do? Find some other group—Tracy Anonymous?"

She laughed softly. "Oh Brian, don't make me feel like I'm driving you away, like I'm something to avoid. You know I love you and want you too."

"Of course I do, Tracy. Believe me, I know what I sound like; I'm pathetic."

Tracy leaned her forehead against his. "You're not pathetic. This is what we both get for not waiting. But it's not a permanent situation." She squeezed his hands. "Please, Brian, don't leave; I don't want you to go."

"Neither do I; I mean, I don't want to go, either." He looked back up at her. "You know, I guess it's like you needing a client."

"What?"

"Last night—you said you needed a client so that you could try your hand at solving another case."

Tracy blinked. "Well—"

"Oh, come on, Tracy. Admit it: it's driving you crazy not being involved."

She nodded. "I think I know where you're going with this."

"Uh-huh. You get involved with three murder cases and you solve them. It gives you a thrill and a high. I know you always wanted to be a detective like your dad. And now you've more or less experienced it, more than once. And once again, you're smack-dab in the middle of another crime, and you can't do anything about it. Admit it: it's driving you nuts!"

Tracy frowned. "Yes, okay, I see your point."

"That's kind of how I feel. We've made love before, and it was exciting and wonderful and I miss it. You're more beautiful to me now than you were to me then, and sometimes I just want to pick you up and take you to the bedroom and play explorer again. I don't know any other way to explain it."

Tracy was blushing. "You've explained it just fine, Brian. The question is, How can I help you deal with it?"

Brian was smiling now. "I think talking has helped. I don't feel like I want to go home, anymore."

Tracy beamed. "Great! You know you can talk to me about anything, anytime you want, right?"

"Sure, Tracy."

"So should I start dinner, then? Are you going to be okay?"

Brian nodded. "I'm fine now. I just had a moment, I guess. I'll get back to the list."

Tracy gave him a quick kiss and headed back to the kitchen to start dinner.

"Uh, Tracy?" Brian asked as she was washing her hands.

"What, hon?"

"What do you think about selfies?"

"Huh?"

"You know, people taking pictures of themselves with their smartphones and such."

"Oh. I don't know. I don't have one of those."

"I do."

Tracy was drying her hands, looking at him curiously. "You want to take my picture with your phone?"

"Well, you could take some pictures." Brian was grinning.

Tracy went pale, her bottom jaw slightly dropped. "If you're asking what I think you're asking, the answer is NO!"

"Why not?"

"Why *not*?" she asked incredulously. "Because those kinds of pictures end up in a cloud somewhere. And sometimes that cloud rains; sometimes people *make* the cloud rain. And then you're all over the Internet for eternity. My God, Brian, if something like happened to me, I could never show my face again."

"Oh, Tracy—"

"No, Brian; no way, now how, no sir. I want to be 100 percent in control of who sees me naked. There is absolutely no way I'm going to say yes to what you're asking. That *is* what you were asking?"

Brian cleared his throat. "It was just an idea to help me get through the engagement period."

"Bad idea, Brian. And, of course, I don't have to tell you that I never *ever* want you to do that, to take a picture of me that couldn't go up on a family's picture wall."

"You've been very clear on the matter; I will never bring it up again."

"Okay."

"Hey, you said I could ask you anything, anytime. Don't be mad."

"I'm not mad, I'm just…surprised, I guess. Now let me attack this chicken." She turned and started tearing away the cellophane from the poultry container.

Brian sighed. "You *are* mad at me. I'm sorry."

"It's fine, Brian," she said, without looking at him. For some reason, he didn't believe her.

Dinner was a mostly quiet affair. Brian had complimented Tracy several times on the meal, but Tracy just said thanks and didn't add much more. Finally, Brian put his fork down, tired of the silent treatment. "Look, Tracy, I'm sorry I offended you. I was only really half-kidding, anyway. You said I could talk to you about anything, and now I took a chance and you're not talking to me. I clearly upset you, and I didn't mean to. How long are you going to be mad at me?"

Tracy finished chewing her potatoes. Then she, too, put her fork down and looked up at him. "What were you going to do with those pictures?"

"Huh?"

"My question was pretty self-explanatory."

"Look at them."

"And…?"

Brian turned red. "Tracy, I'm sorry."

"Having pictures of me is not the same as being with me."

"I know that."

"Then how can pictures of me tide you over, or whatever it was you said?"

"Tracy, I'm sorry. I didn't mean to suggest it was the same thing."

"Brian, I take my sexuality very seriously."

"I know, Tracy."

"You know you're the only man I've ever been with."

"I know that too, Tracy."

"It's not like I haven't had offers, you know."

Brian gulped. "I don't pretend that there haven't been other men in your life the past 10 years or so."

"Yeah, well, I didn't sleep with any of them."

"I didn't mean to suggest that you did. And even if you had, it wouldn't have mattered. We're back together, now. *You're* the one who told me I should forget the past."

"I'm not just a *body*, you know."

Brian snorted. "Tracy, I don't get you. You *know* I don't think of you as just a body. I can't help it if you happen to have a great one and I like seeing it. I mean, a couple of weeks ago you were asking about fantasies and teddies. And now, suddenly, you're getting upset over some nonexistent pictures."

Tracy glared. "Oh, are you saying your fantasy is to have naked pictures of me on your phone that you can pull up anytime you want?"

"Oh for crying out loud, Tracy, that's not what I meant." Brian leaned back in his chair. "Tracy, I think there's something else going on here. Did I strike some kind of nerve or something? You know I love you—mind, body, and everything else. What's going on?"

Tracy relaxed her shoulders and looked at her plate. "I'm sorry, Brian. I guess I am overreacting a bit. I mean, you're right, I told you to feel comfortable asking me anything, and when you do I freak out."

"Why did you freak out, Tracy? Did something happen to you?"

Tracy pursed her lips, a solemn expression on her face. "Well, I went to the beach with this guy when I was, 25, I guess. He seemed nice. We had been going out for few months, and when summer rolled around, he said we should take a day trip to Ocean City. You remember how much fun we had when we would go there and stay at your beach house?"

"Sure, Tracy."

"Well, he had a house down there too. I said okay. And I go into the bathroom at his beach place to change into my suit. Well, I get this weird feeling; I mean, something doesn't feel right, because one minute he's talking to me through the door and then it's suddenly quiet. I start looking around the room; I see what looks like a hole in one of the flowers on the wallpaper."

"Oh, no…"

"So I immediately open the door and go around the side, and this prick is standing there with a telephoto lens or something."

"Oh, Tracy, I'm so sorry."

"Not as sorry as *he* was. I left the house immediately, and when I was outside I called the police. I filed an official complaint, and it turned out this guy had done this sort of thing to at least nine other women. I filed an invasion of privacy lawsuit on their behalf, and we took this guy to the cleaners, financially speaking. He lost his photography job and who knows what else."

"Tracy, I didn't know. You never told me this."

"I was lucky; he didn't get one shot of anything of me."

"Tracy, I'm sorry. You can't be thinking I'm like him, though. Or do you?"

Tracy shook her head. "No, Brian, of course not. I know you're not like that. But you're a guy, and guys like to look, right?"

"Uh, I don't know how to answer that."

Tracy smiled. "You don't have to. You've been honest with me, and I shouldn't have been so miserable to you during dinner." Brian sighed with relief. "But that still doesn't mean you can take those pictures."

"I know that, Tracy; I'll never bring it up again, I promise. And I'm really sorry that happened to you."

"People can be so deceptive sometimes. They seem nice and say and do all the right things. And then—WHAM!—you find out who they really are. First you feel hurt, maybe some shame, and then anger, not just at the person but at yourself, too, for being such a sucker. I hate feeling like a sucker."

"Don't be so hard on yourself, Tracy. You've always been a sweetheart, and that means you don't think the way this creep you just told me about does. You tend to be trusting. And people are going to take advantage of that. I'm really sorry that happened to you."

"Thanks. I'm fine. I hadn't even thought about it in forever."

"It's funny, though, you don't like feeling like a sucker, but you love magic shows. Isn't the whole purpose of those things to make everyone feel like suckers?"

Tracy laughed. "Oh, Brian, that's different. People *willingly* go to those. They all know what they're seeing are illusions and tricks. I myself love wondering: how did they *do* that? It's fun. The performers are not there to make the audience feel stupid or bad."

"Oh, I know that. I was just pointing out that sometimes the circumstances can influence how you feel. One person does something, it's fine; another person does it, it's not."

Tracy looked at Brian. "You're absolutely right."

Brian tilted his head. "Tracy, what's going on now? You have that faraway look in your eyes again."

"Huh? Oh, nothing. I was just wondering about something."

"About what?"

"Believe me, you don't want to know."

"Oh, the murder last night, I bet."

"Don't worry, Brian. As you have pointed out, I don't have any right to be poking my nose in the thing."

"I'm glad you realize that."

The couple exchanged smiles and then finished what was now cold chicken, mashed potatoes, and carrots. Tracy was taking her empty plate to the sink when she heard the humming. "What's that noise?" Brian asked.

"I think it's my cell phone." Tracy moved in the direction of the noise and picked up her mobile phone, which was right next to her immobile one. "Tracy Brubaker," she answered.

"Hi," the unfamiliar voice said.

"Hello. Who is this?"

"It's Woody Williams. Remember me?"

Tracy rolled her eyes. "Yes, I remember you. Why are you calling me?"

"Well, I remembered you were a lawyer. And I find myself in need of a lawyer."

Tracy's mouth went dry. "Why do you need a lawyer, Woody?"

"Uh, they just arrested me for killing that guy found in the tank last night."

Chapter 4

Be careful what you wish for, the old saying goes. That's what Tracy was thinking about as she pulled into the Central Booking and Intake Facility where Woody Williams currently resided. She quickly made her way to the room in which her prospective client was being held. She sat down and waited for the guard to close the door before she spoke. "How are you doing, Woody?"

"Seriously? Do you ask all your clients *that*?"

"You're not my client, yet, Woody. I agreed to speak with you and advise you; that's it, for now."

Williams shook his head. "You're a real charmer, you are."

Tracy sighed. "Why did they arrest you, Woody?"

"Because they got no one else to, I guess."

"Woody, come on, answer my questions or I'm outta here. I have a fiancé waiting, and he's none too happy with me right now."

Williams shook his head. "Alright, well, they found some people who saw me arguing with that guy."

"Zachary Granger."

"Yeah, that's what they said his name was."

"Why were you arguing?"

"…Because I saw him backstage."

"Really, when?"

"I had just got my beer from the bar; I was heading back to my dressing room. I talked to a couple of people along the way, I think. Anyway, I decide to sneak a peek behind the curtain on Montado's side. That's a no-no, of course. I'm almost there, when this guy—this Granger fellow—comes out. And I'm like, 'Hey, who the hell are you?' He doesn't answer; he practically pushes me, and I spill some of my beer. So I yell some more at him, when he just walks away. Maybe I push him back. But I don't have time to deal with him properly, because I have to go on in a few minutes, at this point. That's it."

"That's it, meaning that was the end of the argument, or that's it, meaning that's all the police have."

"The argument; I never saw the guy again."

"What else do the cops have?"

"Uh, well, they know I was monkeying with the tank."

"What does that mean?"

"I was curious, is all. I lifted the tarp and was trying to see if there was a trapdoor in the bottom or something. Then I heard some noise and hurried away. I mean, no one's allowed back there except the magic crew."

"Did someone see you?"

"No. I think they found my prints on the glass."

"Ah. What time was this when you were doing your spying?"

"Earlier in the day, maybe around dinner time."

"So without anyone to corroborate your earlier monkeying, the police have assumed your prints got on there when you supposedly dumped the body."

Williams blinked. "Yeah, I guess that's right."

"Anything else?"

Williams cleared his throat. "Well, I have a record."

Tracy sighed. "Tell me some of your greatest hits."

He looked at her and grinned. "Hey, that's pretty good. Hit records, hit people."

"From the sound of it, I'm assuming you have some assaults in your past."

"Yeah, I got into some fights earlier in my career. People would be buying me drinks; inevitably, some asshole would pick a fight telling me I wasn't funny. And then I'd insult him, people would laugh, and then he'd swing at me, and then I'd swing back. So, there it is."

"Hmm. It's pretty clear what the police think happened. Where were you during the last 10 minutes of Montado's show? This would be between 11:20 and 11:30 p.m., more or less."

"At that point, I was probably in my dressing room; it's on the right side of the stage."

"Right side if you're looking toward it."

"Yeah. I was having some private cocktails."

"And by private you mean no one was with you."

"Yeah."

"Do you usually stick around after you do your final act for the night?"

"Yeah, after the show is over I mingle a bit. Sometimes, at some of the clubs I work at, I'll go out with some of the workers. I'm a night person, so I'm up real late."

"I see. So you have no alibi, your prints are on the tank, you were seen arguing with the victim, and you have a record of bar fights. Did I miss anything?"

"Only the part where I told you I didn't kill this guy."

　　　Practice to Deceive

"Uh-huh. But it's not like you would have told me you did, is it?"

Williams sighed. "You don't like me, do you?"

Tracy blinked. "That's not true, Woody. Your comedy may not be my cup of herbal, but that doesn't mean I dislike you as a person."

Williams shook his head. "Those assaults were a long time ago. I've stayed out of trouble since then."

Tracy nodded. Something in Williams' voice told her he was being sincere. "Is there someone I should call for you, Woody? A wife, a girlfriend?"

"Nah. My ex doesn't want to hear about this. And I don't want her to know, anyway. That's all she'd need to keep me from seeing my little girl, once and for all."

Tracy closed her eyes and then opened them. "You have a daughter, Woody?"

"Yeah—Stacey. She's six."

"Where is she? I mean, where does she live?"

"California; that's where I'm from. The East Coast is fine, but I'm a West Coast guy."

"You tour a lot, I imagine."

"Yep, life on the road—as lonely as it ever was."

"How long have you been divorced?"

Williams scratched his head. "A little more than three years. I should have known better than to marry a fan. Most fans are fair-weather ones. When you start repeating your material, they start looking for new stuff in other places."

"Did your ex-wife remarry?"

"Last year; married a soap opera actor, if you can believe *that*."

"I'm sorry, Woody."

"Sorry, nothing; no more alimony. I don't mind paying the child support; she's my daughter, and Helen can't change that. And I ain't letting Ivory boy adopt Stacey."

Tracy nodded. "This Granger person—had you seen him before, or was your brief confrontation the first and only time?"

"First and last."

"Did the police tell you what they think you did to him? I mean, did they kind of lead you through what they think might have happened?"

"Uh, they think I hit him with something, like a beer bottle maybe. Actually, it was more like they asked me *what* I hit him with. How do you answer that question? I didn't hit him with anything."

"And, to your knowledge, they have no witnesses to you actually assaulting him or putting the body in the tank?"

"They *can't* have any witnesses to that; I didn't kill the guy!"

Tracy leaned back in her chair. And then she smiled. "Okay, Woody. I'll help you."

"You will? Oh, that's great!"

"Well, I should give you the bad news."

"There's more?"

"Unfortunately, because it's the weekend, your bail review hearing can't be until Monday. And, to be honest, with your record and the fact you have no ties to Maryland, I'm not sure you're going to be granted bail."

"What? I can't stay in here!"

"I'm sorry, Woody, I really am. I'll start working on your case right away, see if I can find something. I'll do whatever I can. But I have to be honest with you: I think you're going to be here a while." She watched as disappointment overcame him. "Do you need anything? Should I call anyone, like your agent, someone like that?"

"I've taken care of all that."

"Okay." Tracy scratched her ear. "Uh, Woody, how'd you get my number? My cell phone isn't listed."

"Oh, one of the detectives gave me your number. I remembered talking to you at the show, remembered you were a lawyer, and mentioned you when they asked if I had any representation. One of the detectives had one of your cards."

"Detective Price?"

"Yeah, her." He started chuckling.

"What's so funny?"

"The look on that other cop's face; man, did he look *pissed*."

Tracy laughed. "Detective Lucas; yeah, he doesn't like me very much."

"Really? Why?"

"Because he arrested the wrong the person once, and I had to step in and fix his mistake."

Williams' eyes widened. "So you *know* this Lucas makes mistakes then?"

"I know of at least two."

"Oh? Did you fix that other mistake too?"

"I plan to." She smiled at him.

He smiled back. "Oh, I get it."

"I'll be in touch, Woody. If you need anything, let me know."

"Okay. Look, I really appreciate this."

"Sure, Woody. I'll see you." Tracy gave him another smile as she prepared to exit. When in her car, she sat there briefly. She smiled and then joyfully pounded her fists on the steering wheel. "Thank you, God! Thank you,

Debbie!" she cried out. And then she thought, "Ask and you shall indeed receive." She *had* her client.

"Hi Mom!" Tracy said after Violetta Brubaker had opened her front door.

"Tracy! Happy Birthday! Give me a kiss, dear child."

Tracy obliged. "Don't forget Brian, too, Mom. He'll most likely be joining me from here on out for my weekend visits."

"Of course, Brian, how are you?" The future in-laws embraced.

"Just fine, Mrs. Brubaker." Shortly thereafter, the engaged couple were seated next to each other on the small living room sofa while Violetta took a seat in the recliner.

"So how was your birthday, Tracy?" her mother asked.

Brian and Tracy looked at each other. "Just fine, Mom. Brian took me out for dinner and then to *Merlin's Manor of Mirth and Magic*."

"What?"

"It's a relatively new place downtown; they have a show where the first part is comedy and the second part is magic. It's incredible! And I got a hat and flowers, too."

"Oh. Well, as long as you had a good time."

"I did."

"And how is work?"

"Oh, just fine; in fact, yesterday I got a new client—a famous one."

Violetta looked at her daughter quizzically. Then she looked at Brian, who looked like he had just swallowed some sour milk. "Famous, huh? How famous?"

"He's a stand-up comedian. He's been on TV."

"Oh? What's his name?"

"Woody Williams."

"Never heard of him."

"You will if you watch the news; his arrest must be all over it by now."

"What'd he do?"

"You mean: *allegedly* do. The police think he killed someone."

Violetta look horrified. "Who'd he kill?"

"Nobody."

"But you just said—"

"I said the police *think* he killed someone."

Violetta frowned. "Stop being so smart; you know what I meant."

"Sorry, Mom; I've got my legal cap on."

"She has for the past two days," Brian said frowning. Tracy turned toward him and frowned back.

"Two days? I thought you said you got this client yesterday."

"He was an answer to a prayer," Brian said unconvincingly.

Tracy slapped Brian's knee. "Stop that." She turned back to her mother. "There was a murder at the magic show Brian took me to on Friday. Yesterday, they arrested the comic for it. He had met me, sort of, during the show, and now he's my client. See?"

"If the police think he did it, why do you think he didn't?"

"Yes, Tracy, your mother asks a *very* good question," Brian snapped.

Tracy looked to the both of them. "The same way I thought Brian was innocent; the same way I thought Max was innocent. Have the both of you developed short-term memory loss or something?" Tracy's cheerful mood was starting to lose its cheer.

"Oh," her mother said. "So, what have you done so far for the wedding?"

Tracy sighed. "We're making lists of possible guests. I brought mine with me so we could go over it together at some point today. Then I'll start looking for a place for the reception." Tracy was smiling again.

"Oh. How big will it be?"

"Uh, maybe 200 people."

"Two hundred?"

"Well, I have a lot of clients who have become friends. And I have kept in touch, more or less, with most of the women I met in college. And Brian, of course, is something of a local celebrity, with his father's business and all. And maybe there are some people you'd like to be there whom I've forgotten about."

"Oh."

"Mom, is 'oh' all you can say? I'm getting married!"

Violetta smiled. "Of course, I'm happy for you."

"Then what's wrong?"

"Nothing."

"Mom, really. Do you want to be more involved in the planning, is that it? You can be, you know; I just got the impression you didn't want to be."

"Well, I have the time."

"GREAT! Then you can help me pick the reception location and the menu."

Violetta smiled. She looked at Brian. "How are you, Brian? You don't look so good."

"He's not happy I got my client."

"That's not true," he said quickly.

 Practice to Deceive

"Tracy, let him answer for himself," Violetta scolded. "So what is it, Brian?"

"It's nothing, really. I just know that when Tracy gets wrapped up in a case like this, it can consume her. Between that and all the planning she's doing, I'm not sure where my place is right now."

Tracy looked at him, stunned. Violetta looked at him sympathetically. "So, what, you think this wedding will take place without planning, that Tracy should stop working?"

"Of course not."

"Then stop feeling sorry for yourself. Your place is to stand by your future wife and help her. And, more importantly, to be understanding of the pressure she's under. You'll be married soon enough, and then you can have her to yourself."

Brian gulped. Tracy looked at her mother, smiling widely. This was the first time, to Tracy's knowledge or memory, at least, that her mother had ever stood up for her like she just had. "Yes, ma'am," Brian said sheepishly. "I just miss her, I guess."

"Miss her? Bah—you see her more than I do. Now enough of this; I thought we were going out to eat." When Violetta finished arising from her seat, Tracy went over and hugged her mother tightly.

"Thanks, Mom."

"What? You don't think I know what's on his mind? Just like your father."

Tracy jerked her head back, as if someone just pulled her hair. "What?"

"Your father, he always—"

"You know what, Mom? Forget I asked. I don't want to hear this." Tracy turned to Brian. "Let's go, Brian. Mom's hungry."

Violetta went over to Brian as Tracy moved toward the front door. "Brian…"

"Yes, ma'am?"

"You love my Tracy?"

"Yes, ma'am, with all my being."

"Then you support her and help her; don't be something else she has to worry about. She loves you, and she's going to be your wife soon. Show her respect and understanding."

Brian nodded. "Of course, Mrs. Brubaker. You're right, Tracy deserves everything you say."

Violetta smiled. "That's better. Now let's go eat; my daughter is hungry."

Tracy and Brian were on their way back to the latter's apartment. She would drop him off and then head to her own home. He knew she would be plunging into her defense of Woody Williams first thing tomorrow. Their weekend was over. There had been little conversation thus far during their return trip. "Tracy," Brian started, "I'm sorry."

"Sorry for what?" she asked.

"I'm sorry for the last couple of days. I don't know why exactly I've been so testy. I mean, I have every reason in the world to be the happiest person on earth. And yet, I feel kind of down."

Tracy sighed. "Do you really think you're not in first place in my life right now?"

"Huh?"

"You said you didn't know where your place is."

"Oh. Maybe I'm just jealous."

"Jealous? Jealous of what?"

"Woody Williams."

"HUH?"

"He's going to be on your mind from here on, until you finish his case. And then someone else will come along, and it will be the same thing. I know it sounds stupid. I remember when *I* was your client, we saw each other a lot. We have so few hours of the day together as it is. And I know you warned me about late hours. I'm jealous. Maybe I should go out and commit some crime and then hire you."

Tracy smiled and looked at Brian quickly. "Brian, you know I'm *always* thinking about you, about us. You *are* in first place."

"I know that in my head, Tracy."

"Well, you need to tell your head to have a talk with your heart, so the two of them can get on the same page of the book of *love*."

Brian laughed. "Oh, really?"

"Really, honest, and for true."

"Tracy, I love you so much, sometimes I can't think straight. I'm sorry for being something else you have to worry about. I don't want to be that."

"Brian, you're only human. Don't beat yourself up too much. But, thanks, just the same. All is forgiven. You know I love you too."

"Sure I do." Brian gulped. "And as for the physical thing, well I'm honored beyond words at being your first and only. I know how unusual such a thing is in today's world. What we have is really special, and it's not fair of me to be so whiny. I'm sorry about all that too."

Tracy felt the tears welling up in her eyes. "Brian, thank you so much for saying that. We'll be together like that again; you know we will. And then, watch out!"

     Practice to Deceive

Brian chuckled. "Alright, let's not delve into that any further."

"Sure, good idea."

When Tracy pulled into Brian's apartment complex, she quickly found a visitor's spot in which to park. She turned off the ignition. "Tracy, why don't I just leave you here? You don't have to come up. It's so hard letting you go once I have you inside." He smiled.

She stroked his cheek. "Okay, Brian." And then she leaned over and kissed him. He kissed her back and put his arms around her. Soon they were locked together. As the intensity increased, she found her commitment to celibacy moving in the opposite direction. She was almost on top of him in the car, when Brian gently pushed her away. They looked at each other, and he knew by her eyes that if he asked her, she would say yes.

"Good night, Tracy," he said, straightening himself up. "Call me tomorrow, and let me know if I can see you."

Tracy closed her eyes and smiled. "Goodnight, Brian. I'll call you tomorrow, promise." He opened the door, gave her a quick smile, and moved quickly to his building. Tracy sat there briefly, staring at her hands. Then she looked back to the building. She closed her eyes again. And then she turned the key in the ignition and began her trek home. She found herself suddenly being jealous of Brian's apartment; that was where *he* was, after all.

Rebecca Dietz, Tracy's secretary and administrative person, and Neal Bennett, her associate, were hanging on their employer's every word as she related the events of the weekend—the nonpersonal events, that is. When Tracy had finished, she folded her arms and awaited their comments.

Neal spoke first. "I think Woody Williams is pretty funny, myself, Tracy. But I can see why you don't find him funny. His humor is more male humor."

"Male humor?"

"Stuff that guys find funny but women don't."

"Humor doesn't have to be gender-driven, Neal. Guys who spend most of their routine ragging on the opposite sex aren't funny to me."

"Well, I wasn't there, so what do I know?"

Rebecca grinned. "So, we have a genuine celebrity for a client? Pretty exciting, Tracy."

"Yeah, I guess it is. His bail review is this morning; I don't think he'll pass muster unless the judge is a fan of *guy* humor." She frowned at Neal. Rebecca laughed. Neal cleared his throat.

"What is the plan, then, oh humorless boss?" Neal said grinning.

"Come with me, and I'll tell you. See ya, Beck."

"Sure, Tracy." Neal and Tracy headed toward the boss's office.

"The police are running, or have already run, background checks on the *Merlin's Manor of Mirth and Magic* staff, as well as the crew of Montado's show. We need to do the same. Granger was supposedly killed while backstage, so unless another audience member also snuck back there, sight unseen, we're most likely looking at an employee."

"Perhaps the mysterious Buzz."

"Possibly. If Buzz walked off with $50,000, Granger probably thinks he's owed something. Or, it could be something as mundane as Granger getting into a fight with a crew member who questioned him, and then Granger gets a bump on the head."

"If that's the case, putting Granger in the tank was a ghoulish touch."

"Yes, I agree. Of course, I don't yet know *if* the bump Detective Price told me about is what killed Granger. Maybe he drowned; right after I'm done with Woody's bail review, I'm going to track down Detective Price. I think she'll tell me everything they have, now that I'm official."

Neal shook his head. "You sure did get lucky there, didn't you?"

Tracy grinned. "What can I say? Debbie and I hit it off."

"*Debbie?*"

"Yup."

Neal smiled and then started jotting notes on his pad. "Okay, so that's Kurt and Ron, the two guys who pushed the tank onstage and are also involved in security."

"Check."

"And then Greg and Karine Bowers; she was onstage."

"Check, check."

"And then Montado himself, I guess."

"Triple check."

"Even though he was onstage when the murder happened..."

"Yup."

Neal took a deep breath. "Now, the *Merlin* staff: we have the manager, Pamela Houston; the ticket taker and assistant announcer, Rose; the announcer, Richard; and the usher, name unknown. Then there's this witness, Harry Lindstrom; the bank fellow, Dan Scarborough; and our victim, Zach Granger, and his partner-in-crime, the late Chris Pyle. And, of course, Woody Williams."

"And a bartender. And the kitchen staff. And then all the technical crew: the guys who operate the lights, and the sound, and all that. But I doubt it's any of those people; they couldn't leave their station without its being obvious they did so."

"Right."

"But the truth is, I'm leaning toward someone on the Montado crew. That area where the tank is kept is off-limits. On the other hand, if Granger could slip back there, so could someone else, I guess. But, on the *other* other hand, Granger bought tickets specifically for a Montado show. Why would he get tickets to a show that had him waiting so long to meet with people he thought owed him something? Still, on the other other *other* hand—"

"Okay, Tracy, I see your point." Neal sighed. "I'll get started, then. I'll touch base with you this afternoon after you get back from your visit with *Debbie*."

Tracy grinned. "That's Detective Price to *you*; she's *my* chum, not yours."

"Uh-huh. Well, I guess I'll make *myself* disappear then." When Neal reached the door, he stopped abruptly. "Hey, bring in that hat you got for your birthday, sometime; I'd like to see one of those things up close."

"I may do better than that; I may let you have it."

"Oh, Tracy, don't give that hat away; someday it will remind you of this time in your life; precious memories, Tracy."

"Are you going to start humming *The Way We Were*, or something?"

Neal sang, "*…Scattered pictures…*"

"Stop! Out!" Tracy said starting to laugh. And he was gone. So, too, shortly was she; she had a bail review hearing to attend.

"Hi, Detective Price," Tracy said smiling as she approached the investigator's desk.

"Oh, hi, Tracy. I hear you are representing Woody Williams."

"Yes, thanks for giving him my number."

"Well, I thought you could just give him some help. I mean, there could be a conflict, though."

"What *do* you mean?"

"You're a potential witness for the state."

"What?"

"You can help establish when Granger went onstage; that helps with the timeline."

"Lots of other people can help with that too; Art better not try to have me kicked off this thing because of *that*."

Price chuckled. "Well, don't get too worked up yet."

"You're right, still lots of time before a trial."

"Did Williams have his bail review this morning?"

"Yeah, denied. I guess he's not a big enough celebrity to get the special treatment they usually do. On the other hand, he got a woman judge; maybe she saw his act."

Price was chuckling again. "I've seen Williams' stuff; he's okay."

"We'll just have to agree to disagree on *that*, Detective."

Price leaned back in her chair. "So I guess, now that you're officially involved, you're here for some more case details."

"Guilty. Do you have time to talk?"

"Sure, Tracy." Price slid a file folder to the center of her desk, grinning.

"Did you have that already waiting for me?" Tracy smiled.

Price didn't answer. Instead, she started reading from the file while Tracy opened her notebook, ready for action. "Let's see: apparent cause of death was drowning; he had water in his lungs. The bump on the back of his head was pretty severe, though; Granger was probably knocked unconscious before he drowned."

"Was he in a fight, maybe shortly before he drowned?"

"Not really evidence of a fight; there were some light, small scratches on his head. But nothing on his knuckles; no bruised cheeks or broken jaw, either."

"Okay, when did the coroner say Granger drowned?"

"Time of death is tricky, since the body was in the water a while, but the 11:20 to 11:30 p.m. time frame works."

"So you think Williams fought with Granger, knocked him down, and then dumped him in the tank."

"Looks that way."

"…Because of his record and the fingerprints on the tank."

"And because Williams is something of a loudmouth. The bartender said he was always hitting on other guy's women, and then insulting the men if they challenged him. We know Williams had been drinking, just like he had been in those previous fights."

"Oh. Were there any other prints on the tank?"

"Sure, most of the crew's were there. And so were Granger's."

"Granger's prints were on the tank?"

"Yes, near the top."

"That's strange."

"He may have touched the tank before he got into the fight."

"Maybe."

"Of course, there was something strange about the prints."

Tracy blinked. "Really? What?"

"His hand was upside down. What I mean is, his fingers were pointing downward toward the floor, as if he was using his left hand to brace himself."

"Like maybe he was getting into the tank himself?"

"Now, why would you say that?"

"He took his jacket off. Why did he do that? It doesn't make sense, unless he took it off in preparation of getting into the tank, maybe."

"Wait—are you thinking Granger was part of the trick, and something went wrong?"

"Not sure; I just learned about Granger's prints from you. I'm just thinking out loud."

"Uh-huh."

Tracy continued pondering aloud. "I wonder why Woody then put Granger in the tank. It certainly wasn't to hide the body so he could then make a getaway. Woody was still in the club when Granger was discovered."

"Who knows?" Price asked. "Maybe he thought it'd be funny."

"Mmm. I guess you talked to Kurt and Ron, and they didn't see anything?"

"No, they didn't see anyone, including Granger."

"Wasn't one of them by the curtain the whole time for security purposes?"

"Yes, for the most part. But they leave the curtain when they have to get ready to bring the tank onstage."

"So there's a period when the curtain is unattended?"

"Yes."

"And Granger picked just that time to sneak back there?"

"He must have."

"And neither Kurt nor Ron saw anything?"

"That's what they said."

"Something doesn't add up here, Detective."

"Yeah," Price agreed. "It does sound like whatever happened must have been super-quick if neither of the Donlevy brothers saw anything."

"Oh, I didn't realize they were brothers."

"Yes."

"And how long have they been with Montado?"

"Eight years."

"Long time."

Price nodded. "The Bowers siblings have been with him longer: almost 11."

"Where was Greg Bowers during the show? Was he backstage?"

"No, he was actually at his hotel room when the show was going on."

A puzzled look planted itself on Tracy's face. "Wait a minute, how did he get inside the building after the murder, then? I had the manager monitor the doors and make sure nobody got in or out."

"Oh, Kurt let him through the back. It's one of those doors that have no handles or anything on it on the outside, a flat surface. So, the only way you can get in that door is if someone lets you in from the inside."

"Oh, so someone called him at the hotel?"

"Yup, Karine called him—let me check my notes—around 11:30 p.m., she told us. He came over, and then Kurt let him in."

"I see. And you verified all this?"

"We confirmed the call with the hotel switchboard, and Karine's cell phone shows a minute-long call starting at 11:33 p.m. Both Kurt and Ron were there when she made the call."

"Wow, she called her brother fairly quickly."

"They're pretty close, from what I gather."

"That doesn't really leave Greg enough time to kill Granger, leave through the back, and then be at his hotel room when his sister called later."

Price nodded. "No. It's a 20-minute walk, and it would have been risky to count on a cab getting him back to his hotel in time to get that call. Plus, he'd risk being identified by a cab driver. Besides, what would his motive be?"

"Not sure, just thinking out loud again."

Price leaned forward in her chair. "Tracy, I know your history and reputation; Jim told me all about it, well what *he* knew, anyway. So let me ask *you* a question: Why are you so certain Williams didn't kill Granger? Or will answering be an ethical dilemma for you?"

"No dilemma, but allow me to answer your question with a question for you. Doesn't it strike you as odd that this ex-con who's been in the joint for 12 years dealing with tough guys, who earlier in the evening had threatened a bank president, who alluded to this same bank president he had someone else to see, allows himself to get bested by some scrawny stand-up comic who's been knocking back cocktails for most of the magic show? According to you, Granger didn't even get a swing in."

Price remained silent for a moment, studying her inquisitive visitor. "When you put it like that, I see where you're coming from. But I'm not the lead detective, and I didn't make the push to have Williams arrested." Price lifted her head so she was looking over Tracy's shoulder. "Speak of the devil…"

"Hello, Detective Price, Tracy," Lucas said. "Having a nice chat, are we?"

"Just seeing what you have with respect to my client, Detective, and maybe swapping some brownie recipes with Debbie here."

Lucas frowned. "You'll get what the state's attorney has when he's ready to turn everything over."

"What the heck, Detective? Williams hasn't even been arraigned, yet. Meanwhile, he's sitting in a cell."

"Where he belongs…"

"Says you."

"Says the evidence."

"You need a new interpreter. Your translation is all wrong."

Price started chuckling. "Are you two done yet?"

"Did you guys check on Scarborough's alibi? Did he leave the club when he said he did?"

"He used the Intercounty Connector—Route 200—when he went home, so we checked his E-ZPass records." Price shared. "So his alibi checks out, unless someone else was driving his car. I'm going to have someone confirm with his wife and kids as to when he got home, just for the record."

"Okay, thanks. How much longer are Montado and his crew here?" Tracy asked. "I hadn't thought to check that until now."

"They're here through Saturday; they leave Sunday," Price answered.

"Okay, now I know what my real time frame is."

Lucas shook his head. "What are you talking about?"

"I think Granger was at the magic show because he wanted to see someone there. Why would Granger wait for so long after being paroled to see Scarborough, unless he had a reason to do so? I think the reason was that he planned to see someone *else*, someone who may have made off with $50,000."

"And who might that be?" Lucas asked.

"Off the top of my head, Buzz or one of his friends or relatives."

"Granger said he barely knew Buzz."

"Exactly, he *said* he didn't know him well. Isn't it just the teensiest bit possible that Granger was—oh, I don't know—*lying*?"

Lucas looked at Price, who looked right back at him. "Alright," Lucas said. "If you're right, and it's the magic group involved, we're probably not going to be able to get anywhere with talking to anyone. That Montado group is tight."

"Tight enough to cover up a murder? Loyalty is one thing; murder is something else. If I were you, I'd see if anyone connected with Montado was in the Gaithersburg area 13 years ago, or has family in the area." Tracy looked at both detectives and then stood up. "I guess I should go, now. Thank you for the recipe, Detective Price. I'll be in touch."

"See you later, Tracy."

Tracy smiled at Price, grinned at Lucas as she passed by him, and then disappeared into the hall.

"What do you think, Jim?" Price asked after Tracy was no longer in their sights.

Lucas sighed. "It's a good thing Greg Bowers can prove he was at his hotel Friday night."

"Why?"

"Because the Bowers family hails from Arlington, Virginia, which as you know is about an hour's drive from Gaithersburg."

Chapter 5

"You're kidding," Tracy said, upon hearing Neal's news about the Bowers parents' location.

"Nope," Neal responded.

"And the robbery happened in October 2002."

"Yes. Thirteen years ago, Greg was 21 and Karine was 17."

"Wouldn't they both have been in school, though?"

"I guess. I haven't gotten that far."

"What about their parents, especially their father?"

"Let me see if I can guess what you're thinking: dad Bowers was the getaway car driver."

"Eh, could be."

"I'll see what I can find. But seriously, if they had $50,000, do you think they'd have hooked up with Montado?"

"Maybe Dad blew all the money; maybe the kids didn't even know what Dad did in his spare time."

"Should we go ask him? He's still alive, you know."

Tracy frowned. "Hmm. Monkey wrench. If Bowers is the driver, why didn't Granger just try to contact him directly instead of going through his kids?"

"Maybe he did."

"Hmm. The cops have to know about this already. Maybe they've already cleared all the Bowers family."

"Possible."

Tracy started massaging her temples. "And Kurt and Ron Donlevy—what about them?"

"They joined up with Montado in 2007. They're from Arizona. They worked for another magician—Leonardo was the guy's stage name—before that. Leonardo retired in 2006. Nothing came up when checking criminal history."

"How about Montado himself?"

"He's been in the business for almost 30 years; 52 years old. There's lots of stuff on him in terms of his professional life; very little on his personal. I'm still looking, in other words."

"A man of mystery, eh? I'm intrigued."

"I can tell."

Tracy looked at her watch. "It's almost quittin' time. Neal, can you can find out where Montado and company were performing in October 2002?"

"The time of the bank robbery; you bet. He's pretty popular, so I'm sure information about his appearances should be relatively easy to track down."

"Supreme!"

"Now, Harry P. Lindstrom III, that witness, owns and manages a hardware store in Baltimore County: Harry's Hardware and Lumber. He, as you may have guessed, is a third-generation owner. He lives with his wife and two daughters not too far from where he works."

"Hmm. I may just pop into the hardware store and speak with him briefly. I think Lucas and Price got everything there was to get, but you never know."

"Yeah. I should have something for you on the magic house's employees before tomorrow afternoon."

"Thanks, Neal. I want to visit *Merlin's* tomorrow—see if I can talk to the Montado team, maybe the magician himself. And, then, maybe *Merlin's* employees, if I can swing it. Not sure if that will all work out, though, since they'll be prepping for the Tuesday show."

"So, are you coming in here first tomorrow?"

"Yes, I can't imagine everyone's there by 9:00 a.m. I'll have to call and hope I get hold of somebody to find out a good time to pop over."

"Okay, then, I'll look forward to seeing your smiling face tomorrow." Neal rose to leave.

"Goodnight, Neal; thanks for your diligence." Tracy sat back in her chair and then reached for her phone. "Beck…"

"Yeah, Tracy?"

"Pick up the receiver."

Rebecca obliged and then asked, "What's up, Tracy?"

"When Neal's left, come back and see me, okay?"

"Sure."

"Thanks."

Rebecca did as instructed and closed Tracy's office door upon entering. "What's going on, Tracy? Are you okay?"

"No, Beck, I'm not. I'm insane."

"What?" Rebecca asked, laughing slightly.

"Or I'm going to drive Brian insane, and he's going to break off the engagement."

"I doubt that *very* much, Tracy."

"I don't."

Rebecca took a seat on the office sofa. "What happened? Why are you upset?"

Tracy joined Rebecca on the couch. "I'm telling him one thing and then acting in a contrary way. It's crazy."

"Tell me the details, and Dr. Beck will help."

Tracy sighed. "Well, I told you, I'm trying to resist temptation before we get married."

"Sure."

"And Brian's been pretty good about respecting my wishes. But on Saturday, he wanted to leave long before he usually does, because he was having some kind of struggle. We talked about it, and things seemed to be okay."

"Alright, I'm with you."

"Then, on Sunday, we went to my mother's for dinner and some wedding stuff. On the way home, Brian apologized and said some really wonderful things."

"Uh-oh."

"Yeah, the more he apologized the…the more I…"

"I get it, Tracy."

"Right. So we get back to his place, and he doesn't even want me to come up. So we start kissing goodnight in the car. And we kept on kissing. And then…well, if Brian hadn't stopped things…"

"Bye-bye resistance."

Tracy nodded. "Beck, he didn't even say 'I love you' as he always does when he leaves; nor I to him. I tell him 'No,' and then I do or say something to get him riled up. It's like that old politically incorrect saying about a girl saying no but meaning yes. I'm setting women's rights back 100 years!" Tracy was on the verge of tears.

"Tracy," Rebecca said soothingly, "I'm sure he understands."

"But we've got more than a year to go, Beck. How understanding can I expect him to be?"

"Tracy, he does not have the *right* to sleep with you. Even when you two are married, that doesn't mean every time he wants it you have to give it."

"I know that."

"Well, then you two are just going to have to ride this thing out. If being alone together is too difficult, meet in a public place. You could meet at a food court in some mall and talk. Do that a few times instead of always meeting at your place or his place. But Tracy, if he loves you like you believe he does, then he'll find a way to cope."

Tracy exhaled. "Well, he did have a thought on that, but I had to nix his idea."

"Really?"

"Yeah, but I'm not going to get into that."

"Oh, okay."

"I'm worried he might start drinking to deal with it. I can't help but wonder if he's substituted me for alcohol, like I'm his addiction now."

"Have you talked to him about this?"

"Yes; he denied it. He tells me it's more of an 'I know what I'm missing' thing."

Rebecca nodded. "That could be part of it."

"That's why we should have waited; we wouldn't be having this problem."

"Maybe, maybe not. But there's no point on dwelling on ships that have sailed, to use the words you did many moons ago."

Tracy smiled. "Yeah, that's true." She twisted her lips. "Maybe I should just sleep with him again, get it over with."

"Tracy! That doesn't sound like a good reason to me. You shouldn't be thinking *that* way."

"Oh, I didn't really mean it. I just don't know the best way to handle this. I don't know that there *is* a best way." Tracy looked back at her confidant. "You didn't wait, did you Beck?"

"No, Tracy. Me and the hubster lived in sin a year before we even got engaged."

Tracy nodded. "You know, the only person I know for a fact waited was my mother. But there's no way I'm talking to her about this."

"Why not?"

Tracy looked at Beck with wide eyes. "Beck, you've met my mother. How can you ask me that?"

Rebecca shrugged her shoulders. "I could always talk to my mom about sex; she was very open and honest."

Tracy shook her head. "My mom had one conversation with me when I was 11, and that was it; all clinical-type stuff that I'd already learned in biology class." Tracy paused a moment. "Actually, that's not entirely true: the night she met Brian, she basically said, in her own way, no nookie before marriage."

Rebecca laughed. "Tracy, your mom was a young engaged woman once."

"I'm not sure about the young part, Beck."

"Tracy, your mom probably went through something like you did. Ask her how she handled it."

Practice to Deceive

Tracy grinned. "You know, before we went to dinner on Sunday, my mom stood up for me: when Brian complained about my busy schedule, Mom basically told him to deal with it. And then she alluded to Dad being like Brian sometimes. But I cut her off there before she shared any details; too much information and all that."

Rebecca nodded. "See, maybe that was your mother's way of telling you that she had information to share. Tracy, you really should talk to her. She may surprise you."

Tracy was nodding now. "You know, Beck, you may be right. It's not like I'd be revealing things she doesn't already know or suspect."

"There you go. Pay her a visit. You know she'd welcome you anytime. In fact, call her tonight. You can tell Brian you need to meet with her about wedding stuff, which wouldn't be a lie, exactly."

Tracy was smiling now. "Yes, yes, I think I'll do just that—call her, anyway. Thanks, Beck. I knew I could talk to you and you could help me. You have retained your crown as Queen of Awesome."

Rebecca rubbed Tracy's knee. "I'm so glad I could help you, Tracy. You know I love you, right?"

Tracy gave her advisor a hug. "I love you too, Beck. Thanks for listening."

"You bet." Rebecca stood. "Good luck, Tracy. Now I'll leave you to make your calls." Rebecca flashed another smile and then left the attorney to her dialing.

"What's wrong?" Violetta, sounding panicked, asked.

"Nothing's wrong, Mom. I just want to talk to you. But it's one of those things I'd rather talk about face to face than over the phone. I want your advice."

"*You* want *my* advice?"

"Yes."

"Something *is* wrong."

Tracy laughed. "Mom, I promise you, nothing is wrong. I am sure what I want to talk to you about has been discussed between millions of mothers and daughters before, just not us yet."

There was silence. "Well, of course you can come over; I have nothing to do over here except talk to Mrs. Raccio or watch television."

"Great, Mom. I'll be leaving here in about 15 minutes, and I'm going to make a stop first. Give me a couple of hours before you start worrying."

"Bah. I'll see you soon."

"Thanks, Mom!" Tracy pushed down the switch hook and then dialed Brian's number.

"This is Brian."

"Hi honey, how are you?"

"Hi Tracy!" he answered excitedly. "I'm great; how are you?"

Brian's exuberance caught her off guard. "I'm great too; you sure sound like you're in a good mood."

"I am. Tracy, before I forget, I'm sorry I didn't say 'I love you' when I left you last night. I was thinking it; I don't why I didn't say it. So, I love you."

Tracy beamed. "I love you too."

"I've been thinking about you all day, not that that's really different from any other day. But, I don't know, I've just been smiling all day."

"Oh, Brian, that's so sweet of you to say. Is there something specific on your mind you want to talk about, maybe?"

"No, not really. I know I was kind of up and down this weekend. But I woke up this morning feeling great. I guess I was just having a mood swing or something."

Tracy laughed. "Brian, I'm so glad you're okay; I must admit I was a little worried."

"I'm sorry, Tracy."

"Well, I have to say I'm sorry, too."

"Why?"

"I'm seeing my mother tonight; I'll be home late, probably."

"Is something wrong with your mother?"

"Oh no, no. Just some wedding-related stuff I need to talk to her about. Nothing to worry about, nothing at all."

Brian sighed. "Well, I won't lie; I'm kind of bummed. I really wanted to see you."

"I'm sorry. This will probably be a one-time thing; making a special trip during the week, I mean."

"Oh, I get it: you're picking out wedding dresses or something."

Tracy paused. She wasn't one to lie, and she rarely even bent the truth. "Uh, it kind of has to do with dressing, yeah."

"Okay, I won't push it."

"Brian, you're not going to become down again, are you?"

"Tracy, I'm good. I'm great. I have *you*, and I love you, and I'm great."

Tracy gulped. "Brian, I'll call you when I'm leaving Mom's. Maybe I could stop by just for a quick hug or something."

"You know you can if you want to, Tracy."

    Practice to Deceive

"I love you, Brian; I'll call you later tonight."

"I love you too, Tracy. I'll be on pins and needles until your call."

"Bye," she said. And then she cradled the receiver. She remained in her chair a moment as her eyes moistened. But these were tears of joy.

Harry's Hardware and Lumber was a smaller store than Tracy had expected. It fit nicely into the strip shopping center of which it was a part. She was so used to seeing the huge warehouse-type hardware stores these days that Harry's relative compactness took her completely by surprise. She considered it a pleasant one, though. When she entered, she had no trouble finding the owner, who was speaking with what appeared to be customers; they were discussing the finer points of primer. Tracy waited patiently, effectively forming a line so she would be next. When the couple left, Harry smiled and approached. "May I help you, ma'am?"

"Hi Harry. I don't know if you remember me from Friday—I'm Tracy."

Harry tilted his slightly, and then his smile returned. "Of course! It was your birthday, right?"

"Yes! And then I spoke briefly with you, along with the detectives, afterward about what you saw."

"Right, right. What a coincidence!"

"Oh, it's not a coincidence that I'm here now, Harry. I stopped to see if I could ask you some more questions. I wouldn't be long; I know you're very busy running your store."

Harry was, thankfully, still smiling. "Anything I can do to help the investigation." It occurred to Tracy that Lindstrom might have thought she was with the police. She decided to be a bit naughty and just go with it. Technically, she hadn't done anything wrong: at no point had she, then or now, said she was a police officer.

"Thank you, Harry. Was Friday your first time at the show?"

"Yes, marvelous, wasn't it? I had seen Montado so many times on television, but they're always cutting away and breaking the suspense. A live show is a completely different animal."

"Absolutely, I feel the same way. It's kind of like that with sports for me, too. I can't sit on a couch and watch a game, but I always have a blast if I'm at the stadium."

"Yes—I certainly see what you mean."

"I didn't see anyone with you on Friday. Did you go alone?"

"Oh, my wife was there, but she was in the lobby using the ladies room when we talked. They need to expand the bathrooms in that place; there was such a line to use the restroom!"

"Yes, that always happens after a show is over, I guess. I know you told us that you didn't see anyone enter or exit the curtain after Conrad snuck back there. But I wanted to be clear on another point: Did you see anyone else enter or exit anytime during the show, including the stand-up part of it?"

Lindstrom shook his head. "No. We got there just as the show was starting, so it was dark when the usher helped us find our seats. I don't remember seeing anyone near the curtains for the entire night until Conrad walked over there."

"Okay, thanks. And you'd never seen Conrad before Friday night."

"No, I don't know anyone named Conrad."

"Actually, the victim's name was Zachary Granger. I believe that started hitting the news on Sunday."

"Oh, well I don't know anyone named Zachary, either."

"I see. How close was Conrad standing to you? I mean, you said he was there about a minute or so before he actually went behind the curtain."

"He was a few feet away from me, but of course it was dark. I might not even have noticed him if he hadn't coughed."

"He coughed?"

"Yes, a couple of times."

"Huh," was all Tracy uttered in response. "Well, thank you so much for your time, Harry. I'll be on my way."

"Oh sure, my pleasure. Anything I can do to help the police…"

Tracy had started to move away when his addendum made her turn around. "Oh, I'm not the police, Harry, just an attorney. Thanks again!" And then she headed quickly for the exit. Lindstrom stood there a moment looking at her as she left. Then he recalled Detective Lucas snapping at her during the initial interview. But he just shrugged his shoulders and then resumed pondering the finer points of primer.

Tracy and Violetta broke their greeting embrace quickly. "Tracy, what's wrong?" her mother asked.

"Mom, I told you, I'm fine."

"I don't even remember the last time you came out here during the week."

"Well, I stopped by quite a bit after your stroke to check on you."

"That was different. You had a good reason to come over. So what is it tonight?"

"I have something to talk to you about. But it's not something bad, really."

"Well, come in and say hello to Mrs. Raccio, and then we'll talk. Or maybe you should eat something."

"I want to talk first."

"Okay, then." Tracy followed her mother into the living room, greeted Violetta's roommate, and then took a chair in the bedroom. Her mother took the matching seat and wasted no time. "So what is so important, but not so worrisome, that you wanted to see me?"

Tracy looked at her mother seriously. "Mom, I need to talk to you about something we've never really talked about before. And I'm kind of uncomfortable with it."

Violetta nodded. "Ah. You and Brian are fighting?"

"No, that's not quite it."

"Then you two are struggling with something else, maybe."

Tracy blinked. "Yes, I guess you could put it like that."

Violetta nodded. "You two want to lie down together."

Tracy sighed and then looked at the floor. "Yeah, Mom, we're wrestling with the physical stuff."

"But you two have already done that, haven't you?" So her mother knew; Tracy gulped. She nodded without raising her head. "Tracy, look at me."

Tracy raised her head and sighed. "You're disappointed in me, aren't you?"

Violetta looked at her daughter sympathetically. "No, Tracy. I've never been disappointed in you. I know things are different today than they were when your father and I were growing up. We were dating in the 1970s; it was a struggle then too."

"Mom, how did you deal with it? I mean, you wanted Dad, right?"

"Of course I did. Your father was the most handsome man I've ever known."

"And, of course, he wanted you too. So, which of you kind of took the lead on…well, waiting for the wedding night?"

Violetta started rocking. "I think you know the answer to that."

Tracy studied her mother. "*You* did?"

"Tracy, who's the one who carries the baby?"

"Oh, is that what stopped you?"

"Most of the time, all I had to do was remember the Lord's command. When that wasn't working, I just imagined what would happen if I had to tell my Papa I was going to have a baby before I got married."

"Grandpop would have hurt you?"

"No, he would have hurt your father."

Tracy laughed. "Grandpop would have gotten on a plane and come to kick Dad's butt, huh?"

"Well, we never got to learn what might have happened, thank the Lord."

"Yeah." Tracy cleared her throat. "So when Dad—I can't believe I'm asking you this—started, um, making his intentions clear, how did you handle it? I mean, if he wanted you and you wanted him and…Well, you know what I'm asking, right?"

Violetta smiled slightly. "Well, the first couple of times I told him nicely that we should remain pure, as the Lord intended. After that, I had to scold him."

"Scold him?"

"Yes. He should have known better than to start touching me in places that he shouldn't have."

Tracy's face looked like a red balloon. "Okay, Mom, I *get* it."

"You're father was very talented with his hands."

"MOM! I don't need *that* much detail."

"What? You think your father and I only did it the one time to have you?"

"Of course not. But that doesn't mean I care to dwell on it…or learn about it."

"It's a good thing we waited, too," Violetta mused smiling. "Because after the first time we didn't want to stop—"

"MOM! HAVE MERCY!"

Violetta laughed, a rarity as far as Tracy knew. "Tracy, don't yell; it's disrespectful." But Tracy's mother didn't sound like she really meant it.

"I'm sorry, Mom, but I really don't want to know all of that." Tracy paused. "So you basically told Dad to knock it off."

Violetta leaned forward in her chair. "I told him if every time he kissed me he was going to get impure ideas, that I wouldn't let him kiss me until we were married. And if that didn't work, I wouldn't let him even see me unless someone else was there. But he understood me, and we still had plenty of nice evenings. Your father loved and respected me enough to do what I asked."

"Okay, enough about Dad. How did you handle your *own* feelings?"

Violetta started rocking in her chair again. "Tracy, if you can't control yourself, how can you then expect Brian to do the same? You have to set the example. It's all about self-discipline. If there are certain times or circumstances that you find yourself weakening, then avoid those times and circumstances in the future. If Brian tries to talk you into something, be firm with him. He will listen to you."

Tracy sighed. "You make it sound so easy."

"I didn't say it was easy. I said it was about discipline."

"I understand."

"Tracy, are you pregnant?"

Tracy straightened up. "No, Mom."

"Have you ever been pregnant?"

"No! I would never get an abortion!"

Violetta smiled. "Have you asked for forgiveness?"

Tracy sighed. "I need to go to confession, I guess, for the last time we...."

Violetta nodded. "Tracy, what are you going to do about your children?"

"What do you mean?"

"Are you going to raise them Catholic?"

"Yes, Brian and I have already talked about this."

"Good, that is good."

"Don't think badly of Brian, Mom; he never forced me to do anything. He's trying to be understanding. In fact, I talked to him before I came over, and he was in really high spirits."

Violetta nodded. "Tracy, I couldn't think badly of him without thinking badly of your father. If he loves you like you believe he does, and if you really want to overcome temptation, you both will be able to. But the two of you can't do that alone. Have you prayed about this together?"

"No," she answered quietly.

"Well, there's part of your problem right there. You think you can do this without a little help from above. The next time you're together and you're thinking about such things, say a prayer together instead."

"I never even thought about that."

"That's the problem with everyone today: they think there's no God, or if there is, they don't need Him. Everybody thinks they know everything."

"Okay, Mom, I understand. And I *know* I don't know everything."

Violetta smiled. "Tracy, you know I love you more than anything else in the world. And it pains me to tell you that your struggles are only beginning. Once you and Brian have children, you will have a whole new list of worries to deal with. That's why it's important now to learn humility. We all need help, sometimes from people right next to you, sometimes from above. You and Brian should act as if you already have children who are watching and observing you; start setting an example now. Are you hearing me, dear child?"

"Yes, Mom. I've heard everything you've said to me." Tracy rose and was soon embracing Violetta. "And I love you too," she told her mother. The talk had been what she needed, if for no other reason than to deepen their bond, something she wanted very much to keep doing. But her mother, being the more practical of the two, spoiled the moment.

"You need to eat something. It's almost eight."

"Mom, I'm fine."

"Let go of me so I can get you something."

Tracy laughed softly and shook her head. "Fine, Mom; you sure do know how to kill the moment."

"Bah."

"Thanks, Mom. Thank you for being such a wonderful mother."

"You can thank me by letting me feed you. Come on."

Tracy pushed the button on the outside console at almost 10:30. Brian buzzed her in promptly, and they were soon embracing inside Brian's apartment. "Did you pick out a dress?" he asked.

"We didn't get that far. We talked, and then Mom insisted I eat. And I wanted to leave early enough so that I got to see you tonight, at least for a little bit. I'll pick something out later; there's time."

"Want something to drink? Water, maybe?"

"Sure."

Brian released her and then moved toward his kitchen cabinets to grab a glass. Tracy followed. He was filling her cup at the sink as Tracy waited patiently by the kitchen's island.

Tracy said, "Can I ask what made you so chipper earlier?"

"Huh?"

"You just seemed to be in a really good mood."

"Why shouldn't I be?" Brian handed Tracy her water.

"Are you okay, Brian? You're acting weird."

He laughed. "I'm just trying to be supportive; to keep a positive attitude. I know this purity thing is important to you, so it's important to me too. You know how much I love you."

"Purity thing?" she grinned.

"Whatever you want to call it, Tracy. I was trying to think of other things we could do together to bide our time."

"Bide our time? Good grief, Brian."

"How about taking a cooking class?"

"A cooking class?"

"Sure, we could take one together at night or on the weekends. That way, we spend time together but we're otherwise occupied."

"Oh. It's not because you think my cooking stinks, is it?"

     Practice to Deceive

"Of course not! If anyone's cooking stinks, it's mine. I can follow directions as well as most, but I can't do anything fancy."

"You don't have to cook anything fancy for me, Brian."

"But I'd like to. How'd you like to come home after a hard day at work to a gourmet meal prepared by your loving husband?"

Tracy smiled broadly. "Okay, you got me. I think I'd love that very much."

"And then a massage while sharing a nice hot bath together…"

"Stop! Stop right there!"

"What?"

"What do you mean 'what'? What do you think?"

"Oh, I'm getting you worked up, am I?"

"Listen, it's a lovely idea, Brian. But my work schedule is such that a class might be difficult."

"I don't want to take one alone, Tracy."

"I understand. Why don't you look into it, then, and see what you find? Maybe we could make it work."

Brian smiled and took Tracy by the hand; they were soon seated on his couch. He stroked her hair while smiling at her. "You're so beautiful, you know that?"

She blushed while smiling herself. "If that's what your beholding eyes see, I won't argue."

He chuckled and then kissed her. "So how long can you stay tonight?"

"Honestly, I should probably leave now. I have a busy day tomorrow."

"Defending the innocent..."

"Yes."

He kissed her again. "How about staying just five more minutes? I'll set the timer on my watch, if you want me to."

Tracy chortled. "Oh, you're so romantic." And she embraced and kissed him. She didn't mind that she left almost half an hour later.

"You were right, Beck," Tracy told her secretary early the next morning. Tracy was pouring her second cup of coffee of the day. "I talked to Mom, and she said some good things. I don't think anything *I* said really surprised her." When Tracy finished filling her mug, she offered to do the same for Rebecca.

"I'm really glad to hear it, Tracy," Rebecca smiled, accepting the offer.

"And I even had time to see Brian for a bit. That went very well too. I really think he understands where I'm coming from, now. He proved that to me in his own way: he suggested taking a cooking class. It was a good night all around.”

“A cooking class, huh?”

“The more I think about it, the more I like the idea. Thanks, Beck.”

“I’ll send you my bill,” Rebecca joked as she headed back to her desk.

At 9:45 a.m., Tracy left her office building on Falls Road and headed toward *Merlin’s Manor of Mirth and Magic*. She had called earlier and managed to speak with a member of the cleaning crew. He had told her people started arriving as early as 10:00 a.m. When Tracy arrived, she parked in the pay lot and banged for a few minutes on the entrance doors. No one came to let her in. Then she went to the back, found a Deliveries Only door, and pushed the outside buzzer. An unfamiliar figure pushed open the door. “May I help you?” he asked. Tracy introduced herself and handed him a business card.

“Is Pamela here yet, by any chance? She knows me.”

The greeter studied her a moment. “Follow me,” he said finally. Tracy obliged and was soon approaching an office door marked House Manager. “You know this lady, Ms. Houston?”

Pamela looked up. Tracy thought she must have just arrived, herself, because she was in the process of closing her purse and locking it in a desk drawer. She had her long, red hair in a ponytail. “Oh—sure. You’re that lawyer, right?”

“That’s me.”

“It’s fine, Luke. I’ll talk to her.”

“Yes, ma’am.”

“Thanks, Luke,” Tracy said as he left them. She turned to Pamela. “Does Luke work for *Merlin’s*?”

“No, he’s part of the contracted cleaning crew. What can I do for you, Ms.—what was it?”

“Please just call me Tracy.”

“Tracy—right.”

“You’ve heard they’ve made an arrest?”

“Yes, I certainly have! I had to scramble to find a substitute comic for the week. He’s no Woody Williams.”

“Of course, that was a stupid question on my part. Well, I’m Woody’s lawyer.”

“You? Really?”

“Yes, just one of those things. He needed a lawyer, he remembered me from the show, and here I am.”

“Alright, what can *I* help you with? I’m very busy, as you can imagine.”

"Of course; I just have some general questions about *Merlin's*, Montado, and how things work around here."

"Oh."

"What time does Montado's crew start showing up to prepare?"

"Oh, anytime now."

"Well, I guess my first question for you is, Do you remember seeing anything strange or unusual on Friday night? Where are you, and what are you doing, when the show's going on?"

"Running around like a madwoman is what I'm doing," Pamela said while taking her seat. She pointed to a chair. "Sit down."

"Oh—thanks."

"This past Friday? Well, before the body was found, the thing I remember most was dealing with that irate customer over his lost ticket."

"Yeah—I remember that too. I happened to be a few places back in line when the guy was complaining. Did you ever figure out what happened?"

"Not really. First time it's ever happened. He had his confirmation number, and he did pay for a ticket. Ultimately, we had to refund his money."

"Could you tell what seat he should have had, based on his confirmation number?"

"Unfortunately, no. But we're going to implement a change so that we will be able to do that going forward. You see, the seat location is assigned internally after payment is received. The confirmation number just shows that a person paid. Payments are collected, and then seats are assigned on a first-come, first-served basis. We're going to have to integrate all that, somehow."

"So you just hold all tickets at the box office?"

"Not necessarily. If you order them early enough, we'll mail them to you, unless you specifically request us to hold them. Or, if you purchase them right at our box office, we'll hand them to you right then and there."

"I see. Well, based on what this guy paid, can you tell the area in which he *should* have been sitting?"

Pamela appeared pensive. "Hmm. You know, now that you ask, I can tell you he would have been up front, fairly close to the stage."

"Really?" Tracy asked, suspending her note-taking. "I don't suppose he, theoretically, could have had the seat that the victim in this case had?"

Pamela started nodding. "Yes, in theory; that was the price of the seats in the area where this Conrad fellow was sitting."

Tracy scratched her chin. "Do you recall if Montado came to the ticket booth at any point during the evening?"

"I can't really say. Rose might know. Montado does mingle sometimes before the earlier show, sometimes even while the comedian is on. But not all the time."

"He's performed here before this current engagement?"

"Oh, yes, he was here last summer for two weeks, shortly after we opened."

"I, of course, saw his show on Friday; supreme stuff."

"He's a favorite; that's why we asked him to come back."

"Do you know if Rose is here yet?"

"She won't be here until about 1:00; that's when we open the box office."

"Any tickets left for tonight?"

"Are you kidding? We had already sold out Thursday, Friday, and Saturday *before* the excitement. Once the murder hit the news, we sold the rest of the week within hours."

"Well, people."

"Tell me about it."

"You don't have shows on Sunday and Monday?"

"During the off-season we don't. From Memorial Day through Labor Day, we have something seven nights a week and matinees on the weekends. We had to cancel last Saturday's matinee, of course, but the evening shows went on as scheduled."

"It must have been *really* crazy on Saturday night, then."

"Totally bananas. I was trying to find a replacement for Woody up until practically the last minute, and people were mobbing the place thinking they could get a ticket at so late a date. Thank God we all had Sunday off to recuperate."

"Tonight might not be much different."

Pamela nodded. "Do you know how many phone messages were in the general mailbox asking if we had tickets tonight?"

"I'd be afraid to hazard a guess."

"Almost 90. And that was since the last time I cleaned the thing out on Monday. Some of those callers: the way they go on and on. Some went ahead and left their charge information. My poor finger was hurting after pounding the erase button so many times."

"I thought you weren't in the office yesterday."

"I can access our voice mail from home. I checked it regularly, given what's happened. I didn't want to come in today with a sudden emergency on my hands."

"I hear you." Tracy looked over her notes. "Can I ask what you did before you started managing this place last year?"

"Oh, I managed a comedy club in DC for several years. Having the connections with the stand-ups helped get me this job."

"How do you like it here as compared to DC?"

"The area's nicer here, being by the water and the Harbor. I love being so close to Phillips Seafood. It's been crazy, of course, but I thrive on craziness most of the time. It's fine."

"Well, I think that's all I have for now, Pamela. Thank you so much for your time. I wonder if I can ask you to take me to the back dressing rooms where Montado and company may be. I don't want to get busted by security or anything."

Pamela sniggered. "I'll take you back there. Let's head on over." Soon Pamela was parting the black curtains and Tracy was following. And, then, Tracy was face-to-face with someone who brought a wide smile to her face.

"Mr. Montado, I'd like you to meet Tracy," Pamela said to that someone.

Montado took Tracy's right hand and kissed it gently. "A pleasure, Tracy." Pamela left them.

Tracy was momentarily starstruck. It was rare that she was at a loss for words; she was frantically trying to find some. "Mr. Montado, you don't know what a huge thrill this is for me," she said, finally, still grinning from ear to ear.

"You honor me, dear lady." Then Montado tilted his head. "Have we not met before?"

Tracy giggled. "You handed me flowers on Friday night."

Recognition caused Montado's eyes to open wide. "Of course, of course! You are Tracy the birthday girl!"

She smiled. "Actually, Tracy Brubaker, the attorney. But, please, just call me Tracy."

Montado chuckled. "Yes, of course. So would you like an autograph?"

"Ooo…could I get one?"

"It would be a pleasure for me."

"Wow, sure, okay."

"You will follow me to my dressing room, then?"

"Yes, Mr. Montado."

Soon Tracy was watching Montado sign a color photo of himself. He wrote: "To My Dearest Tracy, On your birthday, May all your days be magical—Montado!" He handed her the prize.

"Thank you so much, Mr. Montado. This will go perfectly with the hat and flowers."

"I am so glad," he said, smiling back.

"Uh, Mr. Montado, I'm actually here to talk to you about Friday night. They've arrested someone for killing the man who was in your tank. And I'm the accused person's lawyer."

Montado leaned back in his chair and started stroking the corners of his mouth with his right thumb and index fingers. "Oh, I see. You are Mr. Williams' lawyer."

"Yes."

"What a horrible, horrible thing that was."

"As bad as it was being in the audience and seeing it, I can't imagine what it was like for you and your people."

Montado shook his head. "Poor, poor Karine. She was so upset, we didn't perform the water tank illusion at all on Saturday."

"Oh, I didn't realize that. I did meet with her briefly Friday after what happened. Thinking of that scream still brings me chills. I felt so bad for her. Imagine turning around and seeing…well, just awful."

"You are so kind for understanding."

"She's been with you about 11 years?"

"That sounds correct. She was so young when she joined. I remember she had tried to be a dancer, but for whatever reason convinced herself she wouldn't succeed. But she still wanted to be on the stage. I was able to offer her a job with me."

"And her brother too."

"Oh yes, Gregory. A fine young man, very close to Karine. It was through him that I met her, as a matter of fact. He was applying to become my business manager—this young *boy*, what confidence he had! I was going to turn him down. But then he told me about his sister. And something told me that if she were working with me, he would of course make good on his boasts and promises. Besides, by that stage in my career I was having no problems getting bookings. So, I took a chance on them. And now look at us, 11 years later!"

"That's really something. Karine's lovely."

"Yes—and graceful—and a quick learner. It pains me to see her so upset."

Tracy nodded. "Yes, that is certainly understandable." She cleared her throat. "I was wondering, Mr. Montado, why you picked Conrad, as he called himself, to come to the stage that night."

Montado laughed. "Oh, it was an easy choice. I look around and I see this man looking so serious, so unpleasant. How can one be this way? I should have been angry with him, myself, insulted by this harsh face. So I realized I must do something about this. I must inspire him! And I did! Did

you see the look on his face as he left the stage? He was not so harsh-look-
ing, anymore, was he?"

Tracy snuffed. "I remember him shaking his head in disbelief. That was
a supreme illusion."

"There is so little magic left in the world today, so few kept secrets. It
has made us all so cynical and serious. It saddens me when I think about it."

"I agree with you completely. I've always loved magic; I still do. I had
such a wonderful time on Friday—up until the murder, of course."

"Thank you, young lady, you are most kind."

"Had you ever seen Conrad before Friday?"

"I don't believe so."

"He was at your earlier show on Friday too."

"Really? This I did not know."

"Well, he was dressed a little differently and had a seat toward the back,
although his friend said Conrad was possibly roaming around."

"Roaming around? I doubt it. They have good security here. You are not
allowed to move about during the show."

"Of course, you're right. You have been to *Merlin's* before and know
how things work. And you have your own personal security in the back."

"Yes."

"Kurt and Ron Donlevy are their names, right?"

"Yes."

"What do they do exactly? I mean, at some point, they push the tank
onstage."

"Yes. They help set up the stage and take it down, load and unload our
van. Once our show starts, one of them is near the curtain entrance while
the other is assisting with the show, dealing with props and such. And they
rotate so they don't get bored doing the exact same thing all the time. Then,
of course, when it comes time for the tank to be brought onstage, whoever is
watching the curtain must leave to put on the mask and assist the other with
the tank. They are supposed to remove the tarp, and then one will return to
the curtain."

"Right, because the next time two figures dressed in black wearing black
masks appear, you turn out to be one of them!"

Montado's head went back as he laughed and clapped his hands together. "Yes!" he cried out in delight. "I must somehow make sure you see this
trick live, since you were denied this pleasure on Friday."

"Thanks, Mr. Montado, I'd love it if you could make that happen."

Montado laughed again. "If you believe in the magic, then anything *can*
happen!"

Tracy smiled and nodded in agreement. She believed, truly believed, what Montado had just said. In fact, despite what had been witnessed by 500 or so people on Friday, Tracy was becoming more and more convinced that Montado may, in fact, have been involved with Zach Granger's death. But how he managed that trick, she hadn't a clue.

Chapter 6

Tracy thanked Montado as she left his dressing room. She saw Kurt and Ron Donlevy by the delivery door, bringing in cases of what no doubt contained Montado's props and paraphernalia. She wasn't going to bother them right now. She noticed that Karine Bowers' door was open, so she poked her head inside. Karine was standing next to a table behind the sofa, pouring from a carafe something most people wouldn't have before lunchtime. She put the glass container down and sipped her drink. She noticed Tracy at the doorway.

"Hi Karine," Tracy said. "Remember me from Friday?"

Karine smiled. "Sure—Tracy. You were so nice. Please come in."

"Thanks. How are you doing today?"

"Oh, this helps," Karine answered raising her glass. "Do you want one?"

"No, thanks."

"Well, please, sit down." Karine put her drink on the table and started removing the clothing that was covering the couch. "I'm sorry; I'm such a slob. You can sit here."

"Thanks, Karine." Tracy smiled as she lowered herself onto the sofa. Karine picked her beverage back up. She saw Tracy watching her.

"I don't usually have one of these this early," Karine said sheepishly. "In fact, I rarely drink at all, really. It's just that I still keep thinking about Friday."

Tracy shook her head. "You don't owe me any explanations, Karine. I can't imagine how you feel."

Karine smiled weakly. "You're very nice. If my brother were here, he'd probably rip this out of my hand."

"Where *is* Greg?"

"He's at the hotel. He'll be bringing lunch for us all in an hour or so. I can call him and have him pick something up for you, if you'd like."

"That's very sweet of you, Karine, but I'm fine."

"Oh, okay. Well, let me know if you change your mind."

"Your brother takes care of the business side of things, does he?"

"Yes. Books the places, oversees the contracts, coordinates publicity, yada yada yada…"

Tracy chuckled. "Is he usually at the shows?"

"It depends. I like him to be here. But sometimes he would rather stay at whatever hotel we're booked in. He prefers peace and quiet to all the noise. And he's seen the act before."

Tracy nodded. "You called him Friday night after what happened?"

"Yeah. I called and told him everything. He came right over."

"Did you talk to him earlier in the day at all, I mean, after he went back to the hotel presumably for the rest of the night?"

"Um…I called him around 7:00 p.m. or so, I think, to see if he was… if he was going out with us after the show. Sometimes we do that; go out together, I mean, for a drink or something. He said he didn't think so."

"I see. This Conrad fellow who came up onstage, had you ever seen him before?"

Karine took another drink from her glass. "No, I don't think so."

"He was there for the earlier show that Friday."

"Oh? I didn't know that."

"Does Mr. Montado make a habit of picking a grumpy-faced patron to come up onstage?"

"Huh? Oh, actually, I usually pick who comes up onstage."

"You do?"

"Yes. But then again, Mr. Montado is always making little changes here and there to vary the act. He doesn't like doing the exact same show each night anymore than someone would probably want to watch the same show over and over again."

"That makes sense. When was the last time Mr. Montado did, in fact, pick the audience participation member?"

"Uh…I'm not sure. I really don't remember. Sorry."

"No problem, Karine."

"Uh, Tracy, can I ask you why you're asking me all of these questions?"

"Oh, I didn't tell you?"

"No."

"I'm sorry. Well, you know Woody Williams was arrested for killing Conrad."

Karine stared into her glass. "Yes."

"Well, he hired me to defend him."

Karine stared at Tracy. "Oh, so you're his lawyer? I didn't realize you were a lawyer. I thought you worked for *Merlin's*."

"I'm sorry. I didn't mean to mislead you."

"But, wait, you were in the audience on Friday."

"Just my luck; I was here for my birthday, and I got a client because of it."

"Oh."

"You're not too upset with me, are you?"

Karine shook her head. "No, of course not. I'm just surprised by it, that's all. I mean, you've been so nice and all."

Tracy looked at her curiously. "Karine, you don't think lawyers can be nice people?"

Karine took another swig. "Not the ones I've dealt with. People are suing Mr. Montado all of the time for ripping off this, stealing that. I get questioned by lawyers about this and that, hoping I'll say something they can use against him. I guess you could say I don't care for them."

"I understand. Well, I'm not here to hurt anybody. I'm just trying to get a good feel for what happened here on Friday night."

"Oh? Do you think your client is innocent?"

"I believe so."

"Well, what's there to get a handle on? The police wouldn't have arrested him if they didn't have reason to think he did it. Right?"

"Yes and no. There's some evidence. But I don't think it's that conclusive. And the timing just isn't working for me."

"What do you mean?"

"Conrad sneaks backstage, presumably has a fight with Woody, and gets dumped in the tank, all during the brief time Kurt or Ron has left to get changed. And neither claims to have seen anything out of the ordinary. At least, that's what they told the police. Something doesn't feel right about it."

Karine pursed her lips. "I guess I see your point."

"I could be wrong, though. It could have happened as I described it just now. I'm not a detective, so what do I know, really?"

Karine looked at Tracy skeptically. "I think maybe you know a lot."

Tracy smiled. "I guess you're going to be rehearsing soon."

"Uh, yeah. I'm going to check my costumes, and then Greg will be here with lunch. And then we'll do some rehearsing."

"I wish I could stay and watch. Of course, even if I had the time, I probably wouldn't be allowed to."

Karine grinned. "No, I don't think so."

"So, do you know Woody Williams at all? Has he opened for you before this particular tour?"

"I don't know him; never met him before this *Merlin's* gig."

"I've heard he fancies himself a lady's man. He didn't make a move on you or anything like that, did he?"

Karine blinked. "No, he didn't."

"Did you see him maybe trying that with someone else, irritating a boyfriend in the process?"

"No, I didn't socialize with him or pay attention to him. When I said we went out after the show earlier, I meant the people involved with the magic show, not Woody's."

"Oh, sure. I just thought if you saw Woody get rough with somebody, that could be important."

"Wouldn't that be bad for your client, though?"

"Maybe, maybe not." Tracy cleared her throat. "Well, I've taken too much time of yours as it is. I didn't mean to. Good luck with the show tonight, and I hope you feel better."

"Sure. No problem. And thanks for…I guess, checking on me."

Tracy smiled as she stood up. "Bye, Karine." And then Tracy left the assistant to stare into her now empty glass.

"I've only got five minutes," Rose told Tracy nervously. "You see that line out there don't you?"

"They think they can get tickets to one of Montado's shows this week?" Tracy asked, not really surprised.

"Exactly, and every 1 out of 10 or so I say no to will want to pick a fight. It's incredible. And I have to just sit there and smile and take it."

"I've seen you in action."

"What?"

"I was there Friday when that guy was going on and on about you losing his ticket, waving his confirmation in your face."

Rose started nodding. "Right, right, right. I don't know what happened with that. That guy just wouldn't leave the line. I don't know what was taking Pamela so long to get this guy taken care of. I called her like three times."

"Well, she was probably putting out another fire."

"Whatever."

"I see they don't make you dress up when you're selling tickets here."

That got a smile from thorny Rose. "No, I'm just me."

"So, do you have any idea what happened to the missing ticket?"

"Nope."

"Okay, let me ask you this: when giving someone their tickets, can you easily tell where the person is sitting, or do you have to open the envelope and actually look at the tickets to know that?"

"Uh—oh, the seat assignments are listed in the top right corner of the envelope. It makes it quicker for me to show someone where they're sitting if they want to know then and there. We have a seating chart at the ticket booth, you know. So I can just look at the outside of the envelope and find their seat and point it out. It's easier than pulling the tickets out and looking for the seat number. Some, though, just wait for the usher to take them. And then, of course, there are the people who have been with us before and know exactly where they're going."

Tracy nodded as she made her notes. "Just one more question, Rose. Did Montado visit the lobby Friday night, maybe between shows?"

Rose looked up at nothing in particular, apparently considering the question. "Well, I remember he was doing some tricks for those still in the lobby during the stand-up act for the first show. Some people skip one act or the other altogether. I think he did come over to say hi to me and flirt; he does that sometimes." Rose grinned.

Tracy smiled back and closed her notebook. "I guess it's about that time."

Rose turned and faced the inside of the pre-sale booth window. "Yeah. Wish me luck."

"I wish you luck," Tracy said. "Thanks, Rose, thanks for your time."

"Sure." And then Rose gulped, entered the booth, and parted the window's mini-curtains. "Can I help the first customer please?" she asked cheerfully.

"Yes," a tall, thin woman said. "I'd like four tickets to tonight's Montado show, please." It was going to be a long afternoon.

After Tracy left Rose to deal with the ever-growing line outside, she saw Greg Bowers talking to Pamela Houston, or rather, arguing with her. "The Saturday afternoon cancellation was not our fault," Bowers was saying. "The police questioned all of us and didn't allow us access to anything until late in the morning. How could anyone have had time to prepare for a 2:00 p.m. matinee?"

"We had to refund everyone their money!" Pamela shouted.

"Yell at the police, not me!"

"I'm not yelling!"

"Look, the contract is clear: any cancellation of one or more of the performances that is beyond our control will *not* result in the refund of any, or all, of our fee. We get the *entire* fee. Go through your insurance company to collect on your loss, if you want to. Now that is all there is to it." Bowers turned hurriedly and almost ran Tracy over. "Oh, I'm sorry," he said, stopping just in time.

"No problem, Greg."

"Do I know you?"

"We met briefly on Friday. I'm Karine's new friend, Tracy."

"Oh yeah, okay. How are you?" he asked insincerely.

"Fine. And you?"

"That depends. Are you looking for Karine?"

"No, actually I'd like to talk to you, if I may."

"Why? What for?"

"Just some questions about Friday."

Bowers was puzzled. "Are you a cop or something?"

"Lawyer."

"Lawyer! Have they got you trying to cover their asses already?!"

"What?"

"*Merlin's*, of course. You work for them, right?"

Tracy shook her head, laughing slightly. "No, Greg. I think you misunderstand. I'm Woody Williams' lawyer."

"Who's he?"

"He's the one who was arrested for the murder."

Realization made its way over Bowers' face. "Oh, of course, how stupid of me. So you're defending *him*, huh?"

"Yes. I'm just here today to ask people who were here on Friday a few questions, to learn what they saw—that kind of thing."

Bowers frowned. "And to find someone else to blame, no doubt."

Tracy breathed deeply. "If you mean to simply pick a name at random out of a magic hat, then, no. I'm interested in facts."

"Uh-huh, sure you are."

"Well, can we make a deal since you're so skeptical? Let me ask some questions. If you don't like them or think I'm out of line, then just tell me to get lost."

"I can tell you to get lost right now and you'd have to. I don't have to talk you if I don't want to. I know my rights. I deal with lawyers all the time."

Tracy had tried to be nice. But if that's the way Bowers was going to be… "Okay, Mr. Bowers, if you want be an ass, fine. But expect a subpoena at some point, because I *will* subpoena you if you won't talk to me now. And you'll have to appear or risk a warrant. And it won't matter where in the country you are at the time, either!" Tracy turned and started walking away.

"Wait!" Bowers called out. He didn't see the grin on Tracy's face, which had faded by the time she had turned back around to face him.

"Yes, Mr. Bowers?" she asked sweet as can be.

He sighed, defeated. "What are your questions?"

"Oh goody," she said moving back toward her subject. "You were at the hotel most of the night on Friday?"

"Yes."

"When did you get there?"

"Well, I had dinner with Karine. We eat early, so I was probably done by 5:30 or so. Then I left before the madness started."

"The noisy patrons."

"Yes."

"So you got to the hotel about what time?"

"Six-ish, I guess."

"And you were there until your sister called you around 11:30?"

"That's right."

"Did you talk to anyone else when you were in the hotel room, such as a business associate or someone like that?"

"Not that I recall."

"So the only call you got that night was from your sister?"

"Yes."

"Hmm."

"What 'hmm'?"

"Your sister said she called you first around 7:00 or something."

"Oh, yes, she did. I got confused; I thought you meant to ask if I had spoken to anyone else except my sister."

"Oh, sorry, didn't mean to confuse you."

Bowers looked at her skeptically. "She did call earlier."

"What did she want?"

"Why do you want to know?"

"Why don't you want to tell me?"

Bowers sighed. "She wanted to know if I was going to join everyone for a drink or something after the show. I told her I wasn't up for it. Satisfied?"

"Oh, I certainly am."

"You…any more questions?"

"So you got the call about the murder, and you came right on over."

"Yes."

"What time did you get here?"

"Around midnight, I think."

"You came by cab?"

"I walked."

"You walked?"

"It would have taken me just as long to hail a cab and get ripped off while we sat in downtown traffic."

"Oh, okay. So how did you get into the club?"

"I just went to the back and rang the bell by the delivery entrance. Kurt let me in; they knew I was coming."

"Did you see anyone hanging around the back? Maybe somebody running or acting suspiciously?"

"No. The police asked me practically the exact same question."

"Okay. Had you seen this Conrad guy before, at another show, maybe?"

"I don't even know what the guy really looks like to answer that."

"His picture's been in the paper."

"I don't have time to read the papers."

"Oh."

"Why do you think I may have seen him before, anyway?"

"No reason, really. It's just that he knew at what time the curtain guard left to get ready for the water tank trick. He was right there waiting to sneak back. So he must have known the routine."

"Oh, I see. You think he may have been at a show earlier in the week."

"Maybe several shows, even. I don't know if one could get a lay of the land with just one show."

"Hmm. Well, that's interesting, but I still can't help you."

"All the *Merlin's* employees knew about Montado and the security, right?"

"Of course."

"So they could have told someone about the curtain guard."

Bowers' eyes narrowed. "If somebody from here said something to that guy—"

"Be careful, Greg. Don't say anything that could be considered slanderous or libelous. I'm a lawyer, remember? You wouldn't want someone from *Merlin's* having cause to sue you for a false allegation."

"Wait—you were the one who suggested it!"

"Suggesting it as a possibility, maybe; I'm not accusing anyone or saying it even happened."

"Well, alright, then. Anything else?"

"I understand your parents live in Arlington."

Bowers eyes narrowed again. "Yes."

"Are you going to see them while you're here?"

"Already did; Sunday."

"I saw my mother on Sunday too."

"Uh…okay."

"Nice visiting family, especially when you need to see a friendly face."

"Right."

"What does your father do for a living?"

"Sells insurance. Why?"

"Just curious."

"I thought you were just interested in facts."

"It isn't a fact your father sells insurance?"

"Isn't…oh, are we done here?" Bowers moaned.

"I guess so. Thanks, Greg. That wasn't so bad, was it?"

All he said was, "Goodbye." He turned and almost bumped into Pamela Houston. Tracy shook her head.

"He's gonna run somebody over one of these days," she thought. "Somebody could end up with a bump on the back of the head." Tracy looked around. Anyone else she could squeeze in today? That's when she recognized the magic house's announcer, Richard, as she had heard him called, coming out of the men's room. "Well, why not?" she asked herself. "Hi, Richard!" she called out.

Richard stopped to look around for the source of his name. He saw Tracy approaching him. When he realized who she was, he smiled. "Tracy, right?"

"Yes, you remember me."

"Sure do. You were terrific on Friday. I felt sorry for your fiancé, though."

Tracy grinned. "Oh, Brian's alive and well; no need to worry about him."

"Out of the toaster, huh?"

"Yeah."

"What did you need me for?"

"Well, Richard, I'm representing Woody Williams."

"Oh yeah! I heard he got arrested."

"Yes, I'm trying to get a handle on what goes on behind the scenes here at *Merlin's*. Can I talk to you about that for a few minutes?"

He looked at his watch. "Sure, I have a few minutes I can spare. Let's get out of the middle of the lobby, though; it's going to be getting busy here real soon." Richard motioned toward the bar and then he hopped up on one of its stools. Tracy did likewise. "What can I tell you?"

"Well, let's start with you, if that's okay. I know you do the opening announcements. What else do you do? What are you doing during the show?"

"In a nutshell, I'm lobby security. Two ushers serve the inside, to help people who have to leave and then reenter—you know, bathroom breaks, getting a refill from the bar. But they can't just go back in at any time. We try to limit reentry to when there's some kind of pause in the show: audience applause, usually."

"Oh, so you keep people out here a bit so they don't create a distraction."

"Yes, the door opening means noise from the lobby could be briefly heard, people in the back get distracted, or, worse, one of our performers could have their concentration broken. So I just politely ask people to wait a moment. It's rarely very long. There are frequent laughs during the comedy and plenty of applause during the magic part."

"Anybody give you a hard time about doing your job before?"

"I can count on one hand without using all the fingers as to how often that's happened."

"Well, that's a good thing. I don't suppose Friday was one of those fingers."

Richard smiled. "No, Friday was fine until the tank thing."

"And you were out here when that happened?"

"Yes. I'm standing there getting ready to open the doors since Montado's nearing the end of his show, and then I hear that scream. I open one of the doors just as the lights come on. Then Pamela shows up. Wasn't that you I saw talking to her almost right away?"

"Yes, I was familiar with police procedure in a case like this, when you have such a large volume of witnesses, I mean."

"Right. I helped secure the doors and then the stage until the police came."

"Okay. And in your travels, did you see anything out of the ordinary, anything or anyone suspicious?"

Richard shook his head. "Sorry, it was just so crazy. I'd never been through anything like that before."

"Of course; very few people have." Tracy made some notes. "Where were you working before *Merlin's*?"

"Oh, with Pamela."

"Oh you worked at the same club she did, huh?"

"Yes, she recommended me to the owner here, and they made a nice offer."

"Pamela's a good boss, then."

"She's fine. She's very business-minded, which means she runs a tight ship. But that means everything that goes wrong is a major crisis. It's always stressful dealing with the public, of course."

"Sure. You don't remember seeing Conrad at any point during the evening prior to his appearance onstage, do you? I mean, did he maybe leave the theater and then have to reenter?"

Richard paused. "No, I can't say that I remember seeing him at all that night." He looked around and called out to a gentleman dressed in a red jacket. "Hey, Barry, find Eddie and the two of you come over here a minute, will ya please?" Barry nodded. Richard looked at Tracy. "Those are the ushers. Let's see if they remember seeing this Conrad."

"Great idea; thanks, Richard." Tracy didn't have to wait long until Barry and Eddie, the latter being the usher she remembered from Friday, joined her and the announcer.

"What is it, Rich?" Barry asked.

"This is Tracy, and she's a lawyer in need of some information. Do either of you remember seeing the Conrad fellow, the guy in the tank on Friday, at any point during the night?"

The two ushers looked at each other. They shook their heads. Tracy asked, "I guess it's next to impossible to recognize faces when you see so many people each night, night in, night out."

"Yeah," Barry said. "You take the tickets, tear them in half, and then give half back to the customer. Sometimes you escort them to their seats; sometimes they just go in to find them on their own."

"Do you keep all the stubs you collect?"

"Yes," Barry told her. "They try to reconcile the attendance. The stubs in the boxes, plus the unclaimed tickets, plus the un-purchased ones should total the seating capacity, which is, I think, 492 or 493, something like that."

"Yeah," Eddie spoke, finally. "I think it's 493."

"And everything worked out on Friday?"

"You'd have to ask Pamela that," Barry answered.

Tracy smiled and closed her notebook. "Thanks, guys! You've been very helpful. Have a great show tonight!" They all smiled and resumed their duties for the pre-show setup. Tracy decided to pop her head in Pamela's office for one quick question. Pamela was just slamming her phone down when Tracy arrived at her doorway.

"Dammed insurance companies," Pamela muttered.

"Hi Pamela. Can I ask you one quick question?"

"Super-quick question."

"Yes: did your ticket reconciliation all work out for Friday's late show?"

"Huh?"

"Were all the tickets accounted for? Used plus unclaimed equaled total seats."

"Oh! Yes, everything worked out."

"Ah, so I guess that guy's lost ticket must have indeed been used by somebody else."

"Yes, otherwise we'd have been short a ticket stub."

"Thanks, Pamela!" Tracy said cheerfully, and then she left the busy manager to her duties. Tracy hadn't eaten, and it was almost 3:00. There were still people she wanted to talk to, but *Merlin's* was starting to buzz with behind-the-scenes activity. The technical group had arrived and was starting sound checks. The replacement stand-up comic—someone she didn't recognize—had also appeared and was reviewing some handwritten notes. The water tank was being filled with liquid; apparently, they planned to perform the trick tonight. Tracy thought she'd come back, hopefully tomorrow, and finish her interviews. The day was passing quickly; time to go back to her office.

Neal was listening as Tracy went through her notes aloud. When she had finished, she looked at Neal, who was pursing his lips. He asked, "So are you thinking that Montado palmed a ticket and gave it to Granger?"

"It does sound like a possibility, doesn't it? I mean, that's the first time a ticket has gone missing, and on the very same night as *that* first, we have a second first: a dead body in the water tank. Pamela said the supposedly missing ticket was used Friday night, so either *Merlin's* double-charged for a ticket or someone stole it. I'm betting on the latter possibility being the case."

Neal considered Tracy's comments. "Okay, so the 'someone else' Granger mentioned to Scarborough is Montado. Montado wants Granger to—what? Stick around until after the show?"

"Maybe. But Granger doesn't have a ticket to the second show; only the first one. So Montado provides the ticket." Tracy leaned back in her chair. "Of course, even if Montado wanted Granger to stick around, why not just tell him to come to the back entrance to be let in when the show is over? Why steal a ticket to a sold-out show and draw attention to that fact? Surely Montado would realize someone was going to complain about the missing ticket. And, anyway, none of that explains why Granger didn't return to his seat after meeting with Scarborough, or why Granger felt he had to don a disguise for the later show. I don't know, Neal, maybe I'm wrong about all of this."

"Plus, Montado was onstage when Granger was killed. Maybe it was someone else Granger was there to see. What about Greg Bowers?"

"Phone records place him in his hotel room earlier in the evening, and just after the body was discovered. Karine called him, remember? Did you find out if he was in school in October 2002?"

"Yes, he was attending Drummond University in Florida."

"Florida? That's, what, a two-hour flight or a 12-hour drive from Maryland?"

"That sounds right."

"And where was Montado, at this point?"

"He was performing in Las Vegas for the entire month of October. He has, or had, some big Halloween show he does."

"So neither Montado nor Greg Bowers was around the area when the bank was robbed. And Karine was 17 and living with her parents."

"*And* she was onstage on Friday night with Montado."

Tracy shook her head. "The most obvious thing right now sounds like either Kurt or Ron Donlevy found Granger poking around, and something happened. Granger gets a bump on the head and a free dip in the pool."

"But why put him in the tank? That doesn't make any sense."

Tracy nodded. "You know, Neal, no scenario makes sense that winds up with Granger in that tank. I can't figure it. I'm baffled."

"Baffled? You?" Neal asked in mock shock.

Tracy frowned. "Instead of sitting there delighting in my frustration, why don't you go back to your desk and find something useful to do? Are you sure the Donlevy brothers don't have some kind of criminal record?"

"Didn't find anything."

"This really frosts my flakes."

Neal smiled. "Okay, Tracy, I'll go be useful."

"Yeah."

"Do you think Lucas has something else on Williams other than what they've told you? The case against Williams sounds awfully weak to me."

"Possibly. They may have made the arrest to keep the masses calm. All the notoriety this case is getting would certainly lead to pressure from the ivory tower folks."

"Uh, yeah." Neal said, and then he rose so he could go rev up his search engine in an effort to help Tracy de-baffle herself. Neal passed Rebecca in the hallway as the latter was hurriedly moving toward the boss's office.

"Tracy," Rebecca said quietly, as she poked her head in.

"What's up, Beck?" Tracy asked, slightly puzzled.

"There's a lawyer by the name of Michael Detweiler out here to see you. He's with—"

"Detweiler, Combs, Lindsey, and Snodgrass," Tracy interrupted. "They're a big deal. What does he want with little ole me?"

"He wouldn't say. He just smiled a lot. Should I tell him you're too busy? He doesn't have an appointment."

"Are you kidding? That might not be a good political move. Better show him on back."

"Okay."

Tracy rose to her feet and brushed off her blouse and skirt. She was coming around her desk when Rebecca re-entered with the smiling visitor. "Can I get you anything to drink, Mr. Detweiler?" Rebecca asked.

"I'm fine, Mrs. Deitz, thank you." Rebecca smiled and left, closing the door as she did so. Tracy approached Detweiler, arm extended.

"Tracy Brubaker, Mr. Detweiler." They shook. "But, please, call me Tracy."

Detweiler smiled. "And you call me Mike. Do you have a few moments to talk? I know you must be busy, and I've shown up here unannounced."

"I can spare some time, sure. Please have a seat." Tracy was moving back toward her desk. Detweiler took a seat as Tracy sat down in hers. "What can I do for you, Mike?"

"Well, to be blunt: I want you working at Detweiler, Combs, Lindsey, and Snodgrass."

Tracy's eyes widened. "I'm sorry?"

Detweiler continued smiling. "I want you to come and work with us. How does Detweiler, Combs, Lindsey, Snodgrass, and Brubaker sound to you?"

Tracy blinked. "Oh, I see."

"I've been hearing things about you and your work for quite a few years now. And then in the past year, I've been hearing about your sudden venture into criminal defense work. I'm very well aware, too, of your trial performance in the Massimo Paganini case; extraordinary."

Tracy blushed; she usually did when unexpectedly being showered with compliments. "Thank you," was all she could think to say.

"In short, Tracy, I and my partners feel you'd be a great addition to our practice. You, in turn, would get a lot more exposure, have many more opportunities available to you. There would be some travel involved; I think you'd find that exciting." Tracy was having trouble focusing on Detweiler's pitch; her head was spinning. But he kept talking. "I recently spoke with Professor Andrew Braxton—he was a law school instructor of yours?"

"Yes," she confirmed.

"Well, he's done some work for us; still does, on occasion. He was bringing me up to speed on that Richmond case; you cleared three murders in a matter of weeks, one of which went back 30 years!"

Tracy gulped. "I got lucky."

Detweiler chortled lightly. "I'm sure it was much, much more than luck." He paused a moment. "Look, I can see this has taken you completely by surprise. Are you available for dinner tomorrow, maybe? I'd like to tell you more about our firm and some of the things we're doing, some of the things we're changing, and where you would fit right in."

          Practice to Deceive

"Tomorrow evening?" Tracy checked her mental calendar. "Well, I guess that would be fine."

"Excellent; would dinner at Wagner House be acceptable? Say, around 7:00?"

"Oh, that would be more than acceptable."

"Excellent." Detweiler stood. Tracy did likewise. There was another shake of the hands. "I look forward to seeing you tomorrow, when we can talk more." Tracy started to follow Detweiler to her office door. "No need to show me out; I've already taken too much of your time. I'll see you tomorrow." Then Detweiler smiled and made his exit. Neal and Rebecca were in their employer's office posthaste.

"Spill," was all Rebecca said. Neal nodded.

"They want me to join their firm; my name along with theirs on the marquee and everything," she told them, still a bit stunned.

"Wow!" Rebecca said. "You just hit the stratosphere!"

"Congratulations, Tracy," Neal said quietly. "This is quite the big deal."

"Thanks."

"What did you tell him?" Rebecca asked.

"Well, nothing, really. He invited me to dinner tomorrow so he could continue his wooing."

"Nice," Rebecca grinned. "Tracy's getting wooed."

"Any idea of what you're going to do, yet?" Neal inquired.

Tracy shook her head. "No, Neal. I'm still processing this. I'd want to make sure you two could come with me before I'd even consider such an offer. I didn't get a chance to ask him that though." They both smiled at her.

"Oh, Tracy," Rebecca said giving her a hug. "Please don't worry about *me*. You know I'll be fine."

"No, Beck, *you* go with me or there's no deal. I *know* you'd find another place, but I *want* you with me." Tracy's unexpected words caught the normally composed Rebecca off guard; so much so that she excused herself. Both Tracy and Neal heard her blowing her nose. "And that goes for you too, Neal. Do *you* need a tissue?"

Neal chuckled. "No, I'll cry behind closed doors." Neal cleared his throat. "Can you at least tell me what your first instinct would be? I mean, assuming we all can head downtown together."

"I…I really don't know. I'm going to have to go home tonight and make the old two-column list: the good on one side; the bad on the other. Then I'll go from there."

Neal nodded. "Yes, you do like your lists, don't you?" Tracy smiled at him. "Do you mind if I share with you *my* first reaction, as irrelevant as it may be?"

"Yes, Neal, I do want to know."

He answered immediately. "Don't do it."

"Why?"

"…Because you're too different from any other attorney out there. I don't think you'd be comfortable in a big tall building somewhere where cases and clients, at least initially, would be assigned to you. You would still be the junior partner, the new girl on the block. Do you think they would want you running around hugging people? Or walking around the office barefoot like you like to do during the summer sometimes? It would be so sterile in a place like that. It would stifle you. To be honest, Tracy, I'm not sure I'd want to be around to watch that happen; it would kill me." Neal stopped and swallowed hard. "I'm sorry, I didn't mean to say that much."

Tracy looked at him mildly surprised. "You think I'm quirky, huh?"

Neal shook his head. "No, I think you have a way about you that makes you approach things differently. It's always more than just the law for you when you take on a client. You…look, if I don't stop I may just need that tissue. I mean, it is your decision, right? It would be, financially speaking, a monumental boost. I know it's never been about money for you. But still, I mean, it's gotta be a factor."

Tracy looked at him warmly, and then went to embrace him. "Oh, Neal, you sweet man; I don't know what to say."

"You don't have to say anything. Just think about what I said." He pulled away from her.

"I will, Neal. I promise."

"Good. Now, enough schmaltz. I have to get back to Operation: De-Baffle Tracy." He smiled, turned, and was soon back in surgery.

Tracy sat back down, feeling overwhelmed. Then she thought, "Lord, I only asked for *one* new client. This a little much, don't You think?" There was no immediate response to her query.

"Holy crap, Tracy!" Brian exclaimed upon hearing the news. "Have you decided what you're going to do?"

Tracy shook her head. "No, I'm going to be wined and dined tomorrow. I'll know more then."

"Wined and dined tomorrow?"

"Yes. I'm afraid you'll have to fend for yourself tomorrow for dinner."

"I don't care about that. I care that I might not see you."

"I think you will see me. I'm going to want to talk to someone afterward. I was hoping it would be you."

Brian smiled and then kissed her. "You know I'll be there for you. You just let me know when you're on your way over."

"Good," she smiled. "Let's eat, then." Tracy and Brian sat at her condo's dining room table and started consuming tonight's simple menu of spaghetti with meat sauce and salad.

"Maybe while you're at your dinner meeting, I'll look into those cooking classes we talked about. I haven't had a chance, yet."

"Okay, Brian."

"Tracy…"

"Yes?"

"Who are you going to ask to be your maid of honor?"

Tracy dabbed her lips with her napkin. "I was thinking of asking your sister."

Brian smiled. "I'm really glad to hear that. I think Crystal wants to be."

"I wanted to invite her to have dinner with us one weekend very soon. I was going to ask her then."

"I guess that's on hold, though, until this case is wrapped up."

Tracy sighed. "Yes; on the other hand, Montado packs up Sunday and leaves. If I don't have something by then, it won't really matter, probably."

"Oh? You think Montado is involved in this?"

"I don't *want* him to be, for obvious reasons." Tracy leaned forward. "Brian, there are some things about this case that make no sense, like the floating jacket and the body being dumped in the tank. And yet, at the same time, they do make sense, if one is looking at them in the right way. I need to figure what that right way is."

Brian smiled and shook his head. "Sometimes, Tracy, I simultaneously understand and don't understand what you're saying. This is one of those times."

Tracy chuckled; she resumed eating. Then her phone rang. She stood up and looked at the caller ID. "Hi Neal. What's up?" Brian leaned forward and watched his fiancée's face go pale. After she slammed down the receiver, she quickly moved toward her television. Soon she was frantically pushing buttons on her remote until she found the 6:00 p.m. news broadcast she was looking for.

"Detective! Detective!" a reporter was calling out. "When did the police find out about this? And why did it take a newspaper reporter to break this story?"

"I can't discuss the specific details of this case, as it is ongoing, as you all well know," Lucas answered her angrily. "Now let me get back to work, will ya?"

The reporter turned toward the camera. "Well, as you can see, Jack and Cindy, this bombshell has the police ducking for cover."

"Yes, we saw that, Jennifer. But the police already have someone under arrest for the Granger murder, don't they?"

"Yes, Cindy, they do: stand-up comedian Woody Williams."

"Do you know if this revelation will be good news for Williams?" Jack asked Jennifer.

"Hard to say at this point, Jack. But you can be sure we will be following up on this shocking turn of events."

"Thank you, Jennifer," Cindy said somberly. Then the blonde, blue-eyed anchor turned back to face the camera. "That was Jennifer Fielding reporting live from the Baltimore Police Department. To repeat the news that broke less than an hour ago, a reporter for the *Baltimore Times* has learned that Louis Purdue, son of Simon Purdue, the officer paralyzed during the October 2002 holdup of Washburn Community Bank, was in attendance last Friday at *Merlin's Manor of Mirth and Magic*, the night that Zachary Granger was murdered. It was, of course, Granger's partner, Christopher Pyle, who injured Purdue, one of the first officers to respond to the silent alarm that fateful October day. That no mention was made earlier of Purdue's presence at the show on Friday now has people wondering if a cover-up is going on, if the police are protecting the son of one of their own. We, of course, will be following this story and letting you know of any breaking developments. Jack…"

Tracy pressed her remote control Off button. Brian was standing next to her. "You didn't know about this, did you Tracy?"

"No," she answered him angrily. "No, I most certainly did *not*."

"You don't look too well. Would you like to sit back down?"

"No." She turned. "Brian, I'm leaving. I'm going to talk to Lucas or Price, the detectives on this case."

Brian sighed. "They probably don't want to see you right now, Tracy. They've got reporters to deal with."

Tracy shook her head. "Oh, they'll see me. Or Jennifer Fielding will find she has a willing interview subject, someone who will have no problem discussing the Granger murder in front of a camera."

Brian put his hands up and backed away as Tracy grabbed her coat and briefcase and then pulled her door open. She didn't look back. Brian shook his head and thought, "Thank God it's not me she's mad at this time." And then Brian sat down to finish his meal. He felt sorry for the detectives who were about to get an uninvited dinner guest of their own.

Chapter 7

"We just found out about this late this morning," Detective Price said, not sounding particularly friendly. "I don't know how that reporter found out so quickly."

"Your walls have ears, I guess," Tracy said flatly.

"So you're here to yell at somebody, then? Bang the conspiracy drum, maybe?"

Tracy sighed. If it had been Lucas she was speaking with, Tracy would have been quick to answer in the affirmative. But she had built up a good rapport with Price and, more importantly, she liked her. "Can I sit down, Detective Price? Suddenly I don't feel like rattling my saber. I guess a lot of us were blindsided by this."

Price gave her a half smile. "Sure, go ahead and sit." Price sighed and took her seat.

Tracy had her notebook open. "You said you found out about Louis Purdue late this morning?"

"Yes. He charged a few drinks to his credit card at the bar shortly before the first show was over. We're still going through the process of checking receipts for tickets, drinks, and food, as well the parking lot credit card charges. Of course, everyone around here had heard about Purdue's father when we reacquainted ourselves with the robbery. So when we saw the same last name, we looked into things a little further."

"You're still investigating, even though you arrested Williams already?"

Price cleared her throat. "There are still some details we're trying to work out. Let's just leave it at that, shall we?"

Tracy nodded. "Sure, Detective. So have you had a chance to speak with Purdue, yet?"

"No. He's coming in tomorrow, voluntarily, with his own lawyer. I think he figured this might be coming. But, please, keep all this to yourself for now."

"Sure, Detective, mum's the word."

Price smiled. "Thanks."

"I guess I can't get a ticket for the interview tomorrow."

"No."

"Well can maybe the two of us talk afterward? If he already has an attorney, then he probably won't talk to me at all."

Price sighed. "I don't know, Tracy; I'll have to get back to you on that."

"So, I guess if Purdue was having drinks at the bar close to the nine o'clock hour, you don't know yet which show he was there to see."

"That's correct. But I think it was the early one."

"I guess he's not much of a suspect, though," Tracy said thoughtfully.

"Why would you say that?"

"Well, if he'd been planning to murder Granger out of revenge or something, he wouldn't have been dumb enough to charge his purchases, leaving a record."

"True. Of course, it could have been an accident, too."

"Right—the bump was on the *back* of the head. No way to know, at this point, if he was hit from behind or he hit his head on the way down to the floor or something."

"Yes. I like the way your mind works."

"Thank you," Tracy said shyly, starting to blush again.

"Your dad was a detective. Any reason you didn't follow in his footsteps?"

"Oh, no one told you?"

"Not about any of the more personal stuff, no."

"Oh. Well, as you know, my dad died on the job. I'm an only child. If I joined the police, I feared that my mother wouldn't be able to handle it. She's the stereotypical Italian mother: she worries if she doesn't hear from me, she worries I'm not eating right. If she finds she doesn't have something to worry about, she's worried that she isn't worried. Basically, she worries 24/7."

Price grinned and nodded. "I see. You thought such a strain would be too much for her."

"Yes. Maybe I didn't give Mom enough credit, though. I never really talked to her about it, except in general terms, until recently, after her stroke. It's because of her that I've started taking on murder defense cases, provided I think my client is innocent."

"Oh?"

"Yes, I could never defend someone I thought committed murder. It wouldn't sit right with me. I loved my dad and respected what he did. I respect what you guys do. I know this sounds weird coming from a lawyer, but I have my own—how shall I phrase it?—code of ethics when it comes to murder cases."

Price was looking at her. "Well, I admit this is a first for me. Thanks for telling me this, Tracy. I knew there was something different about you; now I understand."

"Um, okay, I guess."

Price smiled. "Tell you what: I'll call you after I speak with Purdue, unless, of course, something he says needs urgent attention or requires secrecy."

 Practice to Deceive

"Gee, thanks Detective. That's very nice of you."

"Sure. I guess that's it for now, then?"

"Well, I did have just a couple of things, since I'm here; they're quick."

"Sure, Tracy, what are your questions?"

"You mentioned the parking lot; do you know if that's where Granger was parked?"

"As a matter of fact, we did find Granger's car parked there, or rather, his father's. We first had to find out if he even owned one, given his recent parole, so we went through the DMV. It turned out the car his father owns was the one that Granger was driving."

"Oh. So Granger was staying with his father?"

"Yes, he has a townhouse in Montgomery County. Granger moved in with him after he was released last year."

"I guess you've spoken with the father."

"Yes, he wasn't very helpful. His son came and went as he pleased, he told us. The father, Jeremiah, let his son borrow the car on Friday."

"When did Zachary get his license?"

"He didn't. He just told his father he did."

"Oh. That was risky of him, driving without a license."

"Yes."

"How did Jeremiah seem to be taking his son's death?"

"Badly; he's one of those parents who still insist his child is innocent in spite of the evidence."

"Gotcha. What about Granger's mother?"

"She passed away while he was in prison."

"Oh, that's very sad. I know Granger was no saint, but still."

"Yes. Zach was an only child, so Jeremiah is in pretty bad shape."

"Did he, by chance, let you look at Zachary's room?"

"Yes, he did, but there wasn't much there. I think the father or mother got rid of a lot of stuff after Zach went to prison. There were clothes, linens, the usual furniture; nothing that really could tell you about a person. You know what I mean?"

"Yes, the room had no personality; no posters on the wall, no magazines and stuff like that."

"Exactly. We went through everything there; Jeremiah even let us look in the attic and basement at some stuff that had been stored. But there wasn't anything we found that seemed related to the robbery, or could tell us anything about Buzz. I'm beginning to think Buzz may have been an associate of Christopher Pyle's. He was the one with the record, after all."

"Mmm. And Jeremiah didn't know anything about his son's plans for Friday?"

"No."

"Where was Zachary working, these days?"

"In the back rooms of a nearby grocery store; cutting meat, doing some overnight restocking."

"I guess you've talked to his coworkers already."

"Yes, Granger barely spoke to anyone. Most of them knew his history and left him alone. They were something less than helpful."

Tracy shook her head. "Well, that explains where Granger got the cash to buy the tickets. I assumed Granger paid cash for his tickets at the box office."

"Uh-huh. He didn't have any credit cards. Of course, he could have borrowed his father's, but we checked on that; he didn't."

"Was there a computer in the Granger house?"

"Yes, the father's. Zachary could have used it, of course, but our technicians went through the Web history and didn't find anything. Then, again, his father said Zach went to the library a lot and probably used the computers there. So that pretty much ends any hope of following a cyber trail."

"I see. Did you ever find Granger's wallet, keys, ticket stubs, or anything else he must have had on his person on Friday?"

"No, we haven't, yet. We checked all the *Merlin's* trash and some of the nearby Dumpsters: nothing, so far."

"That's weird. I wonder if the killer was looking for something Granger had on him? That could explain why the coat was off."

"Possibly." Price looked at Tracy, who was turning the pen back and forth in her fingers, a thoughtful look on her face. "Anything else?"

"No, you're busy and you're dealing with a potentially ugly PR situation. I'll be on my way." Tracy rose and then shook hands with Price. "Thanks again, Detective."

"I'll call you tomorrow, then. Cell phone okay?"

"Yup, perfect. Please leave a message if I don't pick up. I tend to turn it completely off if I'm going into a meeting or interview. Quite frankly, I don't like mobile phones too much."

Price nodded. "Goodnight, then." And then Tracy, sword firmly sheathed, retreated to friendlier terrain.

"Thanks for cleaning up, Brian," Tracy said as she noted the clear table. She had just returned and was hanging up her coat.

"Hey, no problem. I washed the dishes, too."

     Practice to Deceive

"Oh, you dear man. Come here and kiss me." She didn't have to give *that* order twice.

"Are you still hungry? I can warm something up for you," Brian offered.

"I'm fine."

"How did it go with the police?"

"Not bad at all, actually. Someone will let me know more tomorrow."

"Okay, good. You looked ready for battle when you left."

Tracy smiled. "I was." Then she took Brian's hand. "Let's sit down. It's almost time for our least favorite part of the day."

"Saying goodbye."

"Um-hmm." The two lovebirds perched themselves on their usual sofa cushions. Pecking and embracing soon followed. "Brian," Tracy said softly.

Brian was kissing her cheek but paused to ask, "Yes, Tracy?"

"Can I show you something?"

Brian pulled back to study her. "Uh—yeah."

She smiled and then left him solo while she went into her bedroom. Brian sat there nervously. "Don't let your imagination run away with itself," he thought. When she emerged, she had an 8 x 10 *something* in her right hand. She sat down and handed the mystery item to him. Brian's eyes widened slightly. The picture was of a couple, probably in their early twenties, facing the camera, cheek to cheek, smiles on their faces. "Who are they?" Brian asked.

"That's my mother," Tracy said pointing to the female.

"*That's* your mom?" Tracy grinned. "My God, she looks like Sophia Loren."

Tracy laughed. "I think some other guys have told me that too."

"And so this fellow must be your father; I barely recognize him."

"That's right."

"Now he…he looks like Rod Taylor."

"You know who Rod Taylor is?"

"Sure: the guy from *The Birds* and *The Time Machine*, right?"

"A-plus," Tracy smiled.

"No wonder you're so beautiful; you're parents look like movie stars. When was this taken?"

"Not too long before they were married. Note the ring on her finger."

"Yes, of course." Brian looked at Tracy, who was smiling warmly while looking at the photograph. "They sure look happy."

"Of course they were happy! They were head over heels."

"Like us."

She looked at him. "Yes, like us."

He kissed her; how could he not when she was so close? "Is there a particular reason you're showing me this?"

"Of course."

"Okay. Is this going to be multiple choice, three guesses—what?"

Traced giggled. "No, no test. You agree that my parents were what you would call attractive people."

"Yes, no argument from me on that."

"They were engaged for nine months, dated for a little over a year before getting engaged."

"Okay."

Tracy was looking into her true love's eyes. "They waited, Brian."

"Huh?"

"They waited until their wedding night. You see what I'm saying?"

Brian gulped. "Yes, now I do." Then he looked at her quizzically. "May I ask how you know this about your parents, given you weren't around to bear witness to this?"

Tracy grinned at him again. "My mom told me."

"Your mom told…you asked your mom about…about *that*?"

"Yes."

"When?"

"Monday night."

"Monday night, as in last night?"

"Yes."

Brian gulped again. "And what, may I ask, brought on this conversation?"

"I did. I asked her how she and Dad were able to deal with…well, you know."

Brian turned red. "What exactly did you tell her, Tracy?" He sounded alarmed.

Tracy smiled and rubbed his cheek. "Oh, don't worry, Brian. I didn't go into any specifics or tell her anything she didn't already know. I sometimes forget how worldly smart my mom is."

"Uh huh."

"Look Brian, I just needed some advice that would help us deal with our…challenge, so that we wouldn't be constantly clashing over it. I didn't want to spend the next year dealing with it every time we're together. Now this, of course, was before I found out about what you were doing on your end to deal with things—the cooking class thing, I mean. But, try as I might, I couldn't think of anyone who waited until they were married."

"Except for your mother, obviously."

"Yes. We had a very nice talk. And, if it makes you feel any better, Dad was dealing with the same stuff you are. So she doesn't think badly of you."

Brian rolled his eyes. "But you told her—"

"I said we were *both* struggling. I did NOT make you the bad guy here. Okay?"

He sighed. "Okay."

"Good."

Brian scratched his neck. "So, uh, what *did* she say?"

"Well, to put it simply: If kissing is going to lead to something else, don't kiss. If you can't be alone together without wanting to kiss, which, in turn, is going to lead to something else, don't be alone together. Ever wonder why some cultures insist on a chaperone during the courting period?"

"Wait, we're not supposed to see each other until the wedding?" he asked incredulously.

"No, silly head. My mom was just making a point. Sort of like, 'if your eye offends thee, pluck it out.' That sort of thing."

Brian gulped a third time. "Good grief, Tracy, you sound like I should… get something else cut off."

Tracy laughed heartily. "Now you *know* I don't want that to happen."

"That's a relief."

"And she also suggested we could pray together about it."

"Oh."

"I'm trying to be a better Catholic, you know."

"Tracy, you've always gone to church every Sunday since I can remember."

"Practicing your faith is more than just showing up at mass every weekend. That's only part of it."

"Yes, okay."

"It's about the way you live your life, day in, day out."

"I understand, Tracy. But I think you live your life in an admirable way."

Tracy shook her head. "I don't pray as often as I should."

"I'm in no position to criticize you."

"Maybe we could try that; praying together, I mean."

Brian shifted in his seat. "Well, I'm not really comfortable with doing that."

"Why not?"

"Well, I've only started going to church again recently; last December, actually. I'm still getting…how shall I put it…reacquainted with everything. I just need some time to be comfortable with everything again. Then…then I'd be willing to try."

Tracy frowned, a look of disappointment on her face. "How can we raise our kids Catholic like we talked about if we aren't able to set an example, an example we should start practicing now?"

"Tracy, I'm not asking for three years or something; maybe a couple of months. Look, nobody in my family, except for my mother, was ever a prayerful person. And when she died, when God took the best person in our family from us, I got mad. I got real mad with God and everything that goes with Him and faith in general. It's only recently that I've started to reconcile it all, to let the anger go."

Tracy embraced him. "Oh, Brian, I'm sorry. I didn't understand that. It's strange; when my dad got killed, I didn't blame God. But maybe that's because there was a *person* responsible. I mean, they got the guy. You didn't have that ability. Blaming cancer isn't the same thing."

"Yeah, I guess. I guess I had to blame *somebody*."

"God's always the default in cases like that, I suppose. I'm sorry, Brian."

"I know you are, Tracy. I am so sorry you never got to meet Mom, or that she got to meet you. I know she would have adored you, and you her." Brian pulled away to face her. "You want to hear something bizarre?"

Another warm smile she gave him. "You know I do."

"Sometimes, in the years just after we broke up, I used to imagine my mom and your dad getting together in heaven. I saw them speaking with each other trying to figure out how to get us back together. Your dad was angry with me, of course, but Mom kept telling him I deserved another chance. After a while, I just forgot about that dream or whatever you want to call it. I guess what I'm saying is that, in my own way, I do pray; at least, I still believe. And soon I know that I'll be comfortable enough to pray with you, but not now, Tracy. I'm just not ready, yet."

Tracy gently kissed him again. She would give him the time he needed, of course, even if she didn't completely understand why he needed it. Then again, she had never watched someone die slowly, being consumed by something so horrific from within. She was not about to say, nor had she ever said to him, that she understood how he felt, because she didn't. He was still struggling with it. Or maybe he was just hesitant to pray to someone he had hated for so long, feeling sheepish about asking for anything. She could understand that.

When they finally said goodbye for the night, it was, as usual, a difficult separation. They held each by the door for longer than they ever had. Finally, Tracy took Brian by the hand and walked him to the elevator doors. She smiled. "We have until the elevator arrives."

                    Practice to Deceive

"It will never get here unless one of us pushes the button." He grinned at her.

"Are we playing elevator chicken or something?" she grinned back.

"How about we push it at the same time?" he suggested.

"Whose finger's on top, though?"

Brian laughed softly and shook his head. "Don't start talking like that."

"Stop setting me up, then; stop making it so easy." The noise of the elevator bell caused them to both turn their heads. Someone exited and smiled as she did so. Brian let the door close.

"Hey, why didn't you get in?" Tracy asked, although she knew the answer.

"I haven't told you I love you, yet."

"Oh."

He kissed her. "I love you."

She kissed him back. "I love you too." And then she pushed the down button. Soon, Brian disappeared behind closing doors.

Back in her apartment, she was once again smiling at the picture of her parents. Movie stars, Brian had called them. Not long ago, Brian had told her he felt like an astronaut without her, that she was his world but he wasn't an inhabitant. Not long after that, she told him he was the brightest star in her bright future. Maybe there was something to what Brian said about his late mother and her late father joining forces. Maybe they were now guiding stars in the sky of Tracy and Brian's collective world. She brought this thought with her as she lay her head down for the night. Soon after, the world went dark for the evening.

Detective Price made good on her promise: she called the attorney shortly after 10:30 Wednesday morning. "Good morning, Tracy."

"Good morning, Detective Price. How did your interview go?"

"Fine, I guess. I can share a few things about it. I also can give you his attorney's name and number if you want to call her and try to talk to Purdue yourself."

"Thank you."

"According to Purdue, he received a ticket to Friday's 7:00 p.m. show anonymously in the mail. There was a typed note with it explaining Granger would be there and that he had information about Purdue's father and the robbery; that it would be a good idea if he was there."

"But Purdue never found out who sent it?"

"No."

"Does he still have the note or ticket stub?"

"He doesn't think so; he believes he may have thrown everything away after what happened."

"Oh, he didn't want to keep anything incriminating lying around."

"Maybe."

"So did he talk to Granger that night?"

"No, he said he didn't get a chance to. He claims he didn't even see Granger there."

"Oh?"

"He got to the show very close to the time it started. He saw Scarborough sitting in the back; Purdue recognized him but didn't do anything about it. Of course, he had no way of knowing Granger was with Scarborough."

"And Scarborough was alone, at that point."

"Yes, at least Purdue didn't see anyone else at the table."

"But he stuck around for the show."

"Some of it; at one point, he left and went into the lobby. He said he wanted to be able to see everyone as they came out. He had some drinks at the bar while he waited. When he didn't see Granger, he left; says he then went back to his home in Montgomery County."

"Did he use Route 200 like Scarborough did?"

"No—he said he took I-95 to I-270."

"Ah. But he still would have been home before the time of the murder."

"True. Unfortunately, he lives alone in his apartment; he doesn't have an alibi."

"I see. Have you guys started showing people at the magic club Purdue's picture?"

"We started doing that yesterday. So far, no one admits to seeing him at all, much less around the time of the murder. Bartender didn't remember him, either."

"Oh well. But he sure does have a heck of motive."

"Yes."

"Anything else, Detective?"

"That's all, I think, Tracy."

"So Woody's still your guy, huh?"

"No one saw Purdue fighting with Granger; Purdue's prints aren't—"

"I see, I see. Well, I may still try to talk to him."

"Sure, let me give you his lawyer's name and number." Tracy heard the shuffle of papers. "Her name is Sandra Abonksi."

"Got it." Price gave Tracy the contact number. "Got that too."

"Good."

"I really wish Purdue still had that stub."

"Me too," Price agreed. "What's *your* reason?"

"Well, when I was at *Merlin's* yesterday, I saw some of the tickets that had been printed. They have a date and time stamp on them so you could tell when they were issued. Any tickets bought at the box office are printed right then and there, so we would know exactly when the tickets in question were purchased. I would like to have compared Purdue's ticket stub to Scarborough's, assuming Dan still has his, of course. I'm curious as to when one was purchased in relation to the other."

"I see, whose was bought first."

"Right."

"But the ticket stubs are just that, Tracy: stubs. You wouldn't have seen everything that was on the ticket."

"But the customer stubs could have been matched up with the other halves that *Merlin's* would still have. *Merlin's* keeps the stubs to reconcile attendance. All of Friday's ticket stubs were accounted for."

"I see. Such an exercise would take some time, though."

"Yes, that's true."

"Still, I think I'll get back in touch with Dan Scarborough and see if he has his stub, and get hold of it if he does," Price offered.

"Okay. Maybe Purdue will end up finding his."

"We should be so lucky. Anything else?"

"No, I guess my curiosity has been satiated for now, Detective."

"Okay. Talk to you later, then, Tracy."

"Thanks, Detective, thanks so much. I owe you one, probably more than that."

"Bring me Granger's killer, and we'll call it even."

Tracy laughed. Then she realized what Price had said, indicating maybe Price didn't think Williams was the killer, either. Price had implied this feeling when the two of them had talked before. Tracy commented, "I may just do that, Detective." She hung up and put her cell phone to the side, and then picked up her desk phone's receiver. "Neal, I need you to look up something for me."

"Sure," he said into the speaker.

"Please look up Simon Purdue's home address and e-mail it to me."

"He's the cop who got shot during the robbery, isn't he?"

"More than that, he's a now-paralyzed cop. Let me know all about that, too. I want to talk to him."

"You think he saw something that day that can help us now?"

"Possibly. But I just learned something that wasn't on the news: his son got a note from somebody regarding the holdup. But what the note said, exactly, I'm not sure."

"Okay—give me a few minutes."

"Sure, *no hay problema*. I'm heading back to *Merlin's* to speak with the Donlevy brothers. I can't put off talking to them any longer."

"Gotcha. Good luck, then."

"Thanks, buddy. See ya!" Tracy gathered her tools of the trade, bid her secretary a fond farewell after advising her of the afternoon plans, and eschewed the elevator for the steps. She had less than five days to determine if Montado or anyone in his crew was connected to the Granger murder. And she still couldn't be certain if they were. The clock was ticking—loudly.

Tracy pushed the doorbell at the delivery entrance of *Merlin's*. She smiled when Kurt Donlevy opened the door. "Hi Kurt! It's me again!"

Kurt smiled. "You thinking of joining the show?" he asked amusedly. "Come on in."

"Thank you."

"Can I take you to someone?"

"Actually, Kurt, I'd like to talk to you and Ron, today. I'm trying to get the timeline down for Friday night, and you're the last couple of people from Mr. Montado's side of things I really need to talk to."

"Oh."

"I promise not to ask you any top-secret stuff, any of Mr. Montado's secrets. I actually prefer *not* to know how it's done, most of the time." She may have been fibbing just a bit.

"Well, I guess that would be okay, as long as you don't mind me eating in front of you. Greg just brought lunch in."

"Oh, not a problem. You eat, and I'll ask my questions."

Kurt smiled. "Alright, follow me." Donlevy led her past the dressing rooms toward the very back of the club. The room they entered was a sterile-looking eating area with white walls, a gray granite floor, and a long gray table surrounded by what looked like seating for 20, with 10 chairs on either side. The only other person there was the other Donlevy brother. "Ron, this is Tracy—the birthday lady from Friday, the one you took to see Ms. Bowers."

Ron stood up and bowed, and then sat back down. He had just taken a bite of his cheese-steak. "Where's everyone else?" Tracy asked.

"Probably eating in their dressing rooms," Kurt answered. "*We* don't have such accommodations." He smiled and sat down. "There's a fridge over there by the sink; help yourself to a drink if you want one."

"Thanks, Kurt. I think I might grab a bottle of water." After she did that, she sat down next to Kurt. His brother was on the other side of the table. "So, you've been with Mr. Montado for eight years or so?" Tracy began as she took out her notepad and pen.

Kurt nodded as he finished chewing a section from his own cheese-steak. "Yes, 2007 sounds right."

"You worked for Leonardo before that?"

"Mm hmm. A good man."

"Yeah," Ron agreed. "I was sorry he retired."

"Why did he retire, exactly? He was on the young side, I believe."

"Yes, he was in his mid-forties. But he had a heart attack and almost died."

"Oh," Tracy gasped. "Now that you say that, I do seem to remember reading about that; a real shame."

"Yes," Ron said firmly.

"Ron really liked Leonardo," Kurt said almost apologetically. "It can be a sore spot."

"Oh, I'm sorry, Ron."

"That's okay. Kurt is exaggerating things."

"I am not."

Tracy smiled. "How close are you two in age, may I ask?"

"Less than two years," Kurt answered. "I'm 46, born in December '68; Ron's 44, born in October '70."

"Do you have any other brothers or sisters?"

"Nope," Kurt grinned. "After Ron came along, the folks had had enough."

Ron was chomping down but scowled at his brother. Tracy giggled. "I sometimes wish I had a sibling; I feel like I missed out on something."

"You can have Kurt, then, free of charge; go ahead and take him with you on your way out." All three of them laughed at Ron's suggestion.

"You know, you two remind me of my relationship with my associate, Neal. We sometimes go at it."

"Really," Kurt said flatly.

"He's the big brother I never had."

"Oh yeah?" Ron asked, sounding completely disinterested.

Tracy took a swig from the water bottle. "Okay, obviously, I'm inter-ested in talking about last Friday. Now, according to a witness, he saw this person—Zach Granger—sneak behind the curtain shortly before the water tank trick was supposed to take place. I'm guessing that Granger picked that short period of time when the one assigned to watch the curtain leaves briefly to get into his hood or whatever. Regardless, neither of you saw Granger backstage that night. Correct?" They both nodded. "Which one of you was on curtain duty during this time?"

"That was me," Ron said.

"And you didn't see Granger?"

"I didn't see anybody who didn't belong backstage."

"Oh, did you see somebody around this time who *did* belong backstage?"

Ron looked at her and started eating a french fry. "Sometimes a technician or somebody like that at the club we're playing has to come back and fiddle with something or other that's not working right."

"Oh. Did something like that happen on Friday?"

"Don't think so," Ron said.

"So, then, you didn't see *anybody* back there?"

"Don't think so."

Tracy thought Ron lacked his brother's warmth. "So, where is your mask kept during the show when you're not wearing it?"

"Around the corner, near the costume trunks."

Tracy furrowed her brow. "Around the corner, huh? So, if you go around the corner to get your mask, would you be able to see the water tank from where you would be standing?"

"Nope," Ron grunted.

"So the tank *was* out of your sight for a bit."

"Well, yeah, but not for long."

"Can you guess how long? A minute? Two minutes?"

"I guess it would depend on how much you had had by that point, huh Ron?" Kurt asked.

Ron scowled at his brother. "I didn't have that much, just a draft beer. I was fine."

"Maybe you put the mask on backward or something and walked right past the guy," Kurt goaded.

"I don't think this is funny; this lady may get the wrong idea."

"Wrong idea about what? About the time you couldn't get the mask on properly because you were so bombed and almost screwed up the entire trick?"

Ron stood up. "That's enough, Kurt!"

Kurt chuckled. "Calm down, calm down." Kurt turned to Tracy. "Don't get the wrong idea; this happened years ago. Ron was still medicating himself over the Leonardo breakup, and he had too much to drink one night. Thankfully, Mr. Montado forgave him and gave him another chance." Kurt turned to face his brother. "You go on all the time about how great Leonardo was; you should be thanking Montado every day for not firing us, then and there."

There was now silence in the room, and Tracy felt the tension. Ron finally sat back down but was still glaring at his older brother. "So, Ron," Tracy restarted, "you put your mask on and joined your brother at the tank."

"No," Ron said. "Kurt, or whichever one of us is helping Mr. Montado, is always getting to the tank just before we bring it up onstage. So, I would have been there first."

"Oh, I see. That makes total sense. So, Kurt gets there, and you two start pushing the tank onstage."

"Right," Ron agreed.

"And this whole time, the black tarp is completely covering the tank."

"Right again."

"And this is how it always is."

"Yes," Kurt stated. "We fill the tank close to dinner. Then the tank is covered until the trick is performed."

"Montado prefers the word illusion," Ron interrupted.

"Fine, the *illusion* is performed. We take off the tarp, the *illusion* is performed, and then we bring the tank back and cover it for the next show."

"And when do you clean out the tank?"

Kurt answered, "Uh, usually after the last show of the night. We drain it, clean it, and let it dry out overnight."

"You said, 'usually.' Friday was different."

"Of course, it was different," Ron said testily. "There was a dead body in the tank. The cops wouldn't let us near the thing while they did whatever it was they needed to do."

Kurt chuckled. "Man, I wished this had happened in Vegas. Maybe we would have seen all those people from the *CSI* show."

Ron shook his head. "You moron, those are actors. You wouldn't have seen any of them even if we *had* been in Vegas."

Kurt glared at his brother. "I know *that*!"

"Sure you do."

"I just meant seeing real CSI people would be cool."

"Uh-huh."

Tracy came to Kurt's rescue: "Where is the ladder kept that's used to climb to the top of the tank if need be?"

"Right against the wall by the tank, next to the ax," Kurt answered.

"The ax?"

"I guess you didn't notice the black x's that are at the center of each of the four windowpanes of the tank," Ron said, sounding annoyed.

"No," Tracy admitted. "I haven't dared ask anyone to allow me to examine the tank. I figured it was off-limits to everyone except the police."

"Good point she just made there, huh Ron?" Kurt said glaring at his brother, obviously not liking Ron's attitude. He looked at Tracy. "The x marks are there so we know just the right place to aim for in case something goes wrong. If Mr. Montado were to get into trouble, we grab the ax and take a whack or two at the nearest x, and then the glass would break."

"Oh, I see. Yeah, you would need some kind of precaution. Have you ever had to use the ax?"

"No," Kurt answered. "So far, so good. But I do worry as he gets older if…Well, like I said, we've never had to use it."

"Okay. Let me ask you both something I'm curious about. Didn't either of you notice that the tank was heavier on Friday when you were pushing it?"

They both looked at her. "Uh, no, I guess I didn't," Kurt answered.

Ron added, "Maybe it *was* harder to get the thing going; I'm not sure. But when that happens, it's usually because Kurt here isn't doing his part."

"Oh, stuff yourself, dickhead."

Tracy started laughing, at which point Kurt went deep red. "Nice going, idiot," Ron scolded. "You know better than to talk that way in front of a lady."

Tracy waved her hand. "Don't worry about it, Kurt. Think of me as one of the guys."

Both Kurt and Ron looked at her, stared at her. Whatever was on their minds suddenly made Tracy feel uncomfortable. And then Tracy started following Kurt's example with the facial shading. "Um, let's now talk about what happened just *after* Karine screamed," Tracy said quickly looking at her notebook.

The brothers looked at each other and grinned. "Sure," Kurt said, finally.

"So the curtain comes down, and then what happens?"

"Well, Mr. Montado puts his arms around Ms. Bowers and tries to calm her down," Kurt began. "He tells Ron and me to put the tarp back on right away, and then he tells us to take Ms. Bowers back to her dressing room.

While we're doing that, the manager—the Houston woman—comes back to see what's going on. She starts talking to Mr. Montado. I think she called the police."

"I did, too," Tracy told Kurt.

"Oh."

"So did the two of you take Karine back to her dressing room?"

"Yes," Kurt continued. "She said she wanted to call her brother, so I handed her cell phone to her."

"Do you remember what she said to him?"

"Uh, something like: 'somebody's been killed, you need to come over here, it was so awful,' and other stuff like that."

"And you guys stayed with her until, when?"

"Well, I think we both stayed there until Mr. Bowers arrived."

"How did he get in?"

"He rang the bell. I heard it and went to let him in. After that, I went back to watch the curtain, and Ron went to see if he could help Mr. Montado."

"That all checks out. How did Mr. Montado seem to you, Ron?"

"Uh, pretty rattled. He was back in his dressing room having a drink. I remember Mr. Bowers came in to get his sister something. Everybody was upset. The *Merlin's* people were keeping an eye on the stage, at that point. Then, the police arrived."

"Pretty crazy, huh?" They both nodded. "But neither of you saw anybody backstage at any point that night who didn't belong there?" They both shook their heads. "And neither of you saw Woody Williams poking around at any point that night or earlier in the day, either?" Mutual headshakes. "Did either of you recognize Granger from the early evening show, or perhaps from earlier in the week?"

The brothers looked at each other. "I don't think so," Kurt said.

"Don't think so, either," Ron added. "Why do you ask that?"

"Granger would have had to know just the right time to sneak in the back. I doubt he would have known that if this were his first night here." The brothers again looked at each other. They shrugged their shoulders almost in unison. "So you two assist with the illusions during the show, provide some security, move things in and out of the vans, set things up and take things down. Is that accurate?"

"Yeah," Ron answered. "We pretty much bring everything back with us each and every day."

"Does that include incidental things, like the costume boxes you referred to earlier, or is it just the illusion items you repack every night?"

"Pretty much everything."

"Do you recall if you brought anything into or out of the building on Friday, or early Saturday morning, that you hadn't before? I mean, was there anything different about Friday's workload?"

"No, not that I noticed," Kurt said.

"Me neither," Ron agreed.

Tracy thought to herself: "Yeah, but neither of you noticed you were pushing a tank that had to be close to 200 pounds heavier." However, she smiled at the brothers. "I think that's all the questions I have, for now, gentlemen. It's been a real treat speaking with the both of you."

The brothers, yet again, looked at each other. "Aren't you going to ask us how Mr. Montado does any of his tricks?" Ron asked.

"She said she's not interested in that stuff," Kurt answered him.

"I find that hard to believe."

"It's true," Tracy said in her own defense. "I like to preserve the mystery. Now, I might try to work out in my own mind how an illusion is performed, now and again. But that's different from wanting someone to give away the secret."

Ron looked at her curiously. "Well, if you say so."

"Knock it off, Ronny." Kurt stood up. "Nice talking to you too, Tracy. You're all right." And then Kurt and Tracy shook hands. Ron remained seated, watching them skeptically.

"Bye!" Tracy said as she left the two brothers to eat, spat, or perhaps both. She looked at her watch: almost 1:30. She next wanted to talk to the eyes in the sky: the people who made sure the sights and sounds dazzled the audience on Friday, as well as at every other show.

But on her way from the back, she decided to sit down in front of the stage, choosing the very same seat she had sat in that fateful night. The Donlevy brothers: an interesting pair. They certainly acted like brothers, from what she understood brothers acted like. They had been, for the most part, helpful and friendly. But something was still off. How did Granger get in a fight and get dumped in the tank in the time Ron had disappeared around the corner? How could he not have heard something, even with all the noise from out front? Kurt's reference to Ron's drinking and the possible ensuing confusion: good-natured ribbing, or convenience? The brothers had no doubt known Tracy was poking her nose around asking questions. They had had time to prepare. Is that what today had been? Had she witnessed a performance, complete with drama and laughs? Tracy scratched her chin. Everyone she had talked to had been gracious and helpful, well, except for Greg Bowers. But Tracy was sure somebody was being less than honest.

                    Practice to Deceive

Somebody was not who they appeared to be. Somebody was deceiving her. The question she couldn't answer right now, of course, was, Who was it?

Chapter 8

"May I come in?" Tracy asked the person seated in the control booth of *Merlin's Manor of Mirth and Magic.*

"Who are you?" he asked her.

"Tracy Brubaker—Woody Williams' attorney."

"Oh yeah—I've been hearing about you. You can come in if you want."

"Thanks. If I ask your name, will you tell me? Because if you will, I'm asking."

The seated gent started chuckling. "Roger Tallis. And you liked to be called Tracy."

"Yes."

"Okay, Tracy, have a seat here and ask your questions."

Tracy sat and pulled out her notes. She looked around the room, which consisted mostly of electronics, knobs, and unfamiliar gizmos. "You don't work all this by yourself, do you?"

"Oh heck no; there are two other people in here with me during the whole show."

"Even during the intermission?"

"Yup. Unless, of course, someone needs a potty break."

Tracy grinned. "What do you three do, exactly?"

"Well, you got your camera and monitors; then you have sound, which includes both music and effects; and then you have your lights and spotlight. Each of us can handle each area; it's a precautionary measure, in case something was to happen to one of us."

"Cross-training; I get it."

"Exactly. And since there's always something going on in those areas, we can't even leave for a bathroom break during the show."

Tracy laughed. "Oh man, that's some hazard pay right there."

Tallis nodded, grinning. "Right on, Tracy, right on."

"Do you guys ever record anything from the show?"

"No, and I don't think we'll be doing any of that in the near future."

"Oh? Why not?"

"The owner of this place doesn't like it. You see, with technology today, once you record something—digitally, anyway—you have no control over where it's going to end up. If someone records the show, they can sell it; worse, they could put it online for all to see for free. What's the point of paying to see the show if you can watch it on your screen at home? So when the buyer had this building renovated, he made sure our little room here didn't have any video recording set up. We can play any sound effect we want, or feed any picture we want through the monitors. But we can't record."

"Gotcha. Now what kind of image would you feed to the monitors?"

"Well, all I meant was, we can move the cameras that are in the auditorium ceiling in any direction, and so we can show anything from the show we want to on the monitors."

"But most of the time the cameras are focused on the stage."

"That's true for the magic show; nobody wants to miss a trick, so to speak. We have a little more flexibility during the stand-up part. If it's not going so well, for example, we try to find people laughing and put *them* on the screen. If people see other people laughing, they may join in."

"I get it: psychological."

"Yes."

"And of course there are pre-show activities sometimes."

"Huh?"

"Like if someone has a birthday."

Tallis studied her a moment and then started laughing. "Hey, that's *right*! Tracy, you were great. You were so fast with the quips and looks. All of us in here were cracking up."

"Really."

"Yup. In fact, quite a few people asked if you were part of the show, especially after you took a dig at Woody Williams. What was it you said: you told him to let you know when he started or something?"

"That sounds like something I might say. I don't like being in the spotlight like that."

"Great stuff, anyway!"

"Thanks; I'm here all week. Now, do you recall anything strange, other than the murder, of course, on Friday from either show? Maybe you saw someone in a flash? Or maybe somebody wasn't where they were supposed to be?"

Tallis scratched his head. "Nothing's coming to mind, other than that body in the tank, like you said."

"Yeah, that's enough to wipe the memory bank."

"We heard that scream up here in the booth; I mean, that noise came through loud and clear, and every hair on my body stood up. If Karine quits this gig because of what happened, she should go into horror movies. I mean, God."

"You haven't heard anything about her quitting, have you?"

"Oh, no. But something like that; well, how is she ever going to be able to turn around and look at a tank again? You know what I'm saying, Tracy?"

"You bet, Roger. What did you guys do after you saw Granger floating there in the tank?"

"Uh, well, I guess it took us a few seconds to realize this wasn't part of the show; I mean, we're staring at the body on the monitor. Then we just hit the kill switch—"

"Kill switch?"

"Yeah, it simultaneously shuts everything down and brings up the house lights. We have it in case of fire or other emergency. Never expected to use it for…you know."

"Sure, I remember now. Suddenly, the sound and monitors cut off, the low lights went out, and the bright lights came on."

"Yes, exactly."

"Do you remember who hit that switch?"

"I did."

"You were pretty fast."

"Well, you have to be. If there's a fire, people have to see where they're going to get out."

"Yeah. Does the kitchen staff, by chance, bring you stuff during the show?"

"No. Too crazy."

"Now, the kitchen is right behind the bar."

"That's right."

"You didn't see any of the kitchen people near the security curtain on Friday, did you?"

Tallis thought a moment. "No, I can't say that I did."

"I didn't think so. What about cleaning staff? Do they have access to anyplace and anywhere at any time?"

"No, they mostly come after the shows are over and work the wee hours."

"What if the kitchen or bathroom trash has to be emptied?"

"Well the bathrooms have those high-powered hand dryers, so that's usually not an issue. The kitchen people just stack the filled bags toward the back."

Tracy looked around the room. "Can I ask where you live, Roger? Are you in the city?"

"No, I live in Howard County."

"No kidding? I'm getting married next year and was thinking of settling down there. Do you like it?"

"Love it. Good schools, lots of restaurants, lots of things you can do if you join the Columbia Association."

"Are those the reasons you picked it?"

"No. My wife works in DC, so it works out travel-wise for both of us."

Tracy nodded. "That's one of the reasons I like it. I love the Smithsonian."

"I hear you."

"So you moved to Columbia when you got married?"

"More or less."

"Where'd you live before that?"

"Montgomery County."

"Really? Where you there in October 2002 when the Washburn Community Bank was robbed?"

"Uh, yeah, I guess I would have been. I'd have been about 23. I lived with my folks until I was 26, when I got married."

"Do you remember the robbery at all?"

Tallis shook his head. "No, I can't say that I do."

"Oh, I thought you may have recognized Granger from news coverage or something."

"No, sorry, wouldn't have known Granger from Adam."

"Okay. Well, thanks, Roger. It's been fun here behind the scenes."

"Hey, no problem. If you want to speak with the other people, they'll be here in another hour or so."

"Thanks, Roger. I'm about to head out, but maybe another day."

"Sure."

"Thanks again."

"You're most welcome," Tallis called out as Tracy started down the steps and toward her auto.

Tracy checked her watch: 3:08 p.m. She sighed. She had wanted to talk to Simon Purdue today. But she had that 7:00 dinner with Michael Detweiler. She could call and cancel that easily enough. But she wanted to meet with him and deal with the whole thing right away. Besides, there was no guarantee Purdue would even talk to her. She really wanted to talk to his son, but that was going to be a trick itself. Get to the son through the father, she thought. No way did she have enough time to take care of that tonight. She called Neal.

"I e-mailed you Simon Purdue's info," Neal told her. "He and his son both live in Montgomery County."

"That makes sense, with the elder having worked for the Gaithersburg bank."

"Son lives close by. He probably keeps an eye on both parents."

"A good son, huh?"

"Yes."

Tracy paused. "And maybe a vengeful one."

"Granger didn't shoot Simon Purdue; Pyle did."

"But Granger was involved, and until recently he was out walking around."

Neal paused. "Yeah, I suppose."

"Anything else exciting or new to report?"

"No, not exactly."

"What does 'not exactly' mean, exactly?"

"I'm looking into Montado a little more deeply. I think there's something in his background that seems a little sketchy. Just a feeling, I guess. There's very little on what he did before he came to the U.S. I've run into this kind of thing before, and usually it's because someone's trying to hide something. That's very hard to do today in the Internet age, but people still try."

"Hey Neal, that sounds promising. Keep at it."

"Yup."

"Anything else?"

"Well, you have that dinner meeting in a few hours."

"Oh, that."

"Yes, that. Have you given the matter any more thought?"

"To be honest, I haven't. Tonight I'm just going to listen to what Detweiler has to say, and then I'll report back to you and Beck."

"Alright."

"Don't worry, Neal. I remember what you told me; I heard you."

"Okay. Well, good luck. It sounds like you're not coming back to the office."

"Not right now. I'm going for a walk."

"A walk?"

"A timing exercise to see how long it would take to walk to the hotel where Greg Bowers is staying."

"Oh, gotcha."

"If it is indeed 20 minutes, then I'll be getting back here close to 4:00 p.m. I may just head home and get ready for the big sales pitch, or purchase pitch, or whatever you want to call it."

"Gotcha again. Well, have a great dinner, anyway."

"Thanks, Neal. Can you tell Beck all the scheduling details?"

"Sure, Tracy. I'll see you later."

"Adios." After hanging up, she got back out of her car, opened her trunk, and pulled out her running shoes she kept in a gym bag. She changed footwear and then timed a walk to the Bowers' hotel: 18 minutes. Okay, the timing works, although she still thought a cab would be faster. She turned and moved briskly back to her auto. Now it was time to dress fancy for her meeting tonight. The butterflies were taking their positions in her belly. "Great," she thought. There wasn't one menu item she could think of that went well with butterflies.

After she had dressed for the evening, Tracy had some time before she needed to leave. She picked up her phone. Soon, the person she called answered. "Crystal Shane."

"Hi Crys, it's Tracy."

"TRACY! Oh I'm so glad you called. I've been meaning to call you forever."

"Me too, Crys. Things have been so crazy. How are you? How's life as a CEO?"

"Busy and busier are the answers. We're looking at several different new approaches to how we market ourselves. I'd like us to increase our visibility out there; looking outside the U.S., too. We may be adding some items to our product line, also, like frozen loaded potatoes that you micro-wave, things like that."

"Sounds yummy."

"Yup, lots happening. How about you? I bet you have more than you can handle, thanks to you being in the news and all; I mean, solving three murders in like a week or something. I knew you were smart, Tracy, but..."

"Well, I have a lot of smart people working with me."

"Tracy, you have one associate and a secretary. Stop with the modesty, will you? It's okay to gloat once in a while."

Tracy laughed. "Hard work pays off."

"So, I guess you're getting more clients than you can handle."

"Well, after you filter out the clients you don't want and the ones who want the impossible, it really hasn't been *too* overwhelming."

"But haven't you thought about expanding? Hiring some new people, or at least getting a bigger office? You know, Tracy, I'm all about expansion. If you let me, I can help you if you want to do something like that."

"Oh Crys, thanks. But I kind of like things the way they are now."

"You need more ambition, girl."

"Maybe."

Crystal changed the subject. "So, my brother finally got up the nerve, huh?"

Tracy giggled. "Yes. You should see the ring he got me. It's obscene."

Crystal laughed loudly. "Oh, Tracy, he could have given you a ring from a Cracker Jack box and you would have thought it was too much."

"Hey, that's silly."

"It's closer to the truth than it is not."

"Maybe. So Crys, we need to get together and talk about this wedding. What does your schedule look like?"

"Hey, Tracy, you let me know what's good for you and I'll *make* it work. That's one advantage of being the boss."

"Hah! Well, how about Sunday, May 3rd? I'd do it this Sunday, but I'm up against a deadline."

"Done. What time?"

"Let's get together early in the afternoon. That way we can spend most of the day together and catch up."

"Sounds perfect. Should we let my brother join us?"

"He'll sulk if we don't," Tracy giggled.

"You care more about that than I do. Sulking is good for him."

"Oh, Crys, be nice. I'll tell him about it and let him decide. If he does decide to tag along, we can kick him out if we have to."

Crystal laughed. "Good answer, Ms. Lawyer. Why don't we plan on meeting at 2:00; your place or mine?"

"Would you mind coming over here? It's cozier."

"I'll be at your place at 2:00 on the third."

"Great, Crys! I can't wait!"

"Me neither! Thanks for calling, Tracy. I miss you terribly."

"Shucks. I miss you too. See you in a week or so." And then the gal pals said goodbye officially. Tracy breathed a sigh of relief. She had been afraid Crystal might have been hurt that Tracy had not called her sooner. It had been almost a year since they had last seen each other, during that awful week that Brian was arrested for, and suspected of, their father's murder. But everything had sounded fine over the phone, although Crystal had unexpectedly taken quite an interest in the future of Tracy's business. Still, it was good to have heard her voice. It had helped with calming down the butterflies. Tracy headed out to her dinner.

Michael Detweiler was waiting in the lobby of Wagner House when Tracy arrived. She had on a sleeveless sequined mesh-back gown and heels.

She had brought a sweater in case it was chilly in the restaurant. She had remembered feeling a little warm during her last visit but was prepared for either extreme this time.

"Tracy, you look lovely," Detweiler said, greeting her.

"Thank you," she said quietly. Good grief, she felt like the shy 16-year-old she used to be, when she was not used to getting compliments. That's what happens when you're a late bloomer, as some of her friends used to tell her. One day you wake up and notice people start noticing you. That's what had happened to her. After all of these years, she still wasn't used to it.

"They're getting our table ready. I hope it doesn't make you uncomfortable it's just me. I thought about having more than one person speak to you. But then I thought that might be a bit much, having two people constantly talking at you."

"Oh, I'm fine." Between the mace in her purse and her first-degree brown belt in judo, Tracy felt like she could take of herself, although her father always believed her mouth was her most lethal weapon. When the maître d' approached, she smiled again as she and Detweiler were led to a table for two. After they were seated, their waiter, Hans, was promptly in attendance and asked for their drink orders. "This water will work for me just fine, thanks," Tracy said. Detweiler ordered a glass of white wine. Given the French-sounding and lengthy title, she imagined it was on the expensive side.

"So, Tracy, what are your initial thoughts? Have you ever considered joining a larger firm? Please, be honest so I know what information I should be giving you tonight. I mean, if you tell me you're in, then we can just enjoy dinner."

Tracy smiled. "Well, Mike, to be honest, I'm still kind of in shock. It's a little weird to realize one day, out of the blue, someone's been watching your career. I'm flattered beyond words."

"You needn't be so modest. I mean, how many times can you best some of the top practitioners in the tri-state area and think you can continue to fly under the radar?"

"Best?"

"Certainly. Now this is mostly in civil matters, but like I told you, I've heard impressive things about your recent forays into criminal work."

"Well, that came about because of a fluke."

"Really? How so?"

"Well, it's a bit boring and involved. But, basically, a man I was involved with in college called me one night saying his father had been killed and he was suspected. Even though we hadn't really seen each other in a while, I took his case. I lucked out and found a blunder the real killer made. So, the charges were dropped."

"Interesting."

"My second case involved a long-time friend of the family. I guess that was a much more challenging case, but I found a way to prove how the killer in that case set my client up."

"And you helped bring down a crooked real estate mogul, too, didn't you?"

"Uh, yeah. That was a little strange. I really wasn't the one who can take the credit for that part of the case."

Detweiler smiled. "Well, that's not how it's being told, but I won't press you on it. What about the triple murder you wrapped just earlier this month?"

"Oh, I got *real* lucky there. I tracked down some witnesses who, after almost 30 years, were able to remember some of the details connected with the earlier crimes. This all factored into the accusations against my client, Colin Richmond. Anyway, the killer confessed after being presented with all of the evidence. Again, I got lucky."

Hans had returned to take the attorneys' orders as well as deliver the wine, after which, Detweiler continued. "You get lucky a lot, then?"

"Yes, plus the people I work with, they're terrific. They're invaluable."

"If you are worried about them, Tracy, you needn't be. They are welcome to come with you."

"Oh, that is good to know. We're sort of a family; I'm the kid sister, but I'm the boss. It keeps us all in check."

Detweiler smiled. "I understand. Plus, being surrounded by unfamiliar faces can be daunting at first, as well."

"Yes."

"So I understand now you are defending the comic Woody Williams?"

"Yes, I guess I made the news, huh?"

"He is a celebrity, after all."

"Yes."

"There aren't too many details about the case in the press. I guess they don't want the case to be tried in advance by the papers."

Tracy sipped from her glass. "Yes, that may be part of it. Or, they may realize they don't have much of a case."

Her companion laughed. "Ah, spoken like a true defense attorney."

Tracy smiled. "I guess. But I think I should explain something about my criminal work, at least as it pertains to violent crime in general, and murder specifically."

"Oh? What is it?"

"Did you know my father, Peter Brubaker, was a detective with the Baltimore Police Department?"

"Yes, I did know that. He was killed in the line of duty, I was sad to learn."

"Yes. And I was planning to pursue a career in law enforcement and follow in his footsteps. But his death changed things, and I ended up, for personal reasons, being an attorney."

"I see."

"But, because I have such respect for the people in blue, and because I am still close with some of the people working the job, I don't take cases involving violence if I believe the potential client is guilty. And if he or she admits to doing it, well, they're shown the door then and there. When it comes to murder, I really have to believe my client is innocent. I can only go with my gut on that, of course. Usually, something about the case doesn't sound right, or maybe I just believe the accused person is telling the truth when they say they're innocent. I guess I'm saying I have no intention of simply just defending accused murderers because the fees are promising. If I were to come with you, that aspect of what cases I take would be nonnegotiable. Did what I say make any sense?"

Detweiler, who had been listening to her intently, smiled and nodded. "I think you were very clear. But tell me, Tracy, what happens the day your gut is wrong and you find, for whatever reason, that your initial impression was wrong? Would you try and drop the case?"

Tracy herself had pondered this question many times since being given her mother's blessing to take on murder cases. Tracy didn't pretend she was infallible. "Well, let me put it this way: If and when that day comes, I will see the case through to the end and live up to my promises; I wouldn't just pull out of the case. And then that will most likely be the last murder case I ever take." Tracy took another sip from her glass.

"I see. So your real passion is for your civil work."

"My passion is for whatever case I'm currently working on. But I built my practice on the civil and business side of law. I have no intention of abandoning it."

Detweiler nodded. "Good, there's no reason why you should have to."

"So, Mike, what is it you hope to gain from my joining up with you and your partners? What would I be doing, and how would I and my people fit in with your firm?"

"Well, Tracy," he began after finishing his wine, "the sky's the limit. You can continue what you enjoy doing: your foreclosure prevention and assistance cases, assistance with low-income persons who get sued by the wealthy, your general business work. Essentially, you would be doing what you're doing now, except you'd have more people to help you, which in turn would free up your time to assist even more clients, or at least concentrate on the more complicated aspects of a case. You would have more opportunities to serve the clientele you want to serve. Our resources become your resources.

"Now, what we'd get in return is you and your reputation. You have strong contacts in the police department and in the state's attorney's office. We know they respect you, even when they're butting heads with you. Quite frankly, we'd like to have more exposure in assisting lower-income families. We of course donate to charities and host some fundraisers. But the people attending those events are well off, so it comes across as wealthy people patting themselves on the back for doing a good deed. With you, you're out there with them, making their struggles your own and doing what you can to help them. We'd very much want you to continue doing that.

"Tracy, I and my partners see this as win-win. We'd get you and what comes with your name. You'd get more help than you've ever had, which would allow you to serve even more of the people you want to help. And, of course, if you want to take a criminal case that you believe in, you can do that too. There are no secret clauses, special circumstances, or surprises. It's just like I'm telling you."

Tracy nodded. She was about to speak when their salads arrived. Suddenly she found herself playing lettuce croquet with her fork and a cherry tomato. "So, in a way, I'll be the social conscience segment of the firm, at least for a while."

Detweiler raised his eyebrows, and then nodded. "I suppose that's an accurate statement. But I do want others within our firm to follow your example. I think we could learn something from your approach. As I said, it's win-win for everyone."

"I see. Would it be all right if I were to visit your offices and talk to some people? Maybe you could show me where I'd be working, that kind of thing."

Detweiler beamed. "Absolutely, Tracy! I *want* you to come and meet with some of your potential partners, coworkers, and staff. Tour our offices. Do what you have to do to get comfortable. Talk to as many people as you want to; get a sense of the office atmosphere."

Tracy stabbed her tomato and disposed of it in her mouth. She then smiled at her host. "I probably couldn't do such a thing until next week, though. I'm going to need the daytime hours to work my current case."

　　　　　Practice to Deceive

"Oh, that would be fine. You can just call me and let me know what day works for you. I have no doubt we can accommodate you."

"Okay, Mike, as soon as I'm done with following up the *Merlin's* leads I'm working on, I'll call you. In the meantime, I'll think of some more questions."

"Perfect."

"However things turn out, though, I want you to know how honored I am by your firm's offer. I keep thinking there has to be a catch somewhere."

"No catch, Tracy. We think we're a pretty great group of attorneys. We think you're a great attorney. And, together, we'd all be even better. It's as simple as that."

"Well, I think you should get to know me a little better. I've been told my style is, at times, unconventional."

Detweiler chuckled. "That's one of the reasons we're here tonight: to get to know each other better. So, Tracy, let's start doing that right now." And, soon, Tracy was in the spotlight again, even if this time her immediate audience consisted of only one member.

"So, what did you talk about in that regard?" Brian asked after Tracy filled him in on the business portion of the dinner. They were seated on Brian's couch, holding hands.

"Oh, I told him about my wonderful fiancé, my mom, some things about Neal and Beck. We talked about my dad a little bit. Mike's very much into the performing arts, and he gets tickets to nearly every single show that comes through the area, whether it's a play, or dance recital, or concert. I'd actually love to do more of that—seeing live shows. So, that would be a nice perk."

"Mm hmm. So you liked this guy?"

"Yeah, I'd say so. Of course, he's recruiting me, so he's got his charm working overtime. But I liked him."

"I'll bet he adored you. Good Lord, Tracy, you look so gorgeous in that dress."

"Oh, stop. He didn't cancel the offer when the night was over, so I know I didn't screw up the dinner, anyway."

Brian shook his head. "Tracy, this is a pretty big deal. I'm so proud of you."

"Thanks."

"But I don't understand why you're not jumping up and down and feeling a little proud of yourself. All your hard work hasn't gone unnoticed. How many attorneys have the opportunity that's just been presented to you?"

"Not many, I guess."

"So why do you seem so, for lack of a better word, down?"

"I'm not down. It's just that this is a major decision, one of the most important in my life. I honestly don't know what to do."

"Oh. So you've bypassed the proud phase and jumped straight into the stress phase."

"I don't think stress is quite the right word."

"Fine."

"Brian, I really just wanted you to listen to me, not try to analyze how I'm feeling."

He blinked. "Well, I'm sorry," he said with more than a hint of sarcasm.

Tracy gulped. "Brian, please don't be like that."

"Be like what?"

"You sound irritated with me."

"Tracy, I admit I get a little tired of your false modesty routine."

Tracy frowned. "What are talking about? I'm not false about anything."

"Remember early in our relationship, how you used to get upset every time I told you how beautiful you were."

"What does how I look have to do with anything?"

"That's not my point. You have a hard time taking compliments, or admitting your own talents. You're always saying things like, 'No I'm not,' or 'I just got lucky,' or things like that. A little self-deprecation occasionally is fine. But you need to give yourself some credit once in a while. It is okay to say 'I'm good at this,' or 'I did good work today,' or 'I'm beautiful.' Do you see what I mean?"

"Brian, I know I'm good at my job."

"You're very good at your job."

"But my job exists because people are getting hurt by someone else. I wish people didn't need lawyers."

Brian looked at her confused. "You've lost me."

"Look, Brian, I like that I can help people doing what I do. But, at the same time, I'm well aware that if people started treating each other like they should be treated, I'd be out of a job. It's the same concept as the need for police: if people stopped committing crimes, then we wouldn't really need much of a police force. The cops would mostly be directing traffic and getting cats out of trees or something. You see what I mean?"

"Not exactly."

"I find it hard to jump up and down for me when the reason I'm doing what I'm doing is because someone else is hurting, whether it's physical or financial. Somebody treated somebody else wrong, and so I show up. I guess that's why I have a love-hate relationship with what I do. Does that make it any clearer?"

Brian sighed. "So, you're telling me you've chosen a profession guaranteed to make you sad for the rest of your life."

"No, of course not. I'm talking in the context of moving to a bigger law firm. Yes, it's an honor and all that. But this whole thing has also reminded me about why what I do is needed. So, yeah, goody-goody for me. Not so goody for others."

"Tracy," Brian sighed, "what about areas of law that are related to business, like drawing up wills, or loan documents, or estate planning, or stuff where you are helping people plan for a future or provide for their families? That's positive."

"But I like that I help people through something difficult."

"You know what? I give up. If you're helping people successfully enough that a peer or group of peers wants you to join them, then what's wrong with being happy that your hard work is clearly making a difference? Why focus on the reasons why your job is needed? You usually take the 'glass is half full' approach. I don't understand it."

Tracy sighed. "Then stop trying to."

"Like I said, I give up."

"That's not the same thing as accepting that you just don't understand how I feel."

"Alright Tracy, I'm sorry. It's just that I *want* to understand how you feel. I really do. Here I'm so proud of you, and thinking what a wonderful thing this is, and you don't seem happy about it at all." Brian narrowed his eyes. "Tracy, I want you to look at me."

"What?"

"You've been looking down at your lap practically this whole time. I want you to look at me."

"Okay," she said meeting his eyes.

"You know what? I think you're deceiving yourself."

"Huh? What does that mean?"

"I think there's something else going on here, and it has little or nothing to do with the psychobabble you just uttered."

"Brian! That wasn't a very nice thing to say."

"Before you get mad, listen to me for a moment and think about what *I'm* going to say. You've been your own boss for quite a while, now. You've built a very comfortable professional life for yourself. It's safe. But if you were to accept this offer, that would all disappear. You'd have other people to answer to, other people who are counting on you. And I know how you hate disappointing people, letting people down. I remember how scared you'd be the night before a test or the day before you turned in some paper or project. And this is what I think is going on here. Instead of thinking what an honor this is, you're thinking of the ways you might screw things up: you might lose a case, or maybe irritate one of your new firm's long-standing clients, or maybe set the office building on fire or something." Tracy laughed gently. "I'm right, aren't I? That's what's really going on here."

Tracy swallowed. "Okay, maybe a little bit of that."

"And, of course, you're worried about Rebecca and Neal, how they would fit in. Or maybe you're afraid they wouldn't, or that they wouldn't even give it a chance."

"Sure, I'm thinking about them."

"Well, all of that I *can* understand. So let me just say one more thing on the matter, and then I'll be done. Tracy, you've never screwed up anything in your life, not severely, I mean. Now, you're going to make mistakes; we all do. But you've given 100 percent to everything that's ever mattered to you. Why do you think if you took advantage of this amazing opportunity that you wouldn't be as successful as you have been with everything else in your life? Give yourself the respect that everyone else seems to have for you."

She smiled. "I respect myself, Brian. I know I'm good at my job. But I also know that a mistake in this job can cost someone else big-time. The more clients I take on, the more chances I have to bollix things. I don't lose the house or go to jail if I screw up; the client does. It's one thing if it's me and me alone paying for the consequences of my actions. You see what I mean?"

"Of course I do. I don't pretend to know the pressure you feel, but I understand the burden. But Tracy, you've got to allow that mistakes can happen and that making a mistake doesn't make you a bad person or a failure or anything like that. It only proves you're human. And you shouldn't let that fear of making a mistake—the fear of being human—stop you from seizing what must be a golden opportunity for you."

Tracy considered Brian's comments. "So you think I should take the offer, then; merge with them?"

"I didn't say that."

Tracy was taken aback. "Wait a minute: are you telling me after all that build-up-Tracy's-ego stuff, you *don't* want me to accept the offer?"

"All that stuff, as you put it, was about trying to figure out why you seem more depressed than excited. It had nothing to do with how *I* felt about it."

"So how *do* you feel about it?"

"I don't think you should take it."

"Why not?" she asked mildly shocked.

"My darling, you are the proverbial square peg that doesn't fit in the round hole. And I mean that as a compliment. You go to one of these big places, one of two things will happen: you'll leave eventually, or your edges will be rounded."

"Oh really?"

"Tracy, why do you think your clients like you so much?"

"Um, because I'm a likeable person?"

"Yes, exactly. You get to be yourself at your own firm. And not just as a person. It's the way you run your office, the way your office looks, and the people you've chosen to work for you. Why do you think Neal and Rebecca have been with you this whole time? Simply because of the work? Of course not. It's because they like *you*. You think that *other* firm is going to want to see you hugging people all the time? Do you think you'd be able to play that joke on Neal that got him so upset that one time? Will it be as much *fun* going to work every day? Your office is bright and cheery and welcoming. It's not some sterile, cubicle-laden place. Do you think your clients would prefer sitting in the lobby you have now, or paying outrageous parking fees so they can climb 10 floors to sit in a waiting area where you have to behave like you're in a library?" Brian took a deep breath. "I think you would lose most, if not all, of that. I'm sure the people at any firm you chose to work at would like you and that you'd do a great job. But, eventually, you'd want your old job environment back."

"But what about the fact I might be able to help *more* people if I had additional staff to help *me*? I could delegate more and then take on more work; that would be a good thing, right?"

"Honestly, I think it would just stress you out even more than you already are. And the inevitable day would come when a mistake would get made, and then you'd blame yourself and maybe have a complete breakdown."

Tracy snorted. "Or maybe I would rise to the occasion and become a more efficient legal machine."

Brian smiled. "Hey, that's the spirit; yes, that is certainly a possibility. And if you truly believe that you can, in fact, become the machine, admit out loud how damn good you are, then I withdraw my earlier negative vote and cast a positive one. Go ahead, Tracy, talk yourself up some more. I want to hear it! Tell me how much you rock!"

Tracy started laughing and then she kissed her cheerleader. "Oh, you're cute."

"I'm serious, Tracy. I want you to be comfortable saying nice things about yourself and realizing how you can do anything you want to do if you believe in yourself."

"I know I can do stuff."

Brian shook his head. "Well, that's a start, I guess. I'll call you Stuff Girl."

She laughed some more. "Don't call me that."

"Alright, if you really don't like it."

"I really don't."

"Okay."

"I really do love *you*, though. Thank you, Brian. I feel better about things now."

"You do? I have no idea what just happened."

Tracy chuckled. "Oh, I think you must have *some* idea. I'm looking at this thing in a more positive way. I guess I do sometimes feel like the nervous student on the night before the test: the potential for failure at the forefront. You know, I've missed not having you around to help me get through those feelings. Like I said, I still have them sometimes."

"Well, I'm back. So you know I'm available."

"Yes, for better or worse, right?"

"Oh, Tracy, I wouldn't place this in the category of 'worse.' If this is the worst thing we have to deal with for the next 50 years or whatever, then we're in for quite an enjoyable ride."

Tracy kissed him again. "But *that* was better, right?"

"I think so. But let me have another just to be sure." She obliged. He was convinced. And then the clock struck one.

"Oh, dear," Tracy said. "I have to go. I didn't realize it was that late."

"Oh, sure, Tracy. Let me walk you down to your car." Soon afterward, Brian was opening her vehicle door for her; she entered.

"Thanks for tonight, Brian. You could always help me get out of those circles that I start talking in."

"Sure, Tracy. And, again, I'm so proud of you. I hope you can be a little proud of yourself at some point."

"Shucks. Give me a kiss and send me on my way." He leaned over and gave her quite a few.

"Goodnight, Brian," she said when he paused. "I love you."

"I love you too, Stuff Girl."

"Hey!"

"Sorry; last time." He grinned and then closed her door. Their eyes stayed locked through the window a bit longer. And then Tracy put her car in reverse, gave Brian one last wave, and left him standing in the parking lot. She could still see him in the rearview mirror when she turned the corner.

When Tracy was back at her condo, now dressed for bed, she sat down at her dining room table and started a two-column list: one for pro and one for con. She jotted her thoughts down, frowned, and then pushed the paper aside. She didn't want to be contemplating this now. She wanted to be focusing on the Granger murder. She pulled her notepad back and turned to another page, where she started writing as things came to her. Montado and Karine: both onstage the whole time. Greg Bowers: at his hotel room. Dan Scarborough: at his home in Gaithersburg. The Donlevy Brothers: opportunity, yes, but no apparent motive. Even an accident in their role as security people wouldn't explain the body in the tank. Who else? Louis Purdue? Motive, but no apparent opportunity. He was first on the list for tomorrow, though. An employee of *Merlin's*, maybe? They would certainly have a lot more flexibility in moving about the building. But what was the motive for one of them? Rats: people who had the opportunity in this case don't seem to have a motive, while the people with the motives don't appear to have had the opportunities.

Tracy shook her head, stretched, and made her way to her sleeping quarters. The clock had more bad news: almost 2:30 a.m. She slapped her pillow a couple of times because it made her feel better. Then she mumbled, "Sorry," and buried her face in the cushion, hoping to black out everything in the hopes it would all go away. She knew she was deceiving herself, though. She could not make her problems disappear or make them reappear on someone else's table. She was no magician. She really wasn't even a detective. She was just Tracy. At sunup, she would again rise to the occasion, like she had done before. But what if she failed, this time? As she had told Brian, she wasn't the one going to jail if she did. Woody Williams would be. And Tracy was sure Woody considered this no laughing matter. Woody wouldn't care how hard she had tried. He'd remember her as the screwup, the one who couldn't do the job—the failure. What would Mike Detweiler and company think of her then?

Chapter 9

"I haven't come to any real decision, yet," Tracy told Neal and Rebecca. "After Montado leaves town, I'll look into scheduling a visit to Mike's office and maybe meet and talk to some of the people there; probably next week."

"Oh," Neal said. "So you're at least open to the possibility of a merger."

"It doesn't hurt to look."

"What did Brian have to say about all of this?" Rebecca asked.

"Oh, how great an opportunity it was and how proud he was of me."

"Good man."

"And then he told me I should turn it down."

"What?" they both asked simultaneously.

"He says I'm a free spirit, I must be allowed to spread my wings and fly; working there would be the equivalent of putting me in cage."

Neal nodded. "That's pretty much what *I* said!"

"Yes, I know."

"So that's two votes no. What do you vote, Beck?" Neal asked.

Rebecca shook her head. "I'll vote for what Tracy wants to do."

"Well, I don't really want to think more about it right now. I want to call Simon Purdue and see if he'll let me talk to him. If I can speak with the father, maybe the son will also talk to me."

"You got my e-mail, then, with the info?"

"Yes, Neal, thanks. Well, I have to make a call. I'll keep you guys up to date on things." Tracy turned and went back to her office. Rebecca turned toward Neal.

"You just don't want to share her," she said tersely.

"What? What are you talking about?"

"You like it just being the two of you."

"Beck, that's not true."

"You come in, sit around doing your research. And then you pop in to joke around with the boss when either of you feels like it."

Neal pursed his lips. "So what if I do like the way things are?"

"Well, you should tell her *that*, instead of making it sound like *she's* the one who wouldn't like a change. And we both know there's probably not another boss like her in the world."

"Yeah, I know."

"Fine."

"Fine."

"Good."

"Why are you mad at *me*, Beck?"

"I'm not mad at you. I'm…I'm mad at myself."

"What? Why?"

"Because I don't want her take the job, either. And it's not fair to be thinking that; it's selfish is what it is. This is an incredible opportunity for her; we both know that. She should think about herself once in a while."

Neal put his arm around his coworker. "Alright, Beck, don't you go getting upset too. You're supposed to be the calm one around here and the voice of reason."

"I need to get back to work." Rebecca pulled away from Neal, quickly took her seat, rested her elbows on her desk, and buried her face in her hands. Neal looked at her a moment longer, and then took to his own office chair. He felt like following Rebecca's example.

"Good morning, Mr. Purdue, my name is Tracy Brubaker."

"Good morning."

"I'm representing a client involved in the Zachary Granger murder."

There was a moment of silence before Purdue commented, "Okay. Why are you calling me? I didn't kill the guy."

"Oh, I know that, Mr. Purdue. I don't know if you've heard about this, but the getaway car driver from the robbery may be involved in this recent crime. They never caught him, as I'm sure you're aware."

"Yeah."

"I'd like to talk to you about the robbery, if I can."

"Why?"

"To go over what happened, see if there's anything I can follow up on."

"Lady, that was like 13 years ago."

"I understand that. But, not to brag or anything, I recently helped solve crimes dating back almost 30 years ago. Maybe you heard or read about the Colin Richmond case?"

She heard Purdue sigh. "That was you, huh?"

"I helped out, yeah."

"You got a cop in trouble."

"No, he got himself in trouble."

"Yeah. Well, okay. I guess you can come over."

"Can I visit with you now? I'd be at your place in about an hour, say close to 10:30."

"That's fine. What'd you say your name was?"

"Tracy Brubaker."

She heard light tapping. "Oh, here you are. You're kind of young."

"Um, I guess so."

"I think I'll read up on you while I wait. I love the Internet."

Tracy cleared her throat. In the five years she had been on her own she couldn't recall ever doing a search on herself. She had no idea what Purdue would find. "I'll see you soon, Mr. Purdue." Purdue didn't respond. She wondered what Web page he was reading now. As she passed Neal's office on her way out, she popped her head in. "Hey Neal…"

"Yeah, boss?"

"Can you do a search on me?"

"I beg your pardon," Neal said, his eyebrows raised.

"Put my name in your favorite search engine and see what you find."

"Oh."

"If you find anything bad, please call me on my cell to give me the heads up. Purdue's checking me out, so I want to know if there's anything unflattering about me in cyberspace."

"Gotcha. I'll let you know."

"Thanks." And then she vanished from his doorway.

"Oh, the fun I could have with this," he thought. He still owed her one for a prank she played on him a few weeks ago. But he thought better of it. He didn't want to give her any reason to say goodbye to this workplace of frivolity and merrymaking—and, of course, the occasional hard work.

Tracy parked her blue Audi on the Purdue driveway in front of the closed two-car garage. She had just raised her arm to ring the bell when the front door was violently pulled open from inside. A young man in a sweatshirt and jeans was standing there, a scowl on his face.

"Uh, hi! Is Mr. Simon Purdue home?"

"You that lawyer?" the young man asked accusingly.

"Are you Louis?" Tracy returned.

"I knew it. It's me you wanted to see, so you went through my pop."

"No, I want to talk to your father about the bank robbery he was involved in."

"Why?"

"Is your father home?"

"Why don't you just get back in your car and leave?"

"Is that the lawyer, Louis?" The elder Purdue called out.

"She's leaving, Pop!"

"Let her in, damn it. Stop treating me like I need protecting."

"Hi, Mr. Purdue!" Tracy shouted.

"Come in, Ms. Brubaker! You have my permission to give Louis a swift kick to the nuts if he won't move." Tracy started coughing to cover up her laugh. Louis' face turned red, and he just turned and moved away from the entrance. By this time, Simon, who was in a wheelchair, had made his way to the large foyer. "Follow me to the study. We can talk in there." Then Simon pushed a button on his handlebar and he was moving toward the meeting room. Tracy followed. And so did Louis.

"Thank you so much for seeing me, Mr. Purdue. And, please, call me Tracy."

"You want something to drink, Tracy? Louis can get it for you."

"No, thanks."

"Louis: get her some water."

"But she said—"

"Get two bottles of water and bring them back here."

"Alright, Pop."

When Louis was out of view, his father said, "Forgive him, please, Tracy. He's a fine young man, but he's angry at the world."

"For what happened to you?"

"Yeah."

"My Mom had a stroke not too long ago. And it was an awful experience. But she, from what we can tell, made a full recovery. I can't imagine what Louis has been going through, or you, for that matter." Louis returned and handed out the water. "Thank you, Louis," Tracy said.

"I've been reading about you," Simon began. "I think you know a thing or two about pain and suffering." Simon turned to face his son. "*You* still have your father around. This young lady here, her father was *killed* doing his job when she was still in school. You hear me? Don't be playing the angry son thing in front of a daughter who trumps whatever you're feeling, pain-wise."

Louis' face went limp, the indignation vanishing quickly. He turned to Tracy. "I didn't know your dad was a cop. I didn't know anything about all that."

Tracy smiled. "How *would* you have known that, Louis?"

"I'm sorry."

"It's okay, Louis. I just want to talk to your father, and to you, too, if that's okay. I'm not here to hurt anybody."

"I know you're not," Simon said. "Like I said, I've been reading about you. You're a pretty clever lady."

"Well, I've had some success. And with this Granger thing, I think the real killer may be the one who drove the getaway car for the Washburn thieves."

"Why do you think that?" Louis asked.

"Granger had met with Dan Scarborough the night he was killed. Do you remember him, Mr. Purdue?"

"Simon, please. And, yeah, I remember him. He was…?"

"A loan officer at the time, he told me."

"Right. Nice guy."

"He's stuck up," Louis added.

"Why do you say that, Louis?" Tracy asked.

"I see him once in a while if I go inside the bank, usually to deposit something for Pop. He knows who I am; he knows damn well what happened to Pop. He barely talks to me."

"Oh. Did you see him Friday night at the show?"

"I saw him, but I wasn't going to go talk to him or anything."

"Was he alone?"

"I think so. I don't remember seeing anyone else there."

"And you never saw Granger on Friday."

"Nope. I figured it was a prank, some elaborate practical joke or something."

"Well, that was a pretty mean trick if it was one."

"Yeah, I guess it was."

"I understand someone mailed you a ticket."

"Yeah, it had a note telling me I should talk to Granger at this magic show. Granger knew something about the robbery that would help my pop. But I don't see this Granger anywhere."

"You knew what he looked like?"

"Yeah, I looked him up on the Internet. I found plenty of pictures and learned he'd been paroled. I would have spotted him if he'd been there."

"Is this why Granger had been in disguise?" Tracy thought. " Did Granger spot Louis Perdue, or find out somehow he was coming? Maybe that's why he never came back to sit down with Scarborough. Maybe he saw Louis and panicked. Wait a minute: Louis is in his 20s, meaning he'd have been in his early teens back in 2002. How would Granger have known what he looked like? On the other hand, Louis looks a lot like his father. Maybe that was enough to spook Granger."

"Are you okay, Tracy?" Simon asked looking at her. "You just stopped talking all of a sudden.

"Oh, sorry about that. I do that sometimes. Well, as I was saying, Scarborough was talking to Granger earlier, and Granger mentioned being there to speak to someone else. Now, if it wasn't you, Louis—and I can't imagine

Granger was the one who sent you the ticket—then it may have been this Buzz person, the driver of the car."

"That's interesting." Simon said. "Granger's pissed off for being left there and goes looking for this guy."

"That's what I'm thinking," Tracy said. "That's why, even though it's been more than 10 years, I wanted to talk to you, Simon. Maybe something you recall from that day could prove helpful."

"I don't mind telling you about it, Tracy. But don't get your hopes up."

"Fair enough." Tracy's note-taking pen assumed its position.

"Well, it was late morning. I was actually by myself, ticketing illegally parked cars, if you can believe it, when the call came over the radio to respond to a silent alarm at the bank. Well I was just a block away, so I responded."

"Were you approaching the bank from the front, the back, or the side?"

"From the back, initially; I was coming around the side when I saw this masked guy heading toward a car parked on the street. I later found out the shooter's name was Pyle. Now, there are already some officers following him; maybe they were just the bank guards. Anyway, he—Pyle I mean— yells something, and I see the car window in the back go down. He yells some more, and then he tosses some bags in the back through the window, and then the son of a bitch turns around and opens fire. I found out later I got hit by a ricochet: Pyle's bullet hit the corner of a bench and then got my spine. The damndest thing."

"I'm so sorry, Simon."

"Thanks. Well, I go down, and as I do I see the car pulling away. Pyle yells something else and then goes down himself. I lost consciousness soon after that. So you see, I can't tell you much."

"Did you see Granger at all during this, or just the shooter, Pyle?"

"Just Pyle. I found out later that Granger had been taken down in the bank by some of the customers. He wasn't armed, you see."

"Right. Pyle wasn't supposed to be either, apparently. Sounds like these guys were total amateurs."

"Yeah. I don't why Pyle didn't… Oh, my God, I can't believe it!"

"What Simon? What is it?"

"Yeah, Pop, what's wrong?"

"Nothing's *wrong*! I just remembered something. I never put it together before."

"Will you tell us, Simon?"

"I just figured out what Pyle was shouting. When Pyle approached the car door, he couldn't open it. That darn fool idiot driver had left the doors locked! So Pyle starts shouting something like 'The door! The door!'—and that moron puts the *window* down! Pyle's telling this guy to unlock the door, and he puts the *window* down! Then Pyle yells something like 'Not that! Not the window!' and then just tosses the bags in. My God, I never put that all together before now. It all sounded like a bunch of nonsense to me." Simon smiled and then shook his head. He looked at Tracy. "You sure have the magic touch, lady. I mean, I don't know how many times people asked me what Pyle said. I guess they were hoping I'd heard a name or something."

Tracy was writing feverishly. "So the getaway guy basically didn't know what the heck he was doing."

"Come to think of it, I think that was a stolen car they were driving. The driver must not have been familiar with the controls, so instead of hitting the auto-unlock button, he hit the window button." Simon started laughing so hard that his son did too. "What a complete idiot."

Tracy grinned at the duo. "Yet Buzz did escape capture."

"Sure he did; it was probably his first job—and his last one. He probably had no record. And nobody was going to give up anything to us, about Granger and Pyle, I mean. They were a couple of loners."

"Yeah, Buzz panicked and fled. I bet he had a car belonging to Granger or Pyle or himself waiting somewhere. You figure they'd want to switch cars at some point."

"Hmm. Good thought there. Buzz just probably took off and never looked back."

"And maybe tried to pull a vanishing act. Up until now, he had pretty much succeeded."

"Maybe."

"Speaking of vanishing acts," Tracy began while flipping to a clean page in her notebook, "do you know anything about the missing $50,000?"

"How's that?"

"Dan Scarborough says Granger accused him of helping himself to 50 large, and then saying the thieves got away with 90 instead of 40; $40,000 was all that was found in the back of the car."

"Well, if that's the case, that would mean this Buzz fella took nothing."

"Yes. Strange isn't it?"

"This whole blasted robbery was strange."

"Did you ever find out who tripped the silent alarm?"

Simon thought a bit. "No, I don't think whoever did it ever admitted to it; probably afraid of someone coming after him."

"Or her," Tracy added grinning.

"Oh sure," Simon grinned back.

"Well, I want to thank the both of you for speaking with me today."

"That's it?" Simon asked. "That wasn't anything."

"I told you, I wasn't here to hurt anybody. Louis, you may want to call Sandra Abonksi and let her know we talked, just so she's kept in the loop. I'm not working with the police or anything, but I feel it would be a courtesy to a fellow attorney."

"Sure, I'll let her know."

"Thanks again, gentlemen."

"Hey, Tracy," Simon said as he followed his guest to the door. "You'll let me know how this all turns out, won't you?"

"Absolutely, Simon. I'll be in touch." Tracy smiled and then closed the door behind her. Simon started laughing again.

"Not the window, the *door*!" Simon said out loud. He would end up spending the rest of his Thursday laughing himself silly over the mistakes of amateurs.

Tracy had put the address of Milton and Elena Bowers in her GPS and found herself outside a rambler with a fenced in backyard. She guessed it probably had three bedrooms: one for the parents and one for each child. Tracy wasn't sure why she was here to bother the Bowers' parents. But they lived relatively close to Simon Purdue, so she had decided to speak with them briefly. Greg Bowers had said his father was in insurance. If he was at work, perhaps Elena would be home and would talk to her. If nothing else, Tracy thought she could eliminate Milton Bowers as the driver who left one of his partners to die and the other to spend 12 years behind bars. Tracy parked on the street and then rapped on the wooden screen door. A five-foot-tall, white-haired woman came to the door. "Yes?"

"Mrs. Bowers?"

"Yes."

"My name is Tracy Brubaker. I'm friends with your daughter, Karine."

"Oh, hello. Karine has not lived here for a very long time."

"Oh, I know. In fact, I saw her at the magic show in Baltimore City last week."

"Oh, yes. Why are you here, then?"

"I would like to talk to you, if I may. You heard about the death at the magic show last week? Greg and Karine probably told you about it when they were here Sunday."

"Yes, of course. Are you a police officer?"

"No, I'm an attorney. I'm working on the case trying to figure out what happened. Can I please talk to you for a few minutes?"

"I suppose so. Let me unlock the door here." The small woman unlatched the screen door so Tracy could enter. "Come in here to the living room. Would you like some tea?"

"No, thank you, Mrs. Bowers."

"Well, sit down then."

"Thanks."

"I don't see much of Greg and Karine, anymore. They were still so young when they joined up with Casper."

Tracy looked at her quizzically. Why had Elena Bowers called the Great Montado by his first name? "Do you know Mr. Montado?"

Elena stopped pouring and then sipped from her cup. "I think you should get to know a man who is going to spend so much time with your children, don't you agree?"

"Of course," Tracy said. "Karine was about 19 when she went to work for him?"

"Yes. I was so glad Gregory was there to watch over her. Show business people have no morals."

Tracy looked around the room. Porcelain knickknacks and picture frames covered every available surface. "Mrs. Bowers, did you work in show business yourself at some point?"

Elena looked at her. "Why would you think that?"

"The way you talked about the people so emphatically, so authoritatively. It sounds to me like you speak from experience."

Elena smiled. "Yes, it is true. I was a dancer for a few years, a very promising one, too. Then, I had a baby: Gregory. Well, that was that. I hoped Karine might someday dance too. But, try as she might, she just was not… not up to the task."

"Oh, poor Karine. She did tell me she wanted to be a dancer."

"Yes. It was my fault. For years when she was little, I filled her head with dreams of dancing, perhaps being a great ballet star someday. But following a dream such as that is a futile task if you don't have the ability. It broke my heart seeing her so disappointed time and time again, so hard on herself."

"She seems happy now, performing with Montado."

Elena sighed. "Yes, I am sure she is happier now."

"Did she and Greg tell you what happened on Friday?"

"Only that somebody died during one of their performances. Karine did not want to talk about it."

"I was there that night. It was horrible. I can understand why she was so upset."

"She hardly spoke the whole time she was here."

"The man who died was someone by the name of Zachary Granger. Have you ever heard of him?"

Elena again sipped from her tea. "No, I don't believe I know that name."

"He may have been a friend of your husband's from about 15 or so years ago, early 2000s."

"I'm sorry."

"Is your husband at work now?"

"Yes."

"Greg told me he sells insurance."

"Yes, that's right."

"Has he always sold insurance?"

"Most of the time I've known him he has. I think he sold something else first; can't remember what it was."

"Hmm. I don't suppose you recall what he was doing in October 2002."

Elena paused a moment. "Uh, I'm not sure."

"It turns out this man who died Friday participated in a robbery that took place on October 17th, 2002, in Gaithersburg. Do you remember anything about that?"

Elena put her cup down and then her face went pale. "*Dios mío,*" she uttered.

"What is it, Mrs. Bowers?"

"That October…that's when they caught him."

"Caught who?"

"The sniper. The man who was shooting people. He and another man were killing people for a long time. We were all so scared, Karine especially. There were days she didn't want to leave the house." Tracy suddenly remembered; she hadn't made the connection. From February to October 2002, John Allen Muhammad and Lee Boyd Malvo had together killed or injured more than 10 people in the Maryland-DC-Virginia area. They were captured on October 24. But during those nine months, the tri-state area lived in fear. Tracy would still see people lock themselves in their car while the gas pump automatically filled their tank. Some of the victims included people who were standing beside their cars at gas stations. Muhammad was eventually executed in Virginia. Malvo would spend the rest of his life in jail.

"You say Karine was so upset she wouldn't leave the house?"

"Yes."

"Do you remember where your husband was working during this horrible time? I guess he worked near here."

"He had a job in Maryland then."

"Do you remember the name of the business?"

"No. I will have to ask him."

"Oh, you don't have to bother with that. Now, you said Karine was so afraid she wanted to stay here. Wouldn't she have missed a lot of school?"

Elena shook her head. "She was never a good student. I knew she had no future in the things they teach you in school."

"Oh, you knew she'd get into something artistic."

"Yes. Gregory was the one with the brains. Karine had the heart. As long as she got her high school degree, I wasn't worried."

"I see. But how did your husband feel? How did he react to Karine's not doing well in school?"

"He yelled, of course. But that just drove her away. She never went to college. One day, she just left home."

"And she joined up with Montado when she was 19."

"Yes."

"How did your husband feel about that?"

"He did not care! He had been driving her away from here for years! There were nights she would not even come home! Did he care? No!" Elena's hands started shaking.

"Oh, Mrs. Bowers, please forgive me. I didn't come here to upset you. I am so, so sorry."

Elena pulled a tissue from her sweater pocket and dabbed her eyes. "No, it is all right. I am a silly woman sometimes."

Tracy felt terrible. She had invaded this woman's peaceful day and brought back painful memories, brought to the surface the anger she still felt toward her husband for driving her children away. "Are you okay, Mrs. Bowers? Can I get you something?"

The hostess shook her head. "I'm fine now, thank you."

"Do you keep in touch with Greg and Karine? They must travel a lot."

"Karine calls at least once from every place she performs. Greg: well, he's always angry about something. He's always too busy to talk. But, I think they are happy. That is what is important."

Tracy smiled. "I hope to have children someday. I certainly hope what they choose to make their life's work makes them happy too, like Karine and Greg."

Elena shook her head. "It is a shame, though, that they will probably never have families of their own."

"Why would you say that, Mrs. Bowers?"

"Because a life like the one they are living is not the life for a family. You need to settle down and plant your roots. Children need stability when they are growing up, not being constantly moved from place to place. And if they were to marry and the children remained with someone else, what kind of life is that for a child: never seeing your parents?"

Tracy thought for a moment and then made some more notes in her small book. "I think that's enough for now, Mrs. Bowers. Thanks for your time. And I'm sorry if I upset you."

"I am fine."

"No need for you to get up, Mrs. Bowers; I can let myself out. Thank you again." Tracy smiled and then moved hurriedly to the door and then to her car. She dialed Neal's cell.

"Hi Tracy."

"Hi Neal. How'd the search on me turn out?"

"You're a super citizen, Tracy. There's some information on you on various 'find a lawyer' sites, and your name is in all kinds of newspaper articles. There was a big write-up in some real estate magazines about Reginald Walters, and you were mentioned. I didn't find anything for you to be ashamed of."

"That's a relief."

"How are you making out?"

"Well, I have a list for you."

"Okay, I have pen and pad in hand. Shoot."

"The Bowers dad worked in Maryland in October 2002; the wife sounded sure of it. See if there's any way to find out *where* he worked."

"Got it."

"Also, Mrs. Bowers used to be a dancer herself; I'm curious to learn just where she danced or whom she danced for. I think I may know the answer, though."

"Really?"

"Yes. Neal, I could be completely wrong here. But I just had an interesting and sometimes weird conversation with Mrs. Bowers. She said some things that got me thinking. I saw some of the photographs of her children when they were younger that were on the tables I was sitting between."

"Okay. Can you tell me what you're thinking?"

"Neal, I think Greg and Karine are more than Montado's business manager and assistant. I think they're his son and daughter."

Chapter 10

"How did you find out?" Montado asked Tracy. He was seated in his dressing room.

"I spoke with Elena. She didn't say anything, but I saw pictures of your children when they were small. Your son looked so much like you at one point."

"You saw Elena, did you?"

"Yes. She went on about how one has to settle down to raise a family; that her dancing career came to an end when she got pregnant with Greg; that show people have no morals. Her husband seemed to have hostility toward the children, not something I really understood. Unless, perhaps, because they were the children of another man."

"Yes," Montado nodded. "Elena's spouse liked them fine when they were small and inoffensive. But children grow up to be their own people."

Tracy sighed. "Mr. Montado, I don't want to hurt you or your children. If this ends up having nothing to do with the Granger killing, then I won't be sharing what I've learned with anyone; neither will my staff. Can you tell me about Greg and Karine, and you and Elena?"

Montado grunted. "I should be rehearsing. It is late."

"I'm sorry, Mr. Montado. But I need to get this cleared up now. Please?"

He smiled. "You are so lovely and charming; how can I refuse you?" Montado smiled again and cleared his throat. "Well, me and Elena: we were in a small variety troupe together in Mexico. She danced, I did magic tricks. She was beautiful, I was handsome. We fell in love."

"Sophia Loren and Rod Taylor, huh?"

"I beg your pardon?"

"Nothing, I'm sorry. Please go on."

"Well, we were both 17 when we started seeing each other. And then Elena got pregnant."

"Right. You're 52, Greg is 34."

"Yes. We moved into a small place together. She stopped dancing while I tried finding work in nearby places like bars, clubs, anyplace I could perform. Later we had Karine."

"Were you two ever married?"

Montado sighed. "No. I was trying to maintain a certain image: the suave dashing master of illusion! I couldn't let people think I was tied down in any way, especially people who might consider me for a tour group. I still wanted a career: to travel, to see the world."

"When did you come to America?"

"I believe Karine was almost two. I found a place for Elena and the children, but I was away most of the time. We kept everything quiet. She, understandably, grew tired of this. Finally, I had the opportunity to perform in a major show that would get me noticed. And it did. And that's when Elena told me I would have to decide what I wanted."

"And you chose to perform."

Montado gulped, and then stood up. He turned his back to Tracy. "I am not proud of it. But I had lived with my dream for so long. And there it was, finally in my reach. I had to at least try. If you had a dream as long as I had mine, you would understand that. Of course, my Elena found someone, this Milton Bowers. She wrote and told me she had fallen in love with a man, and he with her, who wanted to take care of the children and her. What could I do? I had no claim on her. The children did not know who I was, really; I had spent so much time away from them. Gregory was old enough when I left to remember he had another father somewhere. But Elena, my beautiful Elena, never said anything to anyone. She promised to keep my secret if I did not interfere with her own happiness or try to take custody of the children." Montado turned back around. He stared at Tracy.

Tracy sighed. This made her sad. Once, her mother had told her that parents make sacrifices for their children, not the other way around. Montado's entire family had sacrificed for *his* dream. Tracy wondered if had been worth it. "So how did Greg and Karine come back into your life?"

"Elena brought them to me one night, unexpectedly. She had waited until the evening's performances had been finished. I recognized her instantly, my beautiful Elena. I went back to her hotel room, and there were my children, my beautiful children…" Montado's voice cracked, and he cleared his throat before continuing. "Things were bad at home, she told me. Karine was so sad, her own dream to be a dancer crushed. Their 'father' wanted nothing to do with them. He had practically insisted Karine leave. Elena could not take it anymore. She needed my help."

"So you brought Karine onto the stage with you."

"Yes. I tried to find her private instructors to help with her dancing, too. But after the third one, it was clear that Karine would never be what she wanted to be. It broke my heart. She could tell how much it did. In spite of our years apart, in spite of us barely knowing each other, we felt close. I never wanted to leave her again, my beautiful Karine."

"And Greg stuck around to keep an eye on her, perhaps not too trusting of the father who left him behind."

Montado took a deep breath. "Yes. I told them both everything; the same things I just shared with you. It was strange; my daughter seemed to understand, and she forgave me instantly. My son: he *still* feels anger toward me. But things have gotten better between us. He is a very smart young man. And he loves his sister. He was probably more of a father to her than either me or Elena's husband."

"Did you see Elena anytime over the last few days?"

He shook his head. "No. She has a husband and her own life. I thought of going with my children when they visited on Sunday. But…"

"You still love Elena, don't you?" Tracy said it more like a statement of fact than a question.

"I have not seen her for years."

"Time doesn't matter if you're truly in love with someone. Sometimes you share something together that forever binds you to them. I know this couple who were in love when they were in college, and then they had a bad breakup. More than 10 years had passed when they saw each other again. And do you know what, Mr. Montado? It's like that 10-year separation had never happened. They're getting married next year."

Montado smiled at Tracy, and then glanced at her left hand. "I see. So you do not think I am a fool for caring for someone who will never belong to me again?"

"No, I don't. I guess it's our penance, in a way, for doing wrong."

"You think I did wrong?" he asked her, not sounding offended.

"I think *you* think you did wrong. If you still love Elena, how can think you did the right thing, leaving her all those years ago?"

Montado once again turned away. "I must rehearse now. I hope we are done."

Tracy sighed. "For now, we are, Mr. Montado. Good luck with your show tonight."

"Thank you, young lady."

"Oh, by the way, is Karine doing any better?"

He turned around. "Yes, each day it is better. But, I must confess, I am looking forward to leaving on Sunday."

"I understand. This stage here is still ripe with that awful memory. But *Merlin's* isn't about to let you out of your contract, what with the sellout crowds and publicity."

"It is not a publicity I ever want again!"

"I understand. Well, thank you, Mr. Montado, for sharing what you did. I hope things get better with Gregory." Tracy put her notebook in her briefcase and then left Montado's dressing room. She heard the door close behind her, and then the sound of weeping. But whose dreams was he crying over: his or Karine's?

"Thanks for staying late, Neal," Tracy said, after she was settled in her office chair.

"No problem, Tracy." And then she told her associate why he was having problems finding anything from Montado's pre-U.S. days.

"We're to keep this quiet for now."

"Sure, Tracy."

"No need to share this with anyone unless we have to."

"Of course."

Tracy leaned forward. "Neal, what kind of criminal history did Granger have before the robbery; just how a bad a guy was he, really?"

Neal flipped through his papers until he came to the ones that would address his boss's questions. "Actually, he had no history."

"Really?"

"Nope. Pyle was the, ahem, master criminal here."

"What's Pyle's background?"

"Juvenile stuff, mostly. He was charged with some convenience store holdups in his early teens."

"Did he work alone?"

"Sometimes. But he was young enough to be charged as a juvenile. He never shot anybody before the Washburn thing, though."

"But he committed multiple crimes."

"Yes."

"Hmm. I wonder if Granger was telling the truth, after all, about not knowing Buzz. Maybe Buzz was Pyle's associate, just like Detective Price thought."

"Sure, that's possible."

"And that would help explain why Granger didn't have a weapon with him; this was his first robbery."

"Not necessarily, Tracy; it could just have been the first time he got caught."

"True, but if Granger had the same kind of mentality that Pyle had, why didn't Granger bring a gun or something?"

"You know I can't answer that."

"I'm just thinking out loud here, Neal."

"Yeah, okay, sorry." Neal paused. "What is it, Tracy? What is it about Granger that has you troubled?"

"Well, a few things. We already discussed that he had no record and was unarmed. And Dan Scarborough told us that a few weeks before the robbery, Granger was applying for a home loan that he didn't ultimately get."

"So maybe that's why Granger picked that bank: for revenge."

"That's not where I'm going with this. Why would Granger even want a house?"

"Um, I think I'll pass and listen to what you're thinking."

"Well, maybe he and Pyle were thinking of getting a place together."

"Oh. Is that what you're thinking; that they were more than friends?"

"Maybe. But if they were moving in together, you'd think they'd be applying for the loan together, and that Scarborough would have recognized *both* of them, not just Granger. But Granger was applying for the loan alone."

"Maybe Pyle didn't have a job, so he had no income to contribute."

"Yes, that's possible. Or maybe they were afraid Pyle's criminal history would get them denied."

"But juvenile records are sealed, at least until the person dies. The bank would never have known about Pyle's past."

"You and I know that Neal, but maybe Granger and Pyle didn't."

"Oh right, good point."

"Granger's father has always maintained his son was innocent. Now I know that parents can sometimes be blindly devoted to their children. But in this case, look at some of the facts. Granger was unarmed; he had no history; he had a steady enough job where he was earning income; and just weeks earlier he was trying to buy a house. Doesn't it seem like we're missing something here?"

"Do you think Granger was at the bank and didn't realize what Pyle was planning to do?"

"I think that we should consider it. Listen: when Pyle finds out about the denied loan, he gets ticked off about it. We know Pyle has the bad history here. So Pyle and his friend Buzz show up to pick up Granger this October day, and they stop at the bank. Pyle tells Granger to come in with him. The next thing Granger knows, Pyle's got a gun and is asking Granger to back him up. Things go wrong. Some of the bank's patrons easily take Granger down; he doesn't really put up a fight."

"That doesn't exactly jibe with the story Granger told the police. He made it sound like they planned it together and things went wrong."

"Yes, I realize that. But if Granger's a newbie to crime, and he's just witnessed his best friend—and maybe more than that—get gunned down, he's not going to be thinking clearly. What's in the official record is what statement Granger ultimately gave. He could have been coached by officers; he could have been told that the trial would go easier for him if he said the robbery was planned instead of saying he didn't know what was happening. The detectives would have told him how unbelievable such a story would be."

Neal was nodding. "Okay, Tracy, I can see clearly where you're coming from. And the witness statements can probably match both scenarios."

"Yes, Granger was a scared young man, whether he was part of the crime from the beginning or just got pulled in on the spot."

"So, now we have a basically decent young man who, because he hung out with the wrong guy, lost this guy and 12 years of his life."

"Twelve years: he probably wouldn't have been the same person when he got out that he was when he went in."

Neal sighed. "I get the sense you feel bad for Granger all of a sudden."

"If I'm right about him suddenly being thrust into an in-progress robbery, I sure do. Sometimes good, decent people do bad things because they love someone, things they would never do otherwise. I find myself wondering if that's what we have here."

"And he saw Pyle get killed while Buzz drove away."

"Yes, a scene he's probably been replaying in his mind every day for 12 years."

Neal cleared his throat. "You want to talk to Granger's father, don't you?"

"Yes. He's the only person I know of who could give us some idea of the pre-incarcerated Zachary. But I don't know if he'd even see me, given I'm defending his son's alleged killer."

"I think he'll see you," Neal said quietly.

"Oh? Why?"

"Because when he answers your knock on his door, you tell him straight away that you think his son isn't the felon the cops have been saying he is for the past 12 years. You tell him the version of the robbery you just told me. You tell him that you think his son's killer is this mysterious Buzz, and that if you can find Buzz, the truth may come out about what really happened that day. You tell him Buzz is the only one left who really knows the truth. You tell him if you find Buzz, you'll make sure the truth about Zach's role will come out. You'll promise him this." Neal looked at her seriously.

"Neal, that's brilliant," she said nodding. "And it's the truth, too; at least it's a possible truth. As you said, Buzz is the only one left who could confirm it." Tracy smiled. "Thank you, Neal. I think I'm going to have to make it a point to see Jeremiah Granger."

Neal smiled back. "I'm glad I could help."

"Neal, you've helped me on each and every case I've ever worked on. You're the best." They both swallowed and broke eye contact; neither felt like dealing with any mushy stuff tonight. "Go home to your family, Neal. I'll see you tomorrow."

Neal smiled as he arose. "Goodnight, Boss," he said, as he left her office. She sighed. The case had quickly taken a 180-degree turn. The formerly villainous Granger had now been recast, possibly as a victim of circumstance, while Montado, a hero to her in some ways, had been revealed as man who abandoned his children. Just how many more reversals were ahead in this case?

The autographed picture, the magic hat from *Merlin's*, and the bouquet of roses sat together on a small tabletop in Tracy's condo. She was looking at the display differently now. She couldn't bring herself to smile at it. Brian was by the sink, drying dishes and putting them away. He was sneaking quick looks at Tracy, standing in front of her recent gifts. She had been quiet during dinner. All she would confirm is that it had nothing to do with Brian, or the recent merger offer. Case-related stuff was off-limits, for the most part. Brian understood this, or at least tried to. But he hated seeing her sad. "Tracy," Brian said quietly, "I really wish you would tell me what's wrong. Maybe you could talk in code like you sometimes do."

Tracy turned to face him. She thought a moment. "Brian if we talk about this, it has to stay between you and me, at least for now. You can't tell anybody, not even Crystal, not your best male pal. Can I trust you, Brian?"

He nodded. "Yes, Tracy. If you ask me to keep my mouth shut, consider it shut."

That brought a smile. "Let's sit down, then." And then she told him; told him the history, or what she knew of it, of Casper Montado, and of Greg, Karine, and Elena Bowers. She even told him of her new position on Granger. When she had finished, she smiled at him shyly. He looked at her sympathetically. "Two people in love, with two different views of how life should be," she summarized. "And the children suffer for it. And Granger, suddenly forced to make a decision that none of us can really appreciate."

Brian nodded. "You think Montado should have stayed with his family." He had no comment to make with regard to Granger.

"Of course I do."

"What about Elena maybe following her husband?"

"But he wasn't her husband, Brian. He never married her. And she was okay with it, because they had a second child. Then, one day, she decides they need to get married and settle down. It's all ass-backward."

"Tracy, you shouldn't judge them."

"I'm not judging *them*. I'm talking about what they *did*."

Brian sighed. "So what are you going to do?"

"What do you mean?"

"Are you going to tell the police about this? Or bring it up in court during your defense of Williams?"

"Brian, I would never make public something like that unless I believed it had a direct bearing on the case. I had this argument with Neal on the Paganini case."

"Wait a minute, Tracy. We're not arguing. I just asked you a question."

"Oh. I'm sorry. I guess I flashed back for a moment."

"It's okay. So what you're saying is, you're not sure yet if this family drama has anything to do with Granger's murder."

"Depending on how I look at everything, the answer changes. I'm missing something here, something obvious. There's something screwy about this whole death; I just can't put my finger on it yet."

Brian shifted in his seat so he could reach Tracy's shoulders. He started massaging them. "Let *my* fingers do some walking here," Brian said smiling. "Maybe I'll release something and your brain will light up like a pinball machine with the answer."

Tracy laughed. "I don't care what my brain does; this feels great!"

"I am the Amazing Cannoli! I will make your tensions disappear!"

Tracy laughed. "Well, keep at it, Cannoli man, because I may have you work on my back, next."

"Any part you wish," he said suggestively.

Tracy giggled. "Keep it clean."

"Tracy, I'm trying. You have had no idea how hard I'm trying."

"I know, Brian. Look, I think your fingers have worked their magic. You can stop."

"What about your back?"

"No, let's not head any farther south."

He sniggered. "All right. You feeling any better?"

"Yes, I am. Thanks, Brian."

"Any time." She turned to reward him the best way she knew how.

"Oh, I forgot to tell you that Crystal and I are getting together a week from Sunday. She's coming here around 2:00. You're welcome to join us."

"I'll think about it."

"Okay," she said quietly. "Brian…"

"Yes, Tracy."

"I'm curious: when did you get the tickets for the show?"

"Huh?"

"We started dating about a month before the show. How did you get such good seats in such a short amount of time?"

"Oh."

"Oh what?"

"I got them before."

"Before?"

"Before we started seeing each other again."

"You got them for you and someone else?"

"No. I knew you loved magic, and I was working up my nerve to call you. Then I just said: what the heck. I got them as soon as they went on sale in February."

"Oh," she smiled. "Planning ahead."

"Yes."

"Optimistic, were you?"

"I guess. I figured if you said no to me, I could give the tickets to Crystal and she could take you out for your birthday."

"Ah. You had a contingency plan, to boot."

"Yes."

"Well, I'm glad it all worked out the way it did."

"Even if I inadvertently got you mixed up in another murder?"

Tracy grinned. "Yes. Even that."

"So when are you going to solve this thing?"

"I don't have much time left. Maybe I won't solve it."

Brian blinked. "Would you be okay with that? Not solving the thing, I mean."

"No, I wouldn't. But I'd have to deal with it."

"Sure, and you'll live to fight another case."

"I guess."

Brian looked at her; then he looked her over. "Tracy: I have to ask you a favor."

"Okay."

"This summer, no bikinis. Only one-piece suits."

Tracy started laughing. "And you'll swear off Speedos, right?"

"When have I ever worn a Speedo?"

"When have I ever worn a bikini?"

"True. Should we just not visit the ocean this summer?"

Tracy made a pouty face. "I want to go. I'll go alone if you won't come with me."

"If you go, I'll have to go and protect you."

"Oh really? From what?"

"Guys wearing Speedos."

She giggled. "Oh, you're cute." And there was more kissing between the non-swimsuit wearing couple before Tracy called it a night. She dreamt later of ocean waves and sandy beaches, boardwalk fries, and miniature golf: memories of warm summer evenings she had spent with Brian Shane. They were both remembrances and previews of coming attractions. She awoke Friday morning with a smile on her face. Her dreams may have been simple. But they were coming true. In fact they were just around the corner.

"You got my message, then?" Woody Williams asked.

"Yes, Woody. I'm sorry I haven't been back to see you. I've been following up on all kinds of possible leads on your case. It's been a crazy week, and the craziness is not over yet."

"Oh sure. I spoke with some guy, Nigel?"

"Neal."

"Yeah. He said you were running around all over the place. So did you find something, yet, or just get a good workout?"

"Hard to say, Woody. I think I have something, or the beginnings of something."

"Well, how long do I have to stay in this place? I don't want to be held over any longer than I have to, if you know what I mean."

"Your preliminary hearing is next week. So if the judge thinks there's not enough against you, you may be sent home."

"That'd be great!"

"Yes, it would be. And quite frankly, that may happen. I'm still a little surprised they even arrested you as quickly as they did. The evidence is weak."

"So you think this is almost over?"

"…Unless the police come up with something. That's why they're actually still looking into things."

"But you're not done digging around, right?"

"Correct. I still have a couple of other things to look into."

"Okay. Well, don't let me keep you."

Tracy smiled sympathetically. "I guess you haven't had any other visitors."

Williams shook his head. "Nah, no friends or family around here."

"I'm sorry, Woody."

"No problem."

"Hey, Woody, can I ask you a question?"

"You just did."

She sighed but smiled. "What's your real first name? It's not Woodrow, is it?"

"You wouldn't believe me if I told you."

Tracy looked at him and then her eyes widened. "It isn't…"

"It is. My legal name is Robin Williams."

"Oh dear. Were either or both of your parents fans of his?"

"My mother. Fell in love with Robin Williams when he played Mork. Can you believe that?"

"School must have been brutal."

"You don't know the half of it. They used to call me Mork, you know? That damn Nick at Nite and those other stations ran *Mork and Mindy* all the time. They'd call out 'Hey Mork, where's Mindy today?' like I had never heard that one before."

"I'm sorry."

"I mean, do I look like a Robin to you?"

Tracy studied him and shook her head. "A finch, maybe."

Williams shook *his* head and laughed. "You're real funny, or so you think."

Tracy grinned. "So where did you get Woody from?"

"Well, I'm a Tom Hanks fan, myself."

"Oh! At first I thought it was a Woody Allen thing. But I love the *Toy Story* movies!"

"Me too. So, I just put the two together."

"Hang in there, Robin Woody Williams. I'm hoping when I'm done, you'll have the last laugh."

"Alright, Tracy, thanks. I mean that."

"Bye, Woody." As Tracy made her way back to her vehicle, she realized she and Woody had something in common after all. She had developed her particular sense of humor in response to the taunts and teases she had dealt with growing up. She had little doubt Williams had done the same thing. She was now defending a fellow survivor of the cruelties of youth. And defend him she would.

Neal was at Rebecca's desk when Tracy returned from her visit with Woody Williams. "What's up, guys?" she asked.

"Mike Detweiler called while you were out," Rebecca said. "He wanted to invite you to visit his offices next Tuesday. I sent you an e-mail with the proposed time and place."

"Oh, thanks, Beck. I thought I told him I'd call *him* back. Oh well."

     Practice to Deceive

"Tracy, that's not all."

"No?"

"You also got a call from Donna Ratzinger."

"She's the managing partner of Ratzinger, Dowel, and Steadman, right?"

"Yes. She wants to have lunch with you."

"Um, did she say why?"

"A business proposal is what she said."

Tracy looked at Neal who hadn't said a word. She looked back at Rebecca. "Okay."

"And then you got a call from Barry Tompkins."

"Hold on," Tracy said. "Is this some kind of joke you two are pulling?"

"No, Tracy," Rebecca said.

"No, Tracy," Neal repeated.

"Then what's going on?"

"I think your handling of Williams has gotten some attention," Rebecca offered. "I mean, he's a genuine celebrity."

"You could open up a satellite office in Los Angeles," Neal said mockingly. "You could be the next lawyer to the stars! Think of it! Your name in lights—"

"Enough already," Tracy said. "You two are pulling my leg."

"Tracy, we're not," Rebecca said.

"Well, I don't understand this."

"What's to understand?" Neal asked. "You're the subject of a bidding war. You're the prize. The world is your oyster."

"Neal, stop. Something's going on."

"What could possibly be going on?" he challenged.

Tracy looked at Neal sternly. "What kind of question is that? If I knew what was going on, then I'd know what was going on!" And Tracy turned and went back to her office. She slammed her briefcase on the desk. Neal knocked on her door soon thereafter.

"Uh, Tracy, we need to talk about Milton Bowers."

Tracy looked at the sheepish man before her. "Oh. Well, come in, then, if you must. But you're on probation until I find out what's going on."

"Tracy I swear—"

"Zip it, Bennett. Just tell me about Bowers."

Neal cleared his throat. "Bowers worked for Amberson Wilkes Insurance Agency for three years, from May of 2001 through September of 2003."

"How did you find out about *that*?"

"The BondTogether business network: BTN, as it is typically called. I found his name on there a couple of days ago and requested us to be 'bonded.' He granted my request this morning. He had his resume right on there."

"You've got to me kidding me."

"No. And I'm only denying *that* one time."

"So where is, or was, this company he worked for?"

"Oh about five miles from Washburn Community Bank."

"WHAT?!"

"Maybe closer to six miles." He paused. "And I have something even better."

"Alright, Neal, your probation period just ended. Now out with it!"

"The getaway car was abandoned in the parking lot right across the street from where the Amberson Wilkes office is located."

Tracy fell into her chair. "Where is Bowers working now?"

"Runyon Hess Gordon Insurers. They're in Charles County."

"I have to talk to Bowers, like, yesterday."

"I thought you might. So I called in and made an appointment for you. I said you were getting married and were looking into reciprocal life insurance policies for spouses. You have a 1:30 appointment; better hurry."

Tracy beamed, ran over and hugged Neal, and then put her coat right back on. She grabbed her case and went to make her appointment with Milton Bowers. After Tracy had left, Neal strolled casually out to the lobby whistling. "I am in her good graces," he told Rebecca. "*You're* the one under suspicion now."

"Go back to your cage and zip it, oh green-faced one."

"Your taunts do not harm me, woman. I got a hug and *you* didn't. *You're* still in trouble." Neal turned his back and sauntered into his office. Rebecca shook her head and grinned. "Boy, do I love this place," she thought, truly meaning it.

Tracy made it with 10 minutes to spare. She sprang from her car and almost ran into the door. She took a deep breath and then slowly pulled open the entrance to the offices of Runyon Hess Gordon Insurers. A receptionist was talking on the phone. Tracy approached the desk. The attendant covered the mouthpiece of the receiver. "Can I help you?" she whispered.

"I'm here to see Milton Bowers. I have a 1:30. My name is Tracy Brubaker."

The receptionist scanned her list. "I have a Tracy Shane—"

"That's me! Or it will be after I marry Bri-Bri." She gave mental kudos to Neal for the clever subterfuge. Bowers may have recognized her proper name if his wife had shared it with him.

　Practice to Deceive

"Bri-Bri?"

"My fiancé."

"Oh."

"But I may keep the last name Brubaker for professional reasons. Or maybe change it legally to Shane but just keep my firm name the way it is."

"Okay. Why don't you have a seat?"

"Oh supreme! Thanks!"

The woman behind the desk looked at Tracy curiously, and then returned her attentions to her call. Tracy continued bouncing up and down slightly on her chair. She wasn't sure if this act of hers was going to work or not, but she believed she needed to catch Bowers off guard. It wasn't long before a short, 50-ish-looking gentleman came toward the excited undercover attorney. "Are you Ms. Shane?"

"No. But I will be Mrs. Shane next year, unless I decide to stick with my maiden name. I guess I confused who ever took the appointment."

"Oh, no problem whatsoever. I'm Milton Bowers."

"Hi, I'm Tracy. Just call me Tracy. *Everybody* calls me Tracy."

"Sure," Bowers said cautiously. "Follow me." Tracy practically skipped as she followed Bowers to his office. He closed the door as she galloped past him. "Uh, are you okay, Tracy?"

"Oh I'm *fiiiine*, Milton! I'm just so busy with all this wedding stuff. And then Bri-Bri calls and asks 'Did you take care of the thing?' and I say 'What thing, sweetie?' and he says 'The insurance thing,' and I say 'Oh that thing, no I didn't,' and he says 'But we agreed you would look into that,' and I said 'I know,' and he says 'Well, can you take care of it today?' and I say 'Sure, honey,' and…well, here I am! I mean I've just been *sooo* busy! Busy like a bee: buzz buzz buzz!"

Bowers stared at her. She was smiling broadly at him. "Why don't you sit right here?" he offered, finally.

"Oh, sure." Tracy sat as Bowers came around the side of his desk to take his seat.

"Are you married, Milton?" Tracy asked sweetly.

"Yes, I am."

"Any babies?"

"I have two grown children."

"I can't wait to have babies. Neither can Bri-Bri."

"I'm sure."

"We can't agree on names, though. He wants boring names like John or Mark. I want exciting names like Roderick or Benedict for a boy, or Bronywn or Ophelia for a girl. What do you think sounds better?"

"They all sound fine to me. So, I understand you want to discuss life insurance policies for each other."

Tracy breathed deeply. She took a tissue out of her pocket and started nodding. "Yes," she said sounding like she was on the verge of tears. "It's so sad thinking of my Bri-Bri no longer here." She dabbed her eyes with her tissue. "I mean, we're not even married, yet, and you want me thinking like a widow." Tracy started huffing and puffing.

"Now there, there, Tracy. This is just precautionary stuff. No need for you to be sad."

"I can't help it," she whined. "I mean, him gone…"

"Well, what does he do?"

"What do you mean?"

"For a living. You see we're going to have figure out what income he would be earning over his lifetime. Factor in expenses and such. Then come up with a figure that will allow you to continue to live the life you were living until he…went to his eternal rest."

Tracy dabbed her eyes some more. "Oh, that's beautiful: eternal rest. He needs rest. The poor thing can't sleep at night. He tosses and turns, and I say, 'Brian: stop that,' and he grumbles, and I say, 'Brian: take a sleeping pill or something'—"

"Look Tracy—"

"You know why he can't sleep at night?"

Bowers sighed. "No."

"Because he takes a nap when he gets home from work. From 4:30 to 7:30, he's on that couch snoring his cute little nose off. I'm there making dinner, and he's—"

"Tracy, I don't mean to be rude. But I do have other appointments today. Now, what does your fiancé make annually?"

"I don't know. But he's a bank manager."

"He is?"

"Yes. It's too dangerous a job."

"It is?"

"Robberies, Milton. All those people today who go around waving their guns in banks…"

"Oh, yes, I guess you have a point."

"That's when this whole insurance thing came up, when I started talking about it: guns in banks, I mean."

"I see."

"You'd think these days they could steal money over the Internet and make things easier on the rest of us. It's just *so* rude and thoughtless."

"I'm sure that day *is* coming."

"Until that day is here, I want my Bri-Bri to find something safer."

"Your Bri-Bri?"

"Brian—my fiancé."

"Of course."

"I *love* nicknames. Do you love nicknames, Milton?"

"Not really."

"I do. I have a friend Rebecca I call Beck, and a friend Elias I call El, and a friend Arthur I call Art, and a friend Crystal I call Crys, and a friend Neal I call—well I just call him Neal since his name is only one syllable."

Bowers stared at her a moment. "I'm sure."

"Do you have a nickname, Milton?"

"No."

"Nobody calls you Milt or Milty?"

"No."

"How about Milty Way? Get it?"

"Tracy—"

"Let me think. Now your haircut there, that looks like a military cut."

"Not exactly."

"Well, it looks like one to me. I think a good nickname for you would be: Buzz. Do you like that nickname, Milton: Buzz?"

Bowers glared at her; she glared back. "Alright, what's going on here?"

"Is that a trick question? If I answer right, do I win a toaster or something? Oh wait, banks give away toasters. Do you give away prizes if I buy a policy from you?"

Bowers stood up. "Listen: either you're a total crackpot or you're up to something! Now, which is it?"

"I guess it depends on whom you ask and the day of the week, Milton."

"Well I'm asking you about today!"

"You remember the robbery that took place in October 2002 at Washburn Community Bank? It was a few miles from where you were working at the time."

"Who ARE you?"

"I told you. I'm Tracy; Tracy Brubaker."

Bowers looked at her a moment. Then his brain freezer light went on. "Are you that lawyer my wife was telling me about?"

"Probably."

"What do you want with us?"

"I want to know why the getaway car used in the Washburn robbery was abandoned in the parking lot across the street from your former place of employment. I want to know why the man who spent the last 12 years in jail visited the magic show where your daughter was performing last Friday, the show your son oversees. I want to know who Buzz is."

Bowers glared at her some more. "I don't know *what* you're talking about."

"The day of the robbery, Mr. Bowers, did you by chance take an early lunch, maybe go home sick?"

"Get out of my office."

"Did you panic and leave your friend to die?"

"I said, GET OUT OF MY OFFICE!"

"Or what: you'll call the police? Let's call them together, shall we? Jim Lucas or Debbie Price, detectives with the Baltimore Police Department."

"I don't know what you're—"

"Yes you do. It's all over your face. It's interesting to watch a person's face. They go from looking relaxed to amused to confused to annoyed to downright panicked. That's what's on your face right now, Milton: panic."

"Please leave."

"Hey, you said the magic word!" Tracy exclaimed, standing up. "Okay, I'll leave. But you better get your own lawyer, Milty—because the police are going to be visiting you *very* soon." And then Tracy turned and left Bowers to process what she had said, most of which was nothing more than innuendo. But she could tell she had struck a nerve. What would his next move be? Go after her? He sure matched the description of Buzz, such as it was. He would have been in his forties in 2002; he was short in stature. Was he at *Merlin's* last Friday night? Things were starting to come together for her, but she'd had to do some pushing. That was dangerous; sometimes, when you push, things can fall on your head.

Chapter 11

"And just what did you hope to accomplish by this stunt?" Lucas asked sternly.

"I just wanted to shake up his beehive."

"His what?"

"Get his bees buzzing. See?"

Price shook her head. "Tracy, that was risky, don't you think? What if he had panicked and attacked you, or cracked you on the skull with something?"

Tracy frowned. "I could have handled *him*. Heck, I have at least an inch on him, height-wise I mean."

"You should have come to us with this first," Lucas continued.

"You guys don't have jurisdiction with respect to the robbery. And no one, until this point, had any reason to look at employees of Amberson Wilkes Insurance Agency. I wanted to see how Bowers would react."

"And you think he's the driver," Price stated.

"He sure acted guilty. You should have seen the look on his face when I asked him if he liked the nickname Buzz."

Lucas and Price looked at each other. "We should notify Gaithersburg about this," Lucas said. "They should be the ones to follow up on this."

"But the robbery has to be tied into Granger's murder," Tracy pleaded.

"I don't doubt that," Price offered. "We'll go back and see if anyone remembers seeing Milton Bowers at *Merlin's* on Friday; maybe take another quick look at credit card receipts."

"If Bowers did this, I doubt he did it alone," Lucas opined.

"You're thinking one of his kids is involved?" Price asked her partner.

"I doubt it," Tracy said. "There is no love lost between Bowers and his kids. I can't see them helping him order a pizza much less helping with a murder."

"How can you be so sure?"

"I spoke with Mrs. Bowers. She told me how Milton was always screaming at Karine. He drove her and her brother away."

"My, you've been busy," Price grinned.

"Busy as a bee: buzz buzz buzz!"

Lucas shook his head. But he was grinning slightly. "Let the department handle Milton Bowers, for now. Seeing him like that wasn't a very good idea, Tracy."

"I appreciate your obvious concern for my well-being, Detective Lucas. But Montado and company leave in two days, and I'm running out of time. I couldn't afford to wait for you guys to fit Milton into your schedule."

"Alright," Price cut in. "What's done is done. We'll get busy on this. Thanks, Tracy. That's some great work you did there."

"Thank my associate, Neal Bennett. He's the great man behind the great woman. But don't tell Bri-Bri I said that."

"Bri-Bri?" Lucas asked confused.

"That's my new nickname for my fiancé. Do you like it?"

Lucas shook his head yet another time while Price chuckled. She said, "See you, Tracy. I'll let you know what we find out about Bowers, if anything—at least as it pertains to Granger's death."

"Thanks, Deb." And then Tracy gave the detectives a wave and left them to become busy bees themselves.

"You know," Lucas said to his partner, "I think I'm starting to like her. What's wrong with me?"

"Should I start in alphabetical order, or list by severity?" Price grinned.

It was going to be another long day. Immediately after leaving her detective friends, Tracy returned to Montgomery County. She wanted to speak with Jeremiah Granger herself. Tracy wanted to stop thinking about Zachary Granger strictly as the body in the tank; she wanted to learn everything she could about him, even if those things would be filtered through the devotion of a loving parent. Again, her GPS had brought her to her destination efficiently and without incident. She found street parking and was soon ringing the Granger home's bell. An average-sized, mostly bald man came to the door. Tracy introduced herself and repeated pretty much verbatim the opening remarks that Neal had advised her to make. It wasn't long afterward that Jeremiah was handing her a glass of ice water as Tracy sat in one of the living room chairs.

"This Buzz fellow," Jeremiah started as he took his seat, "didn't just kill my son, he killed my wife too."

Tracy looked at him with great sympathy. "She died while your son was in prison I understand."

"Yes, she died because she couldn't stand Zach being in that place when he shouldn't have been. It killed her."

"What did the doctors claim it was that killed her, if I may ask, Mr. Granger?"

"Heart problems. Trouble with blood circulating or something. It was her heart all right, but not for the reasons the doctors said."

Tracy nodded. "Zach was a good kid; I know he was never in any trouble before the robbery."

"Never in trouble a day in his life; not at school, not at home, not anywhere. I know the police think I'm just saying all that because I'm his father. But it's the truth."

"Do you know how Zach ended up being friends with Chris Pyle, the one who got Zach into all that trouble?"

Granger sighed. "Well, Zach got picked on a lot in school. He was a shy kid, not real smart, either. But he had a good heart. This Pyle kid was nice to him, for some reason. Well, they became close friends."

"When was this? I mean, when did they become friends?"

"In elementary school. He seemed like a nice enough kid. But my wife said Pyle was getting Zach to ditch school sometimes."

"Oh. And then Pyle got into some more serious trouble later."

"Yeah. Zach and Chris didn't end up going to the same high school, so they didn't see each other as much. Then that Pyle kid got into some bad trouble. And then Zach just sort of clammed up again."

Tracy reached for Granger's hand. "I'm sorry. How did the two of them meet up again?"

"The way I remember it, when Pyle got released from the kiddie-con place they put him in, he looked Zach up. Then they were best friends again."

"Oh. I guess you weren't too happy about that."

He shook his head. "No. But Zach was smiling all the time again. I told him to be careful. And he told me and his mother that he knew what Chris had done but that he could be a good influence on him. You see, Ms. Brubaker, my son wanted to be a positive thing in this Chris Pyle's life, not some criminal partner."

"Yes, Mr. Granger, I can see exactly what you're saying. So what was Zach doing with his life up until he got arrested?"

"Well, he worked a lot of manual-type jobs: a busboy in restaurants, a stock boy in all kinds of stores. He worked with a landscaping company one or two summers. He was working hard, saving his money. He did a little drinking during the weekends, but nothing so bad as to worry about."

"And he was living here the whole time?"

"Yeah, me and Marianne were happy to have him. Like I said, he was a good boy."

"I understand that Zach, shortly before the robbery occurred, was looking to buy a house. Were you aware of that, Mr. Granger?"

He shifted in his seat. "Yeah, I remember him talking about it."

"Were he and Chris Pyle planning to buy a house together?"

"Pyle? No, I don't think so. He had met some girl."

"What girl?" Tracy felt her heartbeat quickening.

"I never met her. I mean, *he* had just met her, by the sound of it. The first girl who's ever been nice to him—and then he's talking about moving in with her."

"Do you remember the girl's name, Mr. Granger?"

He shook his head. "I don't think I ever gave Zach the chance to tell me her name or much about her, really."

"I'm sorry?"

"Well, as soon as he asked to borrow some money to put down on the house, I told him, in no uncertain terms, I wouldn't do it. He'd have to marry her before I would help them live *that* way."

"Your son wanted a loan from you?"

"Yeah, that's exactly what he called it: a loan. Said he'd pay me interest on it if I wanted. The boy was just 22 years old, and suddenly he wants to buy a house and have a girl move in with him. I told him I wasn't a bank. He got upset with me and left the dinner table."

Tracy breathed in deeply. "Mr. Granger, please forgive me for asking this, but didn't it occur to you that maybe Zach went along with Pyle on this robbery to get enough money to put down on a house? Were you aware that Zach applied for a loan just a few weeks earlier at the very bank that was robbed, and that they turned him down?"

Fury took over Granger's face. He stood up and started yelling. "What are saying?! Are you saying that it was *my* fault?! Are you saying that if I'd given him the money, none of this would have happened?!"

Tracy was afraid this would be his reaction. She knew her time here was most likely over. "No, of course not, Mr. Granger. I think Zach may have told Pyle about his problems, and Pyle suggested they rob the bank. Or maybe Pyle never even told your son what he was planning to do, and Zach suddenly found himself in that awful situation. Please, Mr. Granger, please—I just have a couple more questions. Can't you see how important it is that I find this Buzz person? Only *he* can tell us what really happened that day."

Granger was still on his feet, red-faced. Tears slid down his cheeks. Tracy remained seated, prepared to leave if he asked her to do so. Finally, he took a deep breath and sat back down. He shook his head. "I've wondered that very same thing every second of every day for almost 13 years," he said without looking at her. "I wish I had given him the money."

"Mr. Granger, you cannot blame yourself for what happened. How could you have imagined such a thing? Everyone involved in the robbery was old enough to know better, old enough to know the difference between right and wrong. I can tell in the brief time we've talked that you raised Zach right, did your best for him. Guilt is such a horrible thing to live with. Let me see if I can help make some of it go away. Help me find this Buzz. Did you hear Zach ever mention someone named Buzz?"

"No. I told you right off when you got here, and I told the cops when they asked me last Saturday, and when they asked in 2002: I never heard Zach talk about someone called Buzz."

"Okay, how about the names of any of Zach or Chris Pyle's friends, then? Buzz was probably a nickname, anyway."

He was shaking his head vigorously the whole time she was speaking. "No, I don't remember *any* names. Believe me, I'd tell you if I knew. I just can't think anymore. I just can't."

Tracy looked at Granger, who was on the verge of tears again. She stood and put her hand on his shoulder. "I think I'll go now, Mr. Granger. I'm sorry I upset you. I'll see if I can find Buzz another way. Thank you for your time, and, again, I'm very sorry." She started to move away when he grabbed her left hand with both of his.

"Please, Ms. Brubaker," he said tearfully but quietly. "Please find out what really happened that day. I have to know the truth, even if it's something I don't want to know." He looked at her pleadingly.

She looked at him, feeling great pity. "Okay, Mr. Granger. I'll do whatever I can." He pressed his forehead against her hand but said nothing. He finally released her and she left him there, still seated and weeping. Tracy now, more than ever, also wanted to know the truth about the robbery, if for no other reason than to put Jeremiah Granger's heart and mind at ease, as if anything would truly ever be able to do that.

Tracy had filled Neal in on the afternoon's events. "I gave you all the credit for the Bowers' discovery. Maybe the cops will start making *you* job offers."

"Are we back to that again?" Neal asked, clearly irritated. "I've nothing to do with all those calls."

"I don't need another puzzle to solve right now, Neal. I'll just have to deal with the case of the inquiring esquires next week, then."

"Fine by me. So you're not calling anybody back?"

"Not today. Did you find out anything else about Milton Bowers, given what we know now?"

"No. He's been bouncing around insurance companies over the years, and has lived in the same house for 20 or so. Frankly, I don't see where he spent $50,000."

"*If* he's spent it; he may still be sitting on it. That would explain why he got so nervous when I brought up the past. Remember, he was a rank amateur. He probably wouldn't know any money launderers or any other way to get rid of the money quickly."

"Yes, I guess that makes sense. But if Granger was going after Bowers, why did he go to *Merlin's* instead of visiting Bowers at his home?"

"Because, Neal, Bowers lives in Virginia and Granger is out on parole in Maryland."

"Ah. Granger can't leave the state while on parole."

"Exactly," Tracy agreed.

"And Granger probably wouldn't have known where Bowers worked."

"I wouldn't think so. Maybe Granger wasn't able to get hold of Bowers by phone or other means to tell him to be at *Merlin's*, so he ultimately mailed the ticket to him just like he did… Hey, wait a minute!"

"What, Tracy?"

"What if Granger did send a ticket to Bowers, and then *Bowers* forwarded the ticket to Louis Purdue?"

Neal's eyes flew open. "Yeah—I like that. Bowers hopes Purdue will do his dirty work for him, so to speak."

"Possibly, or at least scare Granger off. If Bowers knew how the young Purdue felt about his father, Bowers could have been hoping for fireworks as an added attraction last Friday." Tracy smiled. "Neal, I think we're finally getting somewhere with this."

"You do?"

"If Milton Bowers does indeed still have $50,000 stashed somewhere, then he could easily offer someone cash to help him. And that means that *everyone* on the *Merlin's* staff just became suspect material again."

Neal nodded. "Because at first you were sure Buzz was connected with the Montado people."

"Right. But if it's a matter of somebody getting some green stuff, then there wouldn't necessarily be any connection whatsoever between Granger and his killer, or Bowers' accomplice, as the case may be. Bowers is nowhere near the club when the crime is committed, and the murderer has no obvious ties to Granger. No one at *Merlin's* is exactly rich, and Montado had been at *Merlin's* last summer; most of the staff would have known Montado's routines and security precautions."

Neal nodded again. "Sure. And it would actually work out better for us if it *is* someone at *Merlin's*, because *they* aren't going anywhere Sunday, while Montado and company are leaving for their next gig."

"Good point."

"What about what Granger's father told you? Anything there?"

"Yes, I think so. I think I know now, more or less, Granger's part in the robbery and why he was there. The only thing I'm not completely sure about is Milton Bowers' role. But we know where we stand with him."

"Okay, then: what next? I know it's already late, but I'll stay if you need me to."

Tracy smiled widely. "Thanks, Neal. But I don't think I can do anything until tomorrow. *Merlin's* will be a madhouse tonight, so I wouldn't be able to talk to anyone if I showed up now. I'll have to plan another visit for tomorrow. I'm sure Lucas and Price are doing everything they can with respect to Milton Bowers. So unless you feel like playing on your computer all night, I can't think of anything else to do right now."

"I don't mind taking another look at the people who work at *Merlin's*. Maybe I'll find someone in need of cash or something."

"That's a great thought, Neal. If you're willing to do that, I'd be very grateful."

"You bet, Tracy. Now, can I ask *you* something?"

"Of course."

"How do you think Granger, Pyle, and Bowers hooked up? The robbers were in their early twenties or so, and Bowers would have been in his forties. They wouldn't be the type of people to hang out together."

"I'm not exactly sure. But Scarborough said Granger had been in the bank looking for a loan. Since Granger was thinking of buying a house…"

"He would have needed home insurance. That would have been a requirement for the loan."

"Yes; that's just off the top of my head, though."

"Okay. I'll stay for a while and see what I can find."

"Thanks, Neal. I think I'm going to bolt. I want to review all of my notes and get a good night's sleep. Tomorrow is going to be yet another crazy one."

"No problem. I'll e-mail you after I'm done, regardless of what I find."

"Thanks, Neal. Have a great weekend." Neal smiled and returned to his computer. Tracy gathered her notes and laptop, and then loaded them into her briefcase. The peace and quiet of her condo would be ideal for collecting her thoughts and working out her strategy. She'd have to send

Brian home early tonight. But it was a necessary sacrifice. She hoped Brian wouldn't mind playing the goat.

"Tracy, you know how much I love you. But please, for the love of God, never, *ever* call me Bri-Bri again."

"You don't like it?"

"I loathe it."

"Why?"

"Why did you hate Stuff Girl? I don't know. It sounds like the name of a poodle or something. Hearing it makes my teeth itch."

"Okay, if you don't like it," she said, clearly sounding disappointed. "But taking my Bri-Bri out for a walk sounds so cute."

"Stop it, Stuff Girl."

"Fine."

"Good." Brian changed the subject. "How's your pizza?"

"Supreme!"

"I know it's a supreme, but how does it taste?"

"Oh, you're cute."

"Good then?"

"Yes, Brian. Thank you for bringing dinner."

"You're welcome. You got home so late tonight." He smiled at her and then took another bite of pie.

"What kind of nickname can you make out of Tracy, I wonder?" she asked him.

"I can't think of any."

"People have called me Trace, as in 'without a'."

Brian nodded. "I was without a Tracy for quite a while myself."

She smiled. "You're not anymore." She leaned over and kissed him.

He stared at her when she resumed eating. "You said it had to be an early night."

"Yes, I need to make some sense out of the facts I've gathered thus far. And Neal may be e-mailing me some stuff later, possibly important stuff. I'm hoping I can find some definitive answers by reviewing everything I have at this point. I hope you understand and won't be mad."

"Of course I understand, and no, I'm not mad; disappointed, sad, and woeful, but not mad."

"Oh stop."

"You don't know how much I look forward to the end of the day, when we get to be together."

She looked at him empathetically. "I do too. That's why I know if I let you stay, I won't get this done. And I *need* to get this done—tonight."

"I'm sorry, Tracy. I'll go in a bit."

"Thanks for understanding, Brian. I wish coming up with a sensible theory for the Granger murder was as easy as coming up with one for that traveling card trick."

Brian blinked. "You have a theory about how that card trick was worked?"

"Sure."

"Well, don't just sit there eating my pizza..."

Tracy laughed. "Brian, it's a *theory* I have. It doesn't mean that's how the trick was *actually* done."

"Stop stalling; stop teasing. *I* want to know your theory."

Tracy grinned at him. "Okay, let's start with the end of the trick—that's easy enough to guess. Montado and his assistant Karine already know what the switched card will be. In this case, it was the two of hearts. So Karine probably has that card concealed and she deftly switches the 10 of diamonds with the two of hearts after Conrad put the former card on the table."

"Hey, *I* guessed earlier that she palmed it."

"Yes, I know. So now, Mr. Smarty Man, how did the 10 of diamonds get back to the deck in Montado's hands?"

Brian cleared his throat. "I'm still working on that."

"Uh-huh."

"Look, Tracy, I readily admit defeat. Come on, will ya?"

She chuckled. "Okay, okay. I think Montado had a second deck of cards on his person that looked exactly like the first deck, except for one difference." She stopped talking.

"Tracy, I swear you love doing this kind of stuff to me."

"Braille markings."

"Huh?"

"Montado was blindfolded, right?"

"Yes."

"So Montado was effectively..."

"Blind!"

"And blind makes one think of braille. So, after Conrad took the 10 of diamonds, Montado very deftly swapped decks, probably while everyone was looking at Conrad showing his card. Then Montado, after learning what the card was, stealthily starts feeling the tops of the cards of his new deck until he finds his 10 of diamonds."

"Okay, but how did he *know* he had to find, using his hands to read the cards, the 10 of diamonds? Conrad confirmed the blindfold was real."

"Ah, that's where Karine comes in."

"Karine?"

"Yes. Remember she has had some dance lessons and is very graceful onstage. Plus, she would have seen what card Conrad put on the table, or maybe she was able to see one of the monitors. Anyway, she has some kind of communication system with Montado whereby they have 52 possible signals, or more likely, a two-tiered set of signals: one to identify the number or face card, the other to identify the suit. I remember her saying something like, 'He's returned to the stage.' That could have been part of it right there: some variation on informing Montado that the person is back onstage. Or, maybe it's the way she puts the table down on the floor. Or maybe she makes certain taps with her feet as she moves about the stage, bringing her dance lessons into play. Or maybe it was some other code. Montado's been doing this a long time, and Karine's been with him quite a few years. They no doubt have great chemistry and have the code down to a science by now."

"Well, okay. When you explain it like that, it sounds so…so obvious."

"Of course it does. If you're going to try and figure out how a magic trick works, you just keep remembering what you're seeing is an illusion; so, if you have a mind to, you just work backward and come up with ideas of how it could be done. Now, I could be completely wrong in what I just told you. It *is* just a theory."

"I like it. You should tell it to Montado and see what his reaction is."

Tracy shook her head. "No, I would never do something like that."

"Why not?"

"I don't want to *know* how the trick was done. I like coming up with my own ideas, but I'll never know if I'm right. I can be content that I *think* I figured it out but preserve the magic, because I'm not *certain*. You get me?"

"I think so."

"And that's how I approach solving a mystery. I try to work backward. You see, once I know, or think I know, who the killer is, it's just a matter of working in reverse, figuring what *had* to have happened for the killer to do this or do that. If I give you a bunch of puzzle pieces but don't tell you what picture you're putting together, it's going to be a long road. But if you know the end result, you know where the pieces must fit to get there."

"Yes, Tracy. I get that."

"Oh, I've told you my puzzle theory before?"

"I doubt it's yours. I'm sure that theory is older than you."

"Well, I didn't consciously steal it, if that's what you're implying."

"No, Tracy, I wouldn't accuse you of something like *that*."

Tracy looked at him skeptically. "Anyway, I want to get this Granger thing over with so I can concentrate on my latest mystery."

"Oh? You managed to take on another client amidst all *this* chaos?"

"No, no. This is something completely different."

"Can you tell me about it? You have me intrigued."

"I'm afraid you'll be disappointed. It's nothing as gruesome as a murder. It's just that within the last few days, no fewer than three of the state's top law firms have contacted me. You know all about the Detweiler thing, but I've since had two more calls. It's so weird, this all happening so close together. Something's going on that I don't know about."

Brian sat straight up and stared at her. "You've been getting calls out of the blue from attorneys?"

"Yes."

"And it all happened this week."

Tracy looked at Brian suspiciously. "Yes," she answered slowly. "Brian, why do I get the feeling that you know something?"

"Tracy, I swear I didn't have anything to with it."

"Brian, now it's *your* turn to spill!"

He gulped. "Kurt Barton is retiring."

"Oh? He's leaving his law firm altogether, or just reducing his presence?"

"Altogether; I think my dad's death may even have had something to do with it. Barton certainly has enough to retire nicely. Anyway, he let us know that he's started the process and that he'd be out by June. He and his wife are moving to Massachusetts. I think she has family there."

"I hadn't heard anything about this."

"Well, there's really nothing official about it, yet. But given his history with Dad and the company, he let us know about it before making any kind of formal announcement."

"I think I'm beginning to see the dawn here."

"Uh-huh. Crystal, as you may remember, had been looking into other law firms in the past couple of years or so. She's been in contact with some of the bigger firms in the area and is soliciting proposals."

"And somehow it also got out, maybe, that I was marrying into the Shane family."

"I guess. Crystal practically issued her own press release when I told her the news about us. I'm not sure how she managed to bring you into the proposal process, though."

"Oh *I* can picture it. 'My brother's marrying a great attorney. It's too bad she has such a small place, because otherwise we'd be using her. We are a family business after all.' Oh yeah, I can see how they would find out."

"Wait: you think Crystal hinted that the winning firm would be the one that managed to bring you into their fold?"

"She probably thought she was doing me a favor, giving my career a boost. Crystal thinks big, she always has. And she thinks everyone else should think big too. She told me on the phone the other day that I lack ambition."

"We *have* been expanding since Crystal took over as CEO. You know, it was thanks to her we started getting picked up in a lot of the wholesale clubs. You know what a big deal it is to get space in those places?"

"Yes, I do. So your company is going to be making their new law firm a lot of salad."

"Yeah. Plus, Crystal is actually looking to expand outside the U.S. I know she's interested in the international experience any prospective law firm has had."

Tracy smiled, rose from her seat, and then, to Brian's utter bewilderment, starting tap dancing on her kitchen floor, a big smile on her face. "Tracy, what the heck?" Then she threw her arms up in the air like a football referee affirming a field goal.

"YES!" she shouted. Then she sat back down, as if nothing had happened, and resumed eating. Brian stared at her cautiously.

"Are you all right? Should I call someone?"

She started giggling. "I'm great. I'm perfect!"

"I've been telling you *that* for years."

She gave him a gentle push to the shoulder. "Not like that. Now I *know* what's going on with all those calls. And now I also know what my answer is going to be."

"Oh. You're not mad that these people were probably trying to use you?"

"I'll be mad later. Even though I was a part of a deeper plan, they wouldn't bring me on unless they thought I was good. I mean, do you think they would offer me a partnership if they thought I sucked? And then, later on, have to somehow fire me after landing the Shane account? Of course not. They did their research and thought it would work well for everyone."

"Oh good, I'm glad that's the way you're looking at this. I was afraid you were going to be depressed over it or something."

"No, it's just business."

"So I take it your answer is going to be no."

"Correct. And it probably would have been no anyway, to be completely honest. I don't want to make a move like that, yet; I like my life—personal and professional—the way it is now. I want to focus on the wedding planning; that's enough to deal with now. And maybe that cooking class you mentioned. Still, maybe someday I'll rethink about going big."

Brian sighed and smiled. "I'm glad to hear that, Tracy."

"So will Neal and Beck, I'll bet."

"They like the way things are too. How could they not?"

Tracy smiled. "Aw, shucks, honey."

"You know it's true, though."

"I can't believe how much better finding out about this has made me feel. On the other hand, I wonder how much I'm worth."

"Uh-oh, your ego is surfacing."

"I don't bring her out that often."

"I know that."

"But she's standing on the shoulders of curiosity, peeking out. You know I'm always curious."

"Yes."

"Maybe I should get all the free meals out of this I can, and then get their offers. And then I could tell the ones that bid the least about the better offers, and then they'd make a counteroffer! Oh, how much fun that might be! And delicious, too!"

Brian started laughing. "Tracy, that's being deceiving, don't you think? Leading them on like that when you already *know* the outcome."

"So what? Detweiler sat there telling me how I was this and how I was that but never mentioned you or the company. I even talked about you a little, and he never batted an eye. Don't you think *that* was being deceptive?"

"Yes, I suppose."

"And there I sat, believing it all. This person I don't know from Adam tells me what I like hearing, and I just buy his act without doubting his sincerity for a moment."

Brian nodded. "He put on a good show."

"I'll say. I should be mad, but I'm not really. I mean, part of it was my own fault: Detweiler had an audience that was just so happy to be there, to be flattered like that, that she turned off her critical-thinking brain parts. And I bought it."

"Well, that's showmanship, Tracy. A good showman can tell or show you anything and make you believe what he wants you to. Just like a magician, I guess."

"I suppose," she repeated.

"Still, I'm real happy to see you taking it all so well. It's a change for the better, I think. For a moment there, I thought the real Tracy had been replaced by a lookalike or something."

"Very funny—not." Tracy continued smiling as she finished the remains of her pizza. In the next instant, her face altered its expression. It was as if she had experienced an epiphany. "That's right," she whispered. Her mental deck of details was suddenly being reshuffled, and a picture started to form—a couple, in fact. She looked at her fiancé. "My God, Brian, I was an accomplice after the fact."

"What?"

"I've been making an assumption this whole time without even realizing how false it was. Of course: I see it now. I saw it then, too, but… How stupid I've been! Of course the jacket was floating in the tank! It HAD to have been!"

"Tracy, what *are* you talking about?"

"Trickery, deception, misdirection: tools of the trade in both magic and murder!"

"Are you going to start dancing again?"

"Brian, I need to go to work now. I'm sorry."

"Tracy, are you sure you're okay?"

"I'm fine. I…Brian I think I know who killed Zachary Granger."

"Tracy, are you serious?!"

"I am. Very. Now I have to figure how I'm going to prove it, because there's a twist to this case that might make that next to impossible."

"Can I help you? Tracy, if I can help you, *please* let me help you!"

She smiled at him. "Okay, Brian, you can stay. But we have to be hands off with each other, because I need to be completely hands *on* with this. You get me?"

"I promise, Tracy. It's my curiosity that's piqued, not my…um…"

She laughed and then gave him his last kiss of the evening. And then she proceeded to dole out the details of the crime, one point at a time. If she had her way, tomorrow there would be an additional matinee performance at *Merlin's Manor of Mirth and Magic*, with a special guest performer. This time, however, the former birthday girl would be center stage, and showing certain spectators her own brand of magic.

Chapter 12

"I'm so excited!" Brian said, almost jumping up and down.

"Brian, you need to calm down," Tracy playfully scolded. "You've seen my act before."

"Yes, but that time I was the main suspect. This time—"

"I understand all that," she said sternly, cutting him off. "You need to do exactly what I tell you to do."

"Yes, Tracy."

"And nothing else."

"Yes, Tracy."

"I'm trusting that you won't give the ending away."

"Yes, Tracy."

"Timing is everything."

"Yes, Tracy."

"And stop saying, 'Yes, Tracy' after everything I say."

"Yes, Tracy."

She laughed. "I set you up for that, didn't I?"

"Yes, Tracy."

"Alright, stop it."

"Yes—"

"Silence! I'll send you home, otherwise." He just smiled. "That's better. Now just stay here and don't move. And don't say anything, either, just to be on the safe side." Tracy turned and headed toward the lobby and found Montado arguing with Detective Lucas.

"This is an outrage! We have a matinee in less than two hours we need to prepare for! How dare you—"

"Hi, Mr. Montado," Tracy interrupted. She smiled at him. "I'm afraid this is my fault. You see, I have something to show everyone."

"My dear, what are you talking about?"

"It's complicated. But I want you to watch my presentation and tell me what you think afterward. In fact, I want your entire team—Karine, Greg, Kurt, and Ron—to watch. They will be joined by several people from *Merlin's*: Pam Houston, Rose, Richard the announcer, and Roger Tallis, who will be assisting us with the technical stuff."

"Oh."

"And I have some special guests, too: Dan Scarborough, Louis Purdue, Harry Lindstrom, and Milton Bowers. Oh, and of course my opening act: Woody Williams. They should all be here shortly. The police will see to that."

Montado gulped. "The police?"

"Yes."

"I see. And why, may I ask, does Milton Bowers need to be here? Are you going to…? You will hurt people."

"The detectives will tell you when the auditorium is ready. I'll see you inside, Mr. Montado." Tracy turned and went to see Price, who was speaking with Tallis. "Hi, Roger. Hi, Detective." They greeted her in return.

"Tracy, what are you up to?" Tallis asked, a grin on his face.

"I'm just giving myself a taste of showbiz. Do you understand what you're supposed to be doing?"

"Yes."

"Great." Tracy turned to Price. "Is everyone on their way?"

"Yes, Tracy," she answered. "People will start arriving any moment."

"Okay. Great."

"Are you doing okay?"

"Yes. I'm always nervous before a performance. But once I get started, I'll be fine."

"You look tired."

"I haven't been to bed; too busy. Buzz buzz buzz."

Price smiled. "Can I get you some coffee?"

"No, I don't want to have to pee while I'm doing my spiel."

Price laughed. "All right. Good luck, Tracy. I hope whatever it is you have planned works out."

"Thank you, Debbie. You know, I never would have gotten this far if it weren't for all of your help during the case."

"You did some helping yourself; I suspect you'll be doing some more very shortly."

"I sure hope so; wish me luck!"

"Good luck!" Price smiled again and headed toward the entrance doors. The guests were starting to arrive.

Tracy went over to Richard, who was reading from a piece of paper. "Can you read my writing, Richard?"

"Oh, sure. This is…this is a little strange."

"I'm a strange person, Richard. Just like the Doors sing about."

"Uh-huh. Okay. This is going to be interesting."

"And don't hold back, either. This is the first, and probably last, time for me onstage, so give it all you've got."

Richard snuffed. "Okay, Tracy. I'll just think of it as a belated gift to the birthday girl."

     Practice to Deceive

"That's the spirit! Now why don't you head backstage, and I'll meet you there shortly." Then Tracy smiled and left him to review his script.

The attorney was headed back into the auditorium when Lucas touched her shoulder. "Tracy, hold up."

"What is it, Detective?"

"This seating chart…"

"What about it?"

"Why are people all over the place?"

"I can talk to people better that way. I don't want people bunched together."

"Oh, all right."

"Anything else?"

"Well, I hope this works out, obviously."

"Me too."

"I'll see you inside, Tracy." And Lucas turned to face the gathering crowd.

"Huh," Tracy thought. "Not a hint of snark; that's progress." Tracy opened the doors to the arena and headed backstage.

It was another 15 minutes or so before the ushers, who looked very much like police officers, started seating people throughout the stadium. Montado, Karine, Greg and the Donlevy brothers were seated close to the stage. Folding chairs had been placed in front of the stage for them so that they were facing the audience. The other patrons were spread out, mostly seated in the back, except for Lindstrom, who was seated in his place from the fateful Friday. Scarborough was seated in the back, to the right and facing the stage, approximately where he had been sitting the night of the murder. Louis Perdue was on the opposite side from Scarborough. Pam Houston and Rose were also seated in the back; Tallis was in the control booth.

Tracy was onstage and witnessed the not-so-warm reunion between Greg and Milton Bowers. "What are *you* doing here?" the younger one asked as he saw the elder being brought down the aisle.

"The cops just brought me here. Do you know where I've been all morning?"

"I don't care."

"You *will* care."

"You're down here, Mr. Bowers," Price said as she took Milton's arm. He sat down a few feet from the stage and then noticed the person on the platform.

"YOU!" he yelled.

"Hi, Milty."

"What the hell is going on here?" Bowers turned to Price, who was now sitting down. "That woman's a lunatic."

"Hey, fella!" Tracy called out. "I'm idiosyncratic, not loony." Then Tracy disappeared behind the curtain. It was almost 12:30. Brian looked at her. She smiled back. "Almost time, honey. You ready?"

"You bet. How about a kiss for luck?" She obliged, and not just with a quick one, either. She pulled away, stroked his face, and smiled.

"On with the show," she told him. And then the lights went out.

"What the hell?" Milton Bowers shouted. Instantly, there was a spotlight on the center of the platform. Everyone's eyes were now on it.

"Ladies and gentlemen," a familiar voice began, "*Merlin's Manor of Mirth and Magic* is proud to present, for the first time onstage anywhere in the world, the lovely, the talented, the mistress of surprises: The Astounding TRACY!" Detectives Lucas and Price started clapping, and then some of the *Merlin's* staff joined in. But after a while, The Astounding Tracy was still not onstage.

Suddenly, a voice called out from the back. "HI, EVERYONE!" The audience turned in their chairs and saw Tracy start making her way down the aisle. "Sorry about that," she said not sounding sorry at all. "I couldn't resist a little misdirection to start the show. There's been a lot of that going around lately." Tracy continued as eyes followed her, until she arrived at the spotlight. She turned so she was facing the gathered. "Okay, Roger, bring up the house lights a little bit, please!" And then the arena's side wall lights came to life while the spotlight disappeared. The stage behind Tracy was also bathed in light.

"Good afternoon, my friends," Tracy said bowing. "Before I begin, I'd like to bring in our special guest. Please join me in welcoming Mr. Woody WILLIAMS!" The entrance doors opened, and a uniformed officer escorted Williams to a spot just in front of the stage.

"Hey, folks!" he called out during his march. "Good to see people dressed in something other than orange, for a change."

"Have a seat right in front there, Woody," Tracy instructed.

"Sure. Where can I get some popcorn, though? I mean, after a week of Detention Center Caterers, I could really—"

"Just sit down, Woody, and leave the jokes to *me* this time."

"Oh, this is a drama, then." And then Woody sat down, looked around, and folded his hands in his lap.

"Okay, that's everyone, I think. Can everybody hear me okay?" Pamela and Rose, the ones farthest away, nodded. "Great. Thanks for coming to my special, by-invitation-only, one-time performance here at *Merlin's*. I hope not so much to entertain, but rather to enlighten." Tracy turned and moved toward the back curtain. "Now, I do have an assistant for the show." Brian heard his cue and emerged from backstage. Then Tracy quickly added, sounding sad, "But, unfortunately, he's mute and deaf and will pretty much just be standing here." Brian glared at her, but she grinned at him. She turned and boomed, "From the Cabinet of The Astounding Tracy, I introduce to you Brian, the Somnambulistic Fiancé!" Detective Price burst out laughing. Everyone else stared with puzzled expressions. "What, no silent movie fans here?" Tracy asked while looking around hopefully. "Jeez, tough crowd." Tracy shrugged her shoulders and returned to the front of the stage.

"I was right, that lady *is* a crackpot," Milton Bowers mumbled.

"Mr. Scarborough, can you see Brian from there?"

"I can make him out."

"That's about where you were sitting for the early show Friday a week ago, so you were probably watching the monitor when Montado performed his card trick with the audience member for the show you saw."

"Yes, that's right."

Tracy turned her attention to Purdue. "Mr. Purdue, can you see my assistant Brian from where *you're* sitting?"

"I can see someone is there."

"Did you see the part of the show where the card trick with the audience member was done, or had you already gone to the bar at that point?"

"I must have already been at the bar. I don't remember the trick you're talking about."

"Okay."

Tracy met the eyes of Milton Bowers. "Is this your first time at *Merlin's*, Mr. Bowers?"

"Yes," he grunted.

"You didn't bring your lovely wife to see her daughter perform at any point during the past two or so weeks?"

"No."

"Okay." Tracy took a deep breath. "Now, of course the monitors would have been on the Friday night of the show. And we'll have them turned on for you in just a few moments." Tracy then reached behind a table, the only nonhuman item visible onstage, and produced a brown paper bag. She pulled out a monogrammed coat, a pair of sunglasses, a wig of black hair, and a false mustache. She placed the items on the table. "Now, it's been all over the papers and the news blogs that the man found in the tank had been wearing a disguise: wig, glasses, mustache, and coat. The coat is important because it was monogrammed." Tracy looked to Purdue. "You weren't here for the later show, Mr. Purdue. Have you seen the news stories about the murder, more importantly, about the disguise?"

"I don't know," Purdue grumbled.

"You don't know? The man who sent you a ticket to the show, the man who was involved with a robbery that resulted in your father's paralysis, is murdered, and you're not following the news reports?"

"I didn't kill the guy!"

Tracy scowled. "How about you, Mr. Scarborough, once you learned who was killed, you must have been following things."

"Yes, of course."

"Do you recall the photographs of the victim that were taken and shown, and what letter was on the coat he was wearing? Or maybe you heard it on the news?"

Scarborough paused a moment. "I think it was an M; yes, that was it: an M."

"Thank you, Dan." Tracy stepped back. "Montado made a point of drawing the audience's attention to that very same M. He even joked that the coat could belong to him because of the initial. In fact, when I first saw the body floating in the tank, I didn't have any idea who it was, until I saw the coat also floating in the tank, and the telltale M. I think I even cried out 'It's Conrad!'—the improvised alias that Zachary Granger used after unexpectedly being called up onstage."

Tracy then moved toward Brian and started dressing him in the wig, glasses, and lip warmer. She continued speaking. "Of course, how do we really know who took the stage that night and assisted Montado with the card illusion? The person was in disguise, after all." When Tracy was done with the facial applications, she stepped back from Brian and turned toward the audience. "If it weren't for the monitors, many of you would be hard-pressed to have any idea of what he looked like. In fact, most of the lights were out." Tracy looked toward the control booth in the back. "Roger, can you dim the lights on the stage, please?" After her request was granted, Tracy put the coat on Brian. She pushed him back a few steps. Then she moved toward center stage.

"Now, earlier I introduced my assistant to you as Brian. But, with the exception of Detective Lucas, I would wager none of you in the audience has probably seen Brian Shane before, unless you remember him from some scandalous news reports about a year ago. So, you have no idea if this man's name really *is* Brian. Or if he is even deaf and mute as I said he is. Basically, you have to put your trust in me. I could tell you anything I wanted to

     Practice to Deceive

about him, and you'd have to take me at face value. And that night, many people—including myself—assumed the man in the tank was the same man who had occupied the stage mere moments before he was found dead." Tracy tuned in the direction of Harry Lindstrom.

"Mr. Lindstrom, you saw Conrad sneak backstage, didn't you?" All eyes were now on Lindstrom.

"Yes. He was by the curtain, and he snuck back there."

"And you didn't see him again, did you?"

"No. Like I told the police, I just thought he was part of the act, so I didn't really think anything of it."

"And this man, this Conrad, even coughed, effectively drawing your attention to him."

"Yes, he coughed," Lindstrom confirmed.

"And, of course, Conrad picked just the right time to sneak back there, the time when Kurt or Ron would be leaving to get ready to push the water tank onstage." Tracy grinned. "But how can we be sure that the man in the tank was the same man who was onstage earlier, the one who then disappeared behind the curtain? Perhaps a switch had been made." Tracy moved toward the assistant onstage. "A switch like *this*!" And then she pulled off the wig and glasses simultaneously with either hand to reveal not Brian, but rather the *Merlin's* announcer, Richard. She heard some gasps while she next removed the mustache.

"Marvelous!" Montado shouted and applauded. "Well done!"

Tracy grinned. "Thanks, Mr. Montado." She faced the amused onlookers. "It was an easy illusion. Before the show, I just made up Richard like I did Brian and had Richard stand behind the curtain with his microphone. Then, when everyone was focusing on what Mr. Lindstrom had to say, Brian and Richard switched places as the three of us had previously plotted; simple misdirection."

"Still, my dear, nicely handled."

"Thank you, Mr. Montado. I really mean that." She looked at him and him at her for a few brief seconds. Then she turned away. She cleared her throat. "I guess my point has been made: Zach Granger was not the man—not this Conrad person—onstage the night he was killed. In fact, he was already in the tank, dead at that point. Time of death was hard to nail down, because the body had been in the water a while before the police fished it out. Detective Price told me there were a few things they were still trying to work out. I suspect time of death was one of them. Anyway, the man Mr. Lindstrom saw sneak back *wanted* Mr. Lindstrom or someone else to see him, to be a witness to Conrad going backstage. After our mystery man knew the Donlevys were otherwise occupied, he went behind the curtain, quickly removed his disguise, including the coat, and then climbed to the top of the tank using the ladder that was leaning against the nearby wall. He dumped everything in the tank and then made his escape before he was spotted. And that's why the coat was left floating in the tank: the man known as Conrad didn't have enough time to put the coat on Granger's body. As it turned out, it was that floating coat that kept bothering me. I can understand the glasses coming off when the body hit the water, or the wig and mustache separating as the glue became wet. But the coat? That didn't make any sense. *Now* it makes sense."

Tracy sighed as she returned her attention to Montado, as he was expecting she would. He was looking at her in return. "Karine told me that she usually is the one who selects the audience volunteers. But that night, Mr. Montado, *you* selected Conrad. And you made it a point to draw attention to the M during the show. You even joked it could be *your* coat because of how it was monogrammed. I think that it *was* your coat, Mr. Montado. I think you gave it to your accomplice and made sure to point out the monogram so that everyone would think it was Conrad in that tank when the coat was noticed."

Montado swallowed hard. He shook his head slightly. "Why would I kill this Granger person? I didn't even know him."

"I didn't say you killed him." Tracy sighed and then took a seat in front of Karine. Then she looked back at Montado. "You didn't kill him. You were protecting someone. You and your accomplice: Greg Bowers."

"NO!" Montado shouted. Greg remained silent.

"I'm afraid so."

"It could not have been Greg!" Montado insisted. "He was at his hotel when all of this happened!"

"I'm sorry, Mr. Montado, but that was a very easy misdirect to accomplish. Yes, Karine called the hotel and pretended to talk to Greg. It would have been nearly impossible for him to make it back to his room so soon to take a call *if* he had left the building after playing the part of Conrad. But Karine didn't really talk to Greg, did she? She was leaving a message on the hotel room's voice mail. She *pretended* to be having a conversation with her brother for the benefit of Kurt and Ron; they would serve as witnesses to the call, and the phone records would back all this up. When Greg returned to his hotel room later, he simply deleted the message. In reality, he was probably hiding outside of the building, not too far away, after he left. Around midnight, he rang the outside bell and Kurt let him in. His alibi was established."

"NO!" Montado insisted again. "This is preposterous!"

Tracy was now looking at Karine Bowers. Karine was avoiding eye contact. "You have a very loyal group here, Mr. Montado. I'm sure it had been a very long time since you used that coat in your act, so long that you figured no one would remember it or recognize it. Of course, one of the crew people may have. Maybe Kurt or Ron *did* recognize it. But you knew they wouldn't say anything. You, of course, did everything to shield them. But if it came down to it, they would be loyal.

"However, loyalty is one thing; covering up a murder is something else entirely. I don't think a person, or several people, would be willing to cover up such a crime, unless there was a very good reason. And I know that men feel very protective of their women." Tracy shook her head. "I don't know why I didn't pick up on it right away. It was literally in my face the whole time, and I didn't see it." Tracy paused and sighed. "*42nd Street*—a classic: a film directed by one of the legendary figures in choreography. A man named Busby Berkeley. Buzz. That was Zach Granger's nickname for you, wasn't it, Karine?"

"Holy crap," Lucas murmured.

"Milton Bowers knew it too, didn't he, Karine?" Tracy turned and gave Bowers a quick look. He lowered his head. "That's why he wanted you gone. He didn't want to break your mother's heart and tell her what he knew, but he didn't want you around his wife anymore, either. So he forced you to leave before you got involved with someone else like Granger. Your mother told me how upset you were around the time of the robbery. She thought it had to do with the sniper who was terrorizing the area at the time. In reality, it was because of what you had done and what you witnessed."

"Don't say anything, Karine," Greg said panicking. "There's no proof of anything."

Tracy continued. "When I went to your dressing room the night of the murder to check on how you were doing, your room was neat and tidy. Your brother had to bring you a drink from another dressing room. But a few days later, when I saw you again, your room was a mess. And you had your own carafe from which to pour a drink. I think Granger showed up in your dressing room Friday night. He left Scarborough alone and then went backstage just after the stand-up show started, before Kurt or Ron would have needed to come on duty. Granger confronted you. During the robbery, you had panicked and left Pyle—Granger's only real friend—to be gunned down, and Granger himself to go to jail. He was there 12 years. You never visited him, you never wrote to him. That must have made him feel incredibly hurt, and then incredibly angry. He felt betrayed. He loved you and wanted the two of you to move in together. When his father turned him down for financial help, he went to the bank. And then they turned him down too. He told Chris Pyle about his problems, and Chris suggested the robbery, a way to get some money and at the same time get revenge against the bank. Zach was a more or less willing participant, although he refused to carry a gun. And I'll bet they didn't even tell you what they were up to. And then it all went horribly wrong, and you left the man who loved you behind. I'm guessing that at some point during his incarceration, while he was being allowed to watch television, he saw Montado's act; he saw you, Karine, and recognized you. As soon as he was paroled, he went to Montado's website, probably using a library computer, to see where the show was playing. But he was on parole; he couldn't leave the state without risking going back to jail. And then he noticed you would be appearing at *Merlin's* in April of this year. So he got himself some tickets. He no doubt knew by now, too, that somebody got away with $50,000. And he wanted his chance to confront you. And that's exactly what he did the night he died."

Tracy stood up and looked around. She looked at Lucas and Price. She continued. "Now I'm guessing during the verbal confrontation, there was eventually some violence. Maybe he hit you, or threatened to hit you. Maybe you pushed him, or maybe he tripped. Whatever the cause, he fell over and hit his head, hit it hard, probably on that back table where the carafe was resting. Montado heard the shouting or the crash, and came in. I suspect, however, he came in *after* Granger was down and out. He…you were like a daughter to him, and he wanted to protect you. His mind worked quickly, thinking of all the illusions he had performed over the years. He then called, or had you call, Greg to tell him to come over. You told the police, and me later, the reason for the call was to ask Greg if he was going to meet up with you after the show. But that wasn't the real reason, was it Karine? Montado told Greg to bring with him a white, button-down shirt and black slacks, the type of outfit Granger was wearing. Who would remember any of the subtle differences in the outfits? And with no recording devices of any kind allowed, there would be no visual record. Greg was a 20-minute walk away, and he *had* to walk. He couldn't risk taking a cab and possibly being identified later, just like he *had* to say he walked after receiving the 11:33 p.m. call, because he knew a cabdriver *wouldn't* be able to identify him. After the call was done, Montado left Karine to go to where the prepurchased tickets were kept. He mingled a bit, but his real reason was to pinch a single ticket for a seat close to the front. Rose will confirm both Montado's presence that night at her booth and the missing ticket. And Pamela Houston will certainly remember the irate customer whose ticket was stolen. Correct, ladies?" The women in the back nodded.

"After Montado had the ticket, he returned to the back. Now, it was probably close to showtime for the magic act, and so Montado sent Kurt and Ron to tend to the stage while he awaited Greg's arrival. He let Greg in, or perhaps left the door ajar. Greg waited in the dressing room while the early show went on as usual. He changed into the shirt and pants that matched Granger's. He probably cleaned everything up, including the carafe that fell to the floor and broke when Granger hit the table. There were some light scratches on Granger's head. Cuts from the broken glass, maybe? Anyway, Greg emptied Granger's pockets of everything, just in case Granger had something incriminating against Karine. It would also delay identifying the body. Greg hid the items instead of throwing them away; he didn't want them to be found just yet. And that's why Granger never returned to Mr. Scarborough. He was lying on the floor in Karine Bowers' dressing room for nearly the entire early performance."

Tracy rubbed her eyes, pausing. She sighed. "Now things had to move quickly when the early show ended around 9:00. After Ron and Kurt returned the water tank to its place in the back, Montado again sent the brothers to tend the stage. Then he and Greg quickly moved Granger's body, using the ladder resting against the nearby wall to dump Granger in the tank, and they replaced the tarp. Next, they went around the corner to the costume box. Montado took out the aforementioned disguise, including the monogrammed coat, and gave Greg the purloined ticket. Montado, who had been at *Merlin's* previously, pretty much knew how things worked, so he probably tore the ticket and surreptitiously returned the stub to the office later to keep the recordkeeping in order. Then, the disguised Greg left the back area to take his seat as people were being let in. At this point, my client Woody Williams was coming back from the bar and saw Greg, now known as Conrad, near the curtain. Right, Woody?"

"That's right. I yelled at him, but he didn't say anything."

"Of course, he couldn't. He wanted to say as little as possible; Greg didn't want a confrontation. He sat down and waited to be called to the stage. It was a very good performance Greg turned in that night: not wanting to go up at first, having to be egged on by the crowd, looking like a man who didn't want to be there, when in fact that was all part of the plan. Montado points out the M and performs the trick. Then Greg sits back down and awaits the final phase of his performance, which I already described. After Greg dumped the costume, he made a quick stop to change back into his original outfit, and then headed for the back door. While he waited to be let in, he may even have tried to find Granger's car and search it; he had the keys, after all. I remember the night you entered Karine's dressing room, Greg, you jingled a bit. It didn't mean anything to me at the time, but I realize now that those must have been *Granger's* keys in your pants pocket. I mean, you didn't have a car here, and hotels now have key *cards*, so what would you need with a set of keys? You weren't searched that night, so you probably just walked out of *Merlin's* with Granger's items in your own pockets, and then got rid of them later." Tracy took a deep breath. "And that, ladies and gentlemen, is how the trick was worked. And it was all about protecting Karine Bowers; it was all about giving *her* an alibi. That's why the body was placed in the tank for all to see. Karine had been onstage from the time Conrad left until the time he was found. And how could Karine have lifted Granger to put him in the tank, anyway?"

Tracy looked at Montado. "I understand why you did it; even though it was an accident, it would probably come out about what Karine had done— her part in the robbery—had she called the police. She would have had to explain why Granger was there, and why he had been angry enough that she felt she was in danger. At least, that's what you were probably thinking when you tried to cover up for her. You were protecting someone you dearly loved."

Greg Bowers stood up. "Don't say anything, Karine; don't you dare say a word. All that this lawyer has spouted are theories and fantasies. She has no evidence, no proof. And there's no way they can tie you to that robbery all those years ago. You think Milton would help them do that? Just keep quiet, Karine, and I'll get you a lawyer; I'll get us *all* lawyers!"

Tracy took Karine's hand and spoke calmly. "The Granger fall may have indeed been an accident, Karine. But letting Woody Williams take the fall for it is *not*. Are you going to let an innocent man go to jail for this, Karine? He has a daughter, you know: a six-year-old little girl named Stacey, who's missing her daddy right now, wondering where he is. Do you want to separate this father from his daughter, Karine? Do you think a daughter would want that to ever happen?"

"Shut up!" Greg Bowers screamed at Tracy. Then he turned to face his sister. "Karine, don't—"

"ENOUGH!" Karine screamed as she sprung to her feet. "Just stop it, Greg; just stop it! Please, just…" Karine sat back down, weeping. "We can't let this happen," she managed to say between sobs.

Tracy moved behind Karine and then knelt down. "I'm sorry about this, Karine. I believe that this *was* an accident. I was there when you screamed, remember? Montado and Greg didn't tell you what they were going to do,

I'll bet. When you turned and saw Granger in the tank, it truly shocked you. That was no performance you were giving when you screamed; you were shocked and horrified. All those tears you were shedding backstage, they were genuine too. Maybe you did love Zach Granger at one point. He was looking to buy a house a few weeks before the robbery. Was that for the two of you, maybe? Is that why he participated in the robbery, to get some money for the both of you? Maybe to pay for some dance lessons too? Your mother said how you never took school seriously, that you missed a lot. You met Zach while playing hooky, right? Maybe at a store or restaurant where he was working?" Karine was crying, but nodding at most of what Tracy was saying. "And then things went wrong that day. I wonder if they even told you what they were planning, Granger and Pyle. Maybe they told you the car you were driving was one of theirs. Louis Purdue's father remembers how the driver didn't have a clue how to operate the vehicle. After it all went bad, you fled and parked near where you knew your father was working. You had nowhere else to turn. And he covered for you."

Karine dried her eyes and cleared her throat. Greg was shaking his head vigorously. "Yes, yes it's all true," Karine admitted. Greg groaned loudly. "IT'S ALL TRUE!" she screamed at her brother. "EVERY LAST WORD OF IT!" Karine turned toward Tracy. "He wanted me back, and he wanted money. After 13 years, he said he still loved me! Can you believe that? He said he was taking me with him, and that Montado would finance us for a while. Otherwise, he'd tell the truth about me, about what I'd done. It would ruin Montado when it came out. He said he would make sure of it. If I didn't come with him, he'd make sure *everyone* I loved would get hurt. He was so mad. He was so, so *mad*! He wasn't at all like I remembered him!" Karine swallowed and sighed. "I told him to get out, and he grabbed me. I pushed him and he tripped over some clothes that were on the floor. He crashed into the table. Mr. Montado came in. You know the rest." Karine lifted her head and looked at Williams. "Mr. Williams, I am so deeply sorry for what we did to you. We never meant for anyone to be blamed for this. We wanted the crime never to be solved. No one else was supposed to get hurt. I want to make it clear in front of everyone here that Mr. Williams had nothing to do with this. *I* did it." Karine turned and faced the detectives. "Please don't do anything to Greg or Mr. Montado. I'll confess to it all, make any kind of arrangement. But please, please don't punish…" Karine turned away and sat back down; Montado held her as she wept on his shoulder. Lucas sighed and rose from his seat. Tracy stood up.

"What are you doing, Detective Lucas?" Tracy asked, mildly confused, as Lucas started moving toward Karine.

"I'm going to take Karine Bowers into custody."

"But I'm not done yet."

"What do you mean you're not done yet?"

Tracy shook her head in frustration. "Detective, haven't you noticed the big problem with what we've just heard?"

At this point, Detective Price stood. "What are you talking about, Tracy?"

"The coroner's report, of course."

Price's eyes flew open. "My God, that's right! Granger had water in his lungs!"

"What does *that* mean?" Greg Bowers asked.

"It means that Granger was *alive* when he was put into the tank, that's what!" Tracy said emphatically.

A look of horror came over the faces of Karine and Greg Bowers, as well as Montado's. "No," Karine started. "No, no, no…*I* killed him!"

"You knocked him unconscious, sure," Tracy told her. "His head wound was severe enough to have done that. Heck, he may have been in a coma. But the actual cause of death was drowning."

"Oh my GOD!" Karine screamed.

"Now wait just a minute!" Greg Bowers hollered. "He was dead when I put him in! I swear to God I thought he was DEAD!"

Karine shook her head. "I knew we should have called the police; I knew it! Now I've made my brother a murderer!" Montado embraced Karine again while Greg stood shaking his head.

Tracy straightened herself. There was some anger on her face now. She looked out to the audience and then back to Karine. "No Karine, you didn't make your brother a murderer, exactly, just an unwitting accomplice."

Lucas looked at Tracy in shock. "What are you talking about *now*?"

"I told you: I wasn't done." Tracy started moving back toward the stage. "Everything that Karine has said is the truth, I believe. Make no mistake about that. What she said happened, happened. I think all the evidence in this case supports her. But there's one more member of our magic troop that needs to be introduced: a secret player, who up until now has pulled the greatest trick of all!" Tracy glared at her target. "I introduce to you now, ladies and gentleman, the *real* murderer of Zachary Granger: the don of deception himself, the master manipulator, the amazingly villainous Mr. Dan Scarborough!"

Chapter 13

There was sudden, total silence in the auditorium of *Merlin's Manor of Mirth and Magic* after Tracy Brubaker's announcement. All eyes eventually shifted to the banker, who was now looking from side to side, wearing a "What? Who? Me?" expression. "What are you talking about?!" he finally said, sounding as offended as he possibly could. "I have nothing to with this!"

Tracy shook her head. "Oh yes, you do; oh yes, you most *certainly* do. Let me enlighten those around us as to how your simple sleight of hand resulted in the death of one person, the arrest of another, and left three people thinking they killed a man or helped cover it up." Tracy looked back at Price. Price gave her a nod.

"You told us, Mr. Scarborough, how Granger and you talked shortly before the show, how he threatened you. What you left out is that he was absolutely right—you *did* steal $50,000."

"NO!" Scarborough bellowed as he stood up.

"According to Simon Purdue and police reports, Granger never made it out of the bank. He was overtaken by several customers. I think while he was being detained by these helpful citizens, Granger saw you do something, observed something that struck him as odd. When he learned about the discrepancy in the money found versus what had been reported stolen, he guessed correctly what you had done. You took advantage of the situation back in October 2002, just like you took advantage of the situation last Friday!"

"NO!" Scarborough repeated, pointing at Karine. "SHE took the money when she abandoned the car!"

"Karine?" Tracy asked incredulously. "That poor 17-year-old kid was so scared, she didn't have the presence of mind to do *anything* except get the hell out of the car as soon as she could. She just confessed to what she thought was murder. Do you think she'd now try and deny stealing the money after she admitted to driving the car?" Scarborough had nothing to say to that; he sat back down.

"As I was saying, after Granger got done threatening you, he moved on to Karine. In spite of what you told us, I think you *did* see where Granger went after he left you. You were uncertain what to do, and so you waited for him. When the show was over and he didn't show up, you got curious. So, while the Donlevys were on the stage where Montado had sent them, you went backstage just in time to see Montado and Greg Bowers carrying, or dumping, Granger's body into the tank. You saw Greg put the ladder back against the nearby wall. Then they disappeared behind the corner, headed toward the costume trunk. And then, Dan, then you saw the tarp *rise*."

"NO! IT'S A LIE!"

"Wrong! I can prove it, too! Granger's fingerprints were found on the *outside* of the tank, fingers pointed downward, the kind of prints that would be made by someone reaching from the *inside* of the tank to grab onto something, anything, to pull himself up. He was covered by a thick black tarp; he was drowning. He was weak and disoriented from the head wound. He was helpless. And then *you* helped him, Dan, helped him to die. You moved the ladder and then climbed it and pushed Granger right back down until he was truly dead."

"I DID NO SUCH THING!"

"Those scratches on Granger's head weren't from broken glass. I'll bet they're fingernail marks made by the person who pushed Granger underwater!"

"*THEY* ADMITTED TO PUTTING THE BODY IN THE TANK!"

"Classic law school question, Dan: If a man jumps from a tall building to his certain death, but gets shot and killed by an intentionally fired bullet through a window he passes on the way down, is the shooter guilty of murder? Of course he is. It doesn't matter what Montado and Bowers did; *you* drowned Granger. *YOU* killed him!"

"*You* have no proof!"

Tracy ignored him and continued. "After killing Granger, you poked your head around the corner and saw Greg being made up by Montado. That's when you realized, having just seen the show yourself, what they were up to; at least you thought you did. And then you left as quietly and quickly as you had come. You probably went to the men's room to use those high-powered automatic dryers to dry off your wet sleeves or cuffs. And then you had a decision to make. You could sneak off and hope no one would remember you. At that point, you hadn't charged anything to your credit card; you weren't the one who bought the tickets. Would anyone remember you? Maybe the waiter who brought Granger his club soda might. Plus, you had made sure that Louis Purdue would be there, and even if you hadn't noticed *him*, he might have seen *you*. He got there just before the show started."

"Wait a minute!" Purdue called out while standing up. "*This* prick sent me the ticket?"

"Of course he did. Haven't you noticed Dan's a man who likes *other* people to do his dirty work for him? He stole money knowing others would be blamed; he murdered Granger knowing he'd be at home when the body was discovered. When he got the invite from Granger, he came to the box office window one day so he could pay cash for a ticket to send to you, Louis. You told me yourself how he paid you no mind at the bank. He knew what a tough guy you were and how protective you were of your father. So Dan took advantage of that, writing that note hoping to get you to *Merlin's* to, hopefully, take care of Granger *for* him. It turned out, of course, he didn't need you."

Purdue's face was a mask of fury. "I'm gonna break your—"

"SIT DOWN, PURDUE!" Lucas shouted, cutting off the hotheaded youth. "Just sit back down, NOW!" Purdue huffed and puffed, but finally obliged.

Tracy cleared her throat. "As I was saying, just sneaking off was risky. You didn't know who killed Granger or what Granger may have said. What if Granger had told whoever had hurt him about you *before* the violence occurred? What if Granger had a compatriot from his prison days in whom he confided? What if Granger had left a note for the police, or something outlining his plan, as a precaution if something *did* happen to him? It wouldn't look good if you said nothing and the police found out you were there that night.

"So you picked the second option: make *sure* people knew you were there. You visited the bar and bought some drinks. You struck up conversations with strangers about the classic comedians, including one friendly attorney, to whom you managed to reveal both your name *and* occupation. Once you were sure you'd be easy to identify, you took off knowing you'd make it home in plenty of time to have an alibi. You knew your E-ZPass would help with that. And then you planned for the eventual interrogation: you told a story as close to the truth as you could, in case someone had told the cops what Granger told you on Friday. I must admit, Dan, you fooled me. The look of horror on your face when you were told it was Granger in the tank: award-worthy. The struggle to tell your story, the implication you were scared that you could be a future victim of the killer: top marks. You fooled me, all right; I felt like a sucker when I realized the truth."

Scarborough looked around. Price and Lucas were standing looking at him. Everyone else was seated but had eyes fixed on him also. Scarborough regained his composure and took a deep breath. "As provocative as your theories and accusations are, you have no evidence against me. You can't prove a word of it."

Now all eyes shifted back to Tracy. She looked around and then back at her suspect. "Yes, I can!" she grinned.

Scarborough moved forward in his seat. "Another one of your lies!"

"Nope," she told him, shaking her head. "No, Mr. Scarborough, I'm afraid you have only yourself to blame for the evidence against you. In fact, before I came here today, I was only 99 percent certain I was right about you. So I had to find out if I was. Thankfully, you've already taken care of that remaining one percent."

"What are you talking about?" Then a smug look was on his face. "You're bluffing."

Tracy put her arms behind her back and started pacing slowly back and forth on the stage. "Earlier this afternoon, I asked about the letter that was on Conrad's coat. You said it was an M."

"So?"

"So, how did you know it was an M?"

"I saw or heard about it on the news."

"No, you didn't."

"I most certainly did!"

"No, you didn't."

"You yourself said it was all over the news!"

"Uh, yeah I did say that, didn't I? The thing is, though, Dan: I was *lying*."

"You *what*?"

"I lied about that. There's been nothing on the news about the disguise, much less the coat. Roger Tallis hit the kill switch almost immediately after Karine screamed. And Kurt and Ron had that tarp back over the tank pretty quickly, so most people at the later show didn't even realize it was supposedly the body of the person who had just been onstage. None of the aired interviews mention anything about the jacket, or much anything else in the way of specific details. The only information thus far that has been released is the victim's name, his criminal history, where he died, and the man arrested for the crime."

Scarborough cleared his throat. "That's right, how silly of me. Now I remember—the detective called me after you all left that day you came to my house and told me about it. She asked if Granger was wearing a disguise. She mentioned the coat."

"No, she didn't."

"She most certainly did call me!"

"Oh, she called you, sure, but she never mentioned the coat. She stopped at the mustache. I know because I was there in the back seat and heard everything she said to you. Strike two, Dan."

Scarborough narrowed his eyes. He licked his lips. Then he smiled. "I saw the letter earlier, when you were disguising that somnambulist person."

"Wait a minute: you could see the coat from all the way back there? The lights were practically off when I put the coat on."

"Yes. I could see the letter M."

"Mr. Scarborough, do you really think that's going to fly, especially after you just offered two other explanations that proved to be lies?"

"I'm telling you I saw it today!"

Tracy shook her head and turned around to face the back of the stage. "Brian, can you come out here, please, darling and stand beside Richard." Brian soon appeared and did as instructed. Tracy turned back around. "Uh, Roger, could you turn the monitors on now for us please? And bring up the lights too!" Roger also did as requested. Images of Brian and Roger were now there for all to see.

"Son of a bitch!" Lucas cried out while smiling. Price started clapping. And Woody Williams gave Tracy a standing ovation.

"She got you *good*, Danny boy!" Williams shouted laughing. "She got you REAL good!"

There on the monitor were Richard and Brian standing side by side, each wearing the exact same monogrammed coat, which looked almost exactly like the coat worn by Conrad the night of the murder—almost. This was a problem for Dan Scarborough, however—a rather large one. The problem was, the left breast pocket did not have the letter M emblazoned upon it. Nay, nay. The letter on the pocket, instead, was distinctly a P.

Tracy grinned a few seconds. And then she started again. "Does that look like an M to you Dan? Because it sure doesn't look anything like an M to me. No, Dan, there's no way you could look at this P and think it was an M. The truth is, I had these two coats commissioned starting in the late, late hours last night. I have a dear friend named Max Paganini, who owns a clothier and tailor shop called Paganini and Sons. That's where the P comes from. When I told him I needed his help in clearing someone who had been falsely accused of murder, Max immediately offered his services. Max, you see, can empathize with a person in such a situation. The coats are almost perfect replicas of the coat Conrad wore the night of the murder, except for the letter on the pocket, of course. And I assure you, Dan, these are the *only* monogrammed coats in this building. I have sworn statements by some of the officers here today to back that up. You, of course, see the problem here."

Scarborough's bottom jaw was as far from his top one as was physically possible. He was practically hyperventilating when he cried out, "You… you…you TRICKED ME! You *hoped* I'd say I saw the coat!"

"You're damn right I tricked you!" Tracy announced triumphantly. "I've been deceived, lied to, tricked, and taken for a sucker enough during the past week or so. And quite frankly, I got tired of it! I thought I should get in on the act. And you know what? It *was* fun! At least it was where you were concerned, Dan. There is only one way you could have known about the M: you had to have seen it when Greg was putting on the coat while backstage, since you were *already* at the bar when Woody left to have his run-in with Conrad. That means you were mere feet away from the tank, right after the body was dumped, right there to see a man trying to escape. And then you killed him. Are you going to tell another lie that you saw Greg or Montado push Granger back down? It won't past muster, Dan: neither of these men would have done such a thing, allowing Karine to believe she killed a man when she had, in fact, not! What a tangled web of lies you've weaved for yourself, Dan. And that last lie you just told is the thread that's going to hang you! Because when the police match your finger span to the scratch marks on Granger's head, they're going to match up *perfectly*! Strike three, Dan – you're OUT!"

Scarborough's face turned red. He shifted in his seat. "I want to speak with my lawyer."

Tracy sighed and pursed her lips. "Yes, Dan, that's probably a very good idea."

Detective Deborah Price looked at Tracy with an expression akin to awe. Then she moved toward Scarborough and advised him of his rights. Several other uniformed officers started appearing from backstage and then commenced leading many of the guests toward the exit doors. Lucas approached Montado and the Bowers siblings. "I'm afraid you all will have to come with me," Lucas said quietly. They all nodded as they arose from their seats.

Montado turned to Tracy, who was standing right next to him at this point. He put his hand gently on her forearm. "Well done, my dear. Well done indeed," he told her quietly. He looked at her, knowing his secret was safe with her. She would keep her promise to him. And then he took Karine's hand in his left one, and Greg's in his right one, and started following the officer who was to guide them to their transportation. Tracy watched sadly as Montado and his children moved away from her. Lucas, seeing how upset she was, went over to her.

"Please, go easy on them," Tracy said with tears in her eyes. "I know they did wrong, but…just…please…"

Lucas put his hand on her shoulder. "I can't make any promises, Tracy," he said sympathetically. "But I'll talk to the SA. We'll need their cooperation to nail Scarborough, after all. I'm sure *something* can be worked out."

Tracy nodded. "Thank you, Detective Lucas."

"So Tracy, tell me: what put you onto Scarborough? I mean, how were so sure you could trip him up?"

"I wasn't *sure*, Detective. But after speaking to Jeremiah Granger yesterday and learning his son had a girlfriend, it was fairly obvious to me that Karine was the lady friend. And that got me thinking about her actions the night of the murder, and then I remembered the poster, and everything sort of fell into place. That meant she probably didn't steal the money; that left Scarborough."

"And so you set up your little trap, hoping he'd slip up about the jacket."

"Yes. I had to find a way to prove he was backstage. The only thing I could come up with was the letter on the jacket. I got lucky he was overconfident and, perhaps, as Louis Purdue called him, arrogant. He was so eager to be cooperative the day we interviewed him; I was hoping he'd be that way today and, without realizing it, give himself away. Now I'm not sure if that's enough to nail him in court, but you can take a closer look at his finances and see if you can track down the money. You have all of these witnesses, including me, who can testify to his lies today. He had motive, and now we know he had opportunity. And then, of course, I'm sure about his fingernails causing the scratches on Granger's head. That may be enough to have his lawyer consider a plea."

Lucas nodded. "Well, I have to admit, Tracy, I'm impressed. I've never seen anything quite like today's…well, I guess you'd call it a performance."

"Gee, thanks, Detective. I wonder, then, if you could do me another favor."

"What's that?"

"Call Jeremiah Granger and tell him about today before it hits the news. He wants to know the truth about the robbery, about his son's involvement. I think you would agree he deserves to know the truth"

"Sure, Tracy. I'll take care of it."

"Thanks again, Detective."

"You can call me Jim, Tracy." He smiled at her and then turned to catch up with the partners in magic and crime. Tracy then felt another hand—a familiar one—on her shoulder. She reached up and clasped it. She breathed deeply and then turned to accept Brian's open arms. He rocked her from side to side briefly.

"How are you doing, superstar?" he asked her.

"I'll be okay. Just hold me a bit while I try to keep it together."

Brian kissed the top of her head. "You truly *were* astounding today, Tracy. I'm so glad you let me help you."

She smiled, although Brian couldn't see her face to notice. "You weren't so bad yourself, Somnambulist Brian. You see how important your part was now, don't you?"

"Oh, sure. If I had moved too close to the front of the stage, someone may have noticed the P on the jacket and maybe blown the whole thing."

"Exactly. Trying to hide a letter without making it look like you're trying to hide a letter is tricky stuff."

"And you trusted me with it."

She pulled away from Brian and looked up at him. "Of course I trusted you. If you're someday going to be my babies' daddy, I'd *better* trust you." He moved his head down slightly so his lips could meet hers. She started stroking the back of his head. She then pulled away and smiled at him. "You know what I'd like to do now?"

"Name it," Brian said while stroking her cheeks with his thumbs."

"I'd like to get some ice cream. I've been wanting ice cream since *last* Saturday. Let's go to the Harbor and get some. I want something sweet."

"Ahem!" A voice said loudly. The lovers turned in its direction.

Woody Williams was staring at them. "I'm sorry to be the third wheel on the love train and everything, but can I get a ride to my hotel room, maybe? The cops just kind of left me here."

Brian looked at Williams confused. "Don't they have to take you back to jail until they formally drop the charges, or something like that?"

"They did that already, love," Tracy said. "Woody was officially discharged late yesterday, thanks to help from my detective friends, Deb Price and Jim Lucas. We all just wanted to keep that detail quiet until my show was over. I'm afraid that deception was necessary to prod Karine into confessing. If everyone knew Woody was free, then Greg may have gotten his sister to keep quiet. Now, of course, Woody you can tell the world the whole story."

"Yeah, sure. I may write a book about it, maybe star in the movie version. I could call it *Shticked and Stoned.*"

"Sure, Woody," Tracy said grinning.

"But you know what I'd *really* like to do right now?"

"Become a comedian?" Tracy kidded.

"Very funny. No, what I'd like to do is have some ice cream."

Tracy laughed. "Oh, would you now? Well why don't you join *us*? Brian's buying!"

Williams slapped Brian's upper arm. "Hey, that's great! You're all right, Bri-Bri."

"What did you just call me?" Brian asked tersely.

          Practice to Deceive

"Let's go, boys," Tracy said taking each one by the arm. "I'm seriously craving, here." They started for the lobby.

On the way out the door, they passed an obviously infuriated Pamela Houston. When she saw Tracy, she came over to her. "Couldn't you have waited until *tomorrow* to do this? How am I supposed to find a replacement act for the magic shows today?"

Tracy gave her a look of mild shock. Then Woody put his arm around Tracy's shoulder. Attorney and client looked at each other, and then they both looked back at Pamela. And then, in unison, they stuck their tongues out at the now-befuddled manager of *Merlin's Manor of Mirth and Magic*. And then the ice cream-bound trio made their way to the happy place where their wishes could be fulfilled in any number of flavors and sizes.

"I think you're making a mistake not even giving us a chance, Tracy," Michael Detweiler told the tired attorney.

"Maybe, but the truth is, I'm not ready for the kind of move you're asking me to make. I'm happy with the way things are right now."

"But Tracy, opportunities like this don't come along but once in a lifetime."

"I hear you. But I'm afraid my answer is still no."

"Forgive me, Tracy. But may I say something before you hang up?"

"Okay, Mike."

"I understand how this can be overwhelming, even scary. But you shouldn't be afraid of success."

"Afraid of success? Forgive me, Mike, but I feel like I'm already successful. I have a job I love, and I work with people who are more like family than employees. I have very good relationships with my clients; I still get Christmas cards from former clients I helped years ago. I just helped the police catch a killer, and not for the first time. And I'm marrying my true love next year, not to mention that I have prestigious law firms such as yours taking me to expensive restaurants and making me job offers. I'd call all these things indications of being successful. But for me, it's not about how much money I make, or how often I can dine out at fancy places, or how many summer homes I have, or working on the 15th floor in a building with a view. It's about feeling like I'm doing something that makes a difference, and being comfortable *where* I'm doing it. My clients like that I'm in this little cozy office suite, where everyone is on a first-name basis and the mood is…well, let's just say chummy. Maybe there will come a time when I want to try something bigger. But now is not that time."

There was silence on the other end. "Actually, we're on the fourth floor."

"Oh," Tracy said sheepishly. "I guess I didn't do all my homework. But my point still remains."

"Yes, yes I think you explained your position very well. I really wish you were joining us, though, Tracy. I think I would really have enjoyed working with you."

Tracy felt familiar warmth come to her cheeks. "I really do appreciate the offer, Mike. I assure you I gave this matter a lot of thought; I really did."

"Alright, Tracy, I won't keep you any longer. Thank you for the call, and enjoy the rest of your weekend. Maybe we'll see each other at some point."

"You may if you get the Shane account."

"The Shane account?"

"Yes, the Shane SnackFoods account."

"What are you talking about?"

"Aren't you proposing to provide legal services for them?"

"No, not to my knowledge."

"Oh, I thought maybe that's why you wanted me to join up with you."

"Tracy, I'm not sure what you're talking about. I told you at dinner why I wanted you with us."

Tracy paused a moment. It appeared that perhaps she had reached the incorrect conclusion regarding the mystery behind at least one business offer. "Never mind, then, Mike; thanks again, and you have a good weekend too. Goodbye." She placed the receiver in its cradle and then sat down next to Brian on the couch. She turned up the volume using the remote.

"But in all seriousness," Woody Williams was telling the smiling reporter, "I want to thank my lawyer, Tracy Brubaker, who kicked ass and took names and maybe saved my life. I'll never forget what she did for me." He looked around. "Well, enough of that. Where do you go in this town to find some action on a Saturday night, huh?"

The scene cut back to the studio, where Jack and Cindy were seated chuckling. "Well, that was Woody Williams, released late yesterday after being held for suspicion of murder," Cindy chirped. "The police have made some additional arrests in that case, the details of which are said to be forthcoming. We'll keep you up to date on the details as we learn them. Jack…" And then the screen went black. Tracy put the remote down and sighed. She stared in the direction of the empty table that just days ago had been topped with a hat, flowers, and autographed photo of the Great Montado. Brian started rubbing her shoulders.

"Are you okay, Tracy? I know you have to be incredibly tired after not sleeping last night."

     Practice to Deceive

"Sure I am. I was just thinking of how people who claim to love each other treat each other sometimes. I mean, Montado seemed to love Elena, and yet left her to pursue a career. Zach Granger tells Karine he loves *her*, but then makes all kinds of horrible threats against her if she doesn't run off with him. Milton Bowers kicks Karine out of his wife's life, even though he knows how it would hurt her. Woody Williams told me about his wife, how she left him when she got bored with him. And then, of course, there's the cover-up of a presumed murder. I mean, some people's definition of love just puzzles me. And it amazes me to think that if just one of the people involved in this case had made a different decision, none of this probably would have happened."

"I hear you, Tracy, but you know there's no point in thinking like that. You can't go back in time; I, of all people, understand that. Like me, they made their decisions; they're stuck with the consequences. And that can be a brutal thing, sometimes."

"Oh, I know that. But remember when I was telling you I had a love-hate relationship with my job? Well, this whole Granger case is a textbook example. I'm certainly pleased that the killer was caught and Woody's a free man. But how can I really be happy knowing that Montado's career is probably over. What will Karine do? I know I seemed to be having a good time today and all. But inside I was really struggling with it, knowing how it all was going to turn out."

"Sure, Tracy, I see what you're saying. Sometimes doing the right thing is hard. But remember what *I* told *you*: that you can be counted on to do the right thing, even if it is the difficult thing to do sometimes, maybe lots of times, in your work."

"Thanks, Brian. I know you mean to compliment me, but I don't want compliments right now."

"Okay, I'll stop." He kissed the back of her neck. "It's almost 7:00; I'll fix some dinner for you, if you want. I still want to cook for you at some point. And now, with the Montado case done, we can take that cooking class like we talked about."

Tracy moved her head from side to side and then up and down. "Maybe, Brian. But as for dinner: that extra-large banana split with extra everything pretty much did me in."

Brian laughed. "I can't believe you ate every last bite of that monster. Woody was speechless, probably a first."

"Hey, I earned that monster!"

"Damn right you did! In fact, maybe you deserve another one."

"Well, as a person who strives to be honest unless trying to trick a killer, I must say I think I *do* deserve another one. Maybe even a third."

"Don't push it, Ms. Astounding."

Tracy yawned loudly. "I'm fading quickly here, Brian. The adrenaline and sugar are abandoning me." She turned around, grinned, and kissed him. "You know, I can't help wondering what I'd do if one of our kids got in a jam like Karine did. She had two fathers trying to protect her, each in his own way."

"Yeah, one kicked her out and one welcomed her back."

"Except the welcoming one abandoned her earlier."

"That's right, Tracy. You suggested it yourself: if Montado had stayed around, maybe Karine wouldn't have gotten mixed up with someone like Zach Granger."

Tracy nodded. "Yeah, maybe. I still wonder what we might have done."

"Well, I can't really consider a similar scenario for us, since *I'd* never leave you and the kids behind. *All* of my dreams involve you somehow."

"Brian…" she whispered. And then she lay back on the sofa as he started kissing her passionately. She pulled him close to her. All at once, she wasn't that sleepy anymore. Eventually, however, Brian pulled back and then turned his head from side to side.

"This is where I'd better get off the love train," he told her. "Otherwise, I'm tunnel-bound."

She grinned at him while sitting herself upright. "Very nicely played, conductor. Are you going home now, then?"

"It's still early. Why don't you let yourself fall asleep in my lap?" She answered by smiling at him and then resting her head on his legs. He started stroking her hair. "What do you think Scarborough did with the money? Any ideas?"

"Mmmm…" she answered. "Probably sat on it a while. Then maybe he made deposits into his account over time in small amounts so as not to have to fill out any paperwork for large deposits. Of course, maybe he has it tucked away somewhere, spending money for a trip he's planning when he retires, a trip to a place that won't ask questions or report serial numbers." She sighed. "Who knows?"

"Maybe he'll tell the cops all about it in exchange for a reduced sentence," Brian said with a hint of bitterness. "I'll bet at the end of the day he gets voluntary manslaughter or something like that. You know, the murder wasn't premeditated, it was a spur-of-the-moment thing, Granger had threatened me earlier and I was scared, yada yada yada…"

Tracy was breathing heavily. "That's a good defense you got there," she said sleepily. "Maybe you should go to law school."

He laughed. "No thanks, one lawyer in the family is enough."

"Okay."

"Tracy, I know how much you loved Montado, as an entertainer, I mean. I hope this hasn't spoiled any good memories you have watching him with your dad."

"Maybe a little."

"I'm sorry, Tracy. But you *do* realize you don't have to leave your home to find there's still magic in the world."

"Oh? Is this where you talk about your magic wand or something?"

Brian chuckled. "No, I'm talking about the simple fact that when two people find each other and fall in love, there's rarely ever any rhyme or reason to it. Sometimes it can be quite irrational and beyond understanding or comprehension. Now that sounds like magic to me. Wouldn't you agree?"

"Uh-huh. Some might also call it a miracle."

"Yes, I suppose so. What would you call it?" She didn't answer him. "Tracy?" Still no answer. He smiled and continued stroking her hair as she breathed in and out softly. He leaned back and looked at the ceiling. And then he closed his eyes. Soon a woman in top hat and tails was spinning around and smiling, saying something that he could not hear. Based on the movement of her lips, he thought she was saying his name. She took off her hat and placed it on a small table. Then, still smiling, she reached her hand inside and took out a heart with a B emblazoned upon it. She pulled the heart closer and closer to her chest until it vanished, as if her own heart had absorbed it. It was clear now that Tracy was indeed the magician who had performed the trick. But it hadn't actually been a trick or an illusion. She really did have his heart, after all, as he had hers. Magic or miracle, as long as he and Tracy were together, Brian didn't care what it was called. Soon he was deep in sleep, his future bride close by him. He was so lucky, and he knew it. He knew that when he opened his eyes in the morning, he'd once again be wide awake and living his dream.

Watch for Tracy's next adventure

Gun in White Satin